PRAISE FOR THE NOVELS OF DELPHINE DRYDEN

"Steampunk erotica at its best." —*RT Book Reviews*

"Something I couldn't resist. Ms. Dryden delivered one hell of a great story!" —*Risqué Reviews*

"Smokin' hot." —*Two Lips Reviews*

"Only Delphine Dryden could pull off a beautiful, funny, sexy-as-sin story like this!"
—Mari Carr, *New York Times* bestselling author

"One of the coolest . . . books I have read."
—*The Romance Man*

"Supersexy!"
—Jennifer Probst, *New York Times* bestselling author

"The plot is captivating, the intimate moments are scorching!" —*Sinfully Delicious Reviews*

"Bravo!" —*Seriously Reviewed*

"I really loved the story." —*Just Erotic Romance Reviews*

"A fun and exciting read that kept me entranced from beginning to end." —*Night Owl Reviews*

"Well-written, sexy . . . and intriguing . . . Highly recommend." —*Romancing the Book*

W9-BMY-603

Berkley Sensation titles by Delphine Dryden

GOSSAMER WING
SCARLET DEVICES

SCARLET DEVICES

DELPHINE DRYDEN

BERKLEY SENSATION, NEW YORK

THE BERKLEY PUBLISHING GROUP
Published by the Penguin Group
Penguin Group (USA) LLC
375 Hudson Street, New York, New York 10014

USA • Canada • UK • Ireland • Australia • New Zealand • India • South Africa • China

penguin.com

A Penguin Random House Company

SCARLET DEVICES

A Berkley Sensation Book / published by arrangement with the author

For information, address: The Berkley Publishing Group,
a division of Penguin Group (USA) LLC,
375 Hudson Street, New York, New York 10014.

ISBN: 978-0-425-26578-9

PUBLISHING HISTORY
Berkley Sensation mass-market edition / February 2014

PRINTED IN THE UNITED STATES OF AMERICA

10 9 8 7 6 5 4 3 2 1

Cover photos: *Couple* © Claudio Marinesco; *Painted Watercolor Background* © Charles
Taylor/Shutterstock; *Railroad, USA* © PHB.cz (Richard Semik)/Shutterstock; *Textured
Vintage Background* © Christophe Boisson/Shutterstock.
Cover design by Rita Frangie.
Interior text design by Kelly Lipovich.

ACKNOWLEDGEMENTS

Thanks to Kate Seaver and the talented team at Berkley for making this series so much more than I ever dreamed. A great big thank-you to my family for their patience and support. And as always, thanks to my wonky crew of pals (both real and mostly virtual) for their help, hugs, laughs and generally reminding me that life is good: Christine, Ruthie, Cara, Kristi, Serena, Charlotte, MaryAnn, Shelley, Shari, Edie, Audra, Amber and most definitely Sarah. Also, about half of Twitter, and all those folks I inevitably forget to include but who still deserve my undying gratitude.

ONE

THE OLD MEN sitting in the front row presented Eliza Hardison with a uniform front of disapproval as she took her place at the lectern. She was accustomed to this and told herself she didn't care. Every time, she told herself this. One day she might come to believe it.

"Ladies and gentlemen," she said firmly, then paused as if to wait for the smattering of polite applause that had greeted each previous speaker.

From out on the street, noises drifted in to fill the silence. A rumbling steam lorry, the honk of a horn. Somewhere in the back rows a man cleared his throat.

"Ladies and gentlemen of the Society, thank you for this opportunity. Today I present for the first time my recent findings on the underpinnings of certain tenacious mythologies in the lower-class working culture, and the very real limiting effects those mythologies can have on behavior and the perception of available alternatives, with a final consideration of who might benefit from—"

It wasn't a throat-clearing. It was a snort, contemptuous

and disruptive. This time, snickers of thinly veiled laughter radiated from the noise like rings in a pool, finally lapping up against the front row in a wave of raised eyebrows and frowns.

"With a final consideration of who might benefit most from what might at first appear to be a harmless superstition." She stared into the back of the lecture hall, waiting for further indirect commentary, then continued when she felt the audience growing restive. "Even in San Francisco, workers who disappear are said to 'go west,' never to return. While some argue that the fanciful term originated from tenant farmers abandoning their home lords' lands to become independent pioneers in the early days of the Dominions along the Atlantic coast, the geographic inconsistency of the term's use along the Pacific suggests that it is purely metaphorical, a subconscious invocation of the great unknown . . ."

She spoke at length, clear and loud, projecting her voice to the back of the hall as she'd trained herself to do. At only twenty-three and fresh from university, Eliza was the youngest member of the Society for the Study and Improvement of Workplace Reform. She knew she couldn't afford to appear frivolous, not even for a moment.

Even now, as she neared the end of her speech and congratulated herself, she noted the mood of the crowd was still tenuous, liable to shift either way. There was some interest, some skepticism. The few old crones in the audience eyed her with the usual suspicion, looking for flightiness. Half the men in the front row were asleep. Of the remaining half, most looked bored, but several wore sour expressions that boded ill for the question-and-answer portion of her presentation.

Two were leering at her. Always the same two. She ignored them and gave her papers a neat tap on the podium to indicate she was finished. "Thank you. At this time I would be pleased to entertain your questions."

There was the usual scuffling, hemming and hawing, a

few hands raised tentatively in the air then lowered just as quickly. Eliza was already preparing to leave. They never bothered with questions. Not for her. They only allowed her to speak because she was Eliza Chen's granddaughter, but she would continue until she had won her own place in the Society's esteem. Or perhaps, she thought some days, she would form her own damn reform society.

"Miss Chen!"

A murmur ran through the crowd with the whisper of wool against upholstered seats as every head turned to the back of the house. A man stood in the next-to-last row, leaning on a cane in a somewhat dandified pose. His bright golden boutonniere caught the light, gleaming against his wine-colored jacket.

"It is Miss Hardison," Eliza reminded him. "Did you have a question for me, sir?"

Even across the many rows of seats, Eliza could see the man's smirk. His entire posture conveyed condescension. Instinctively, she braced herself.

"For the Society at large, rather. I came here today expecting to learn information beneficial to my business, from like-minded gentlemen with experience in industry. Instead, I apparently stumbled onto some sort of recital for children. To whom do I apply for a refund?"

The crowd's outburst ranged from horrified gasps to outright giggling, and Eliza could feel her control of the room slipping away as though it were palpable, a rope being yanked from her hands while she scrambled for purchase on treacherous ice.

"I say! I say! Order!" One of the senior members, the Duke of Trenton and Drexel, pounded his walking stick on the floor repeatedly, to no avail. "Order!"

"Did you have a question about the topic of my presentation, sir?" She lifted her voice, straining to be heard over the uproar. It was difficult to unclench her teeth enough to speak. The temptation to hurl insults was almost overwhelming.

The man chuckled, leaning to one of his companions to share something, then straightening and raising one indolent hand for silence. The crowd granted it, and Eliza knew with a sick certainty that she had lost any hope of salvaging the situation. Whoever he was, he had the audience now, and she could be no more than the punch line of whatever horrific joke he had planned.

"Tell the truth, Miss Hardison. You didn't do any research. You just had your nursemaid tell you some bedtimes stories, didn't you?" Over the laughter, he called out, "Do be careful on the way home, miss. You wouldn't want the bad men to get you and go west forever!"

The tide had turned for good. Anything she might say could only make things worse, and the only thing she could salvage was enough poise to make a dignified exit. With shaking hands, Eliza gathered her notes and made her way offstage, fumbling for a moment to find the gap in the velvet curtains. Her eyes were full of unshed tears, anger and mortification vying for control. She had bitten the inside of her cheek so hard she tasted blood.

When the hand curved around her elbow, she jerked away, ready to fight.

"Easy. Easy there, Miss Hardison. Stand down, it's only me."

She blinked rapidly, clearing her sight enough to recognize the man beside her. "Mr. Larken."

The mild-mannered elderly gentleman had been in charge of lecture arrangements since the Society's beginnings. He gave her an encouraging smile and, to her fierce gratitude, said nothing of her heckler.

"This way, please."

Eliza let him lead her swiftly from the wings and out a side door of the lecture hall. The noise and smell of the street rose up to greet them, harsh and acrid despite the cool spring air.

"What are we doing out here?" Eliza tried to catch the

heavy door but it latched behind her before she could reach it. "Who *was* that man? I'd planned to have him ejected."

"His Grace asked me to make sure there was no trouble. To see you made it outside the building without further . . . harassment."

Of course. The Duke of Trenton and Drexel was a powerful patron to the Society, but shunned like the plague any hint of controversy. Larken hadn't been sent to secure her safe departure, but her quiet one. No public ejection of the heckler, no formal complaints. Bad enough the press would report the incident itself, no need to add ruffled feathers on top of that. She could almost hear the Duke's pompous, lugubrious voice speaking the words.

An ornate steam carriage pulled up before them on the cross street, hissing and creaking to a halt. As she and Larken rounded the corner, Eliza realized it was one in a long line snaking down the street. She glanced at the lecture hall's doorway, half a block away. Her presentation had been the last of the day, and the attendees were starting to emerge.

"This is perfectly ridiculous. Are you going to let me back into the hall at some point? I've left my satchel and scarf inside, along with my driving things."

"Oh. By all means, miss. My apologies."

Eliza stopped again, just yards away from the entrance, when the next group issued from the door with her persecutor at their head. Sunlight caught his glistening boutonniere much as the light in the hall had, this time forcing Eliza to squint against the reflected glare. His companions wore similar fripperies, all in the latest style. No simple rosebuds, but elaborately enameled and jewel-encrusted flora limned in gold or platinum, often with tiny mechanisms that opened the petals of the "blossom" at the flick of a switch to reveal a secret compartment or offer up a flame suitable for lighting a pipe.

"Do you know him?" she asked Larken. "The one with the gilded pansy whatsit in his lapel."

"I don't, Miss Hardison. He was the guest of one of the

less regular members, and the name escapes me at the moment."

No name had escaped Larken's memory since his birth, Eliza was fairly certain.

"You're not planning to accost him, are you, miss?" the gentle old fellow asked in a quavering voice.

Eliza hadn't moved from her spot to the side of the entrance, nor did she intend to until the man left. Eliza might petition to have him tossed out on his ear, but she was no ill-bred harpy or impetuous child waiting to fling harsh words on the open street. Much as she might wish to. Instead she bit the much-abused inside of her cheek once again, forcing back the many unladylike sentiments she longed to hurl at the heckler's sleek top-hat-covered head. The man's dull brown, silver-streaked hair was long, clubbed back with a black velvet ribbon, and she noted uncharitably that the rakish style did not flatter his narrow, unremarkable features. It was too much for him, like his flashy suit and flashier jewelry, almost as though he were all costume, no content.

"Of course not, Mr. Larken. That would be begging for trouble, and I assure you I want none."

The man and his cohorts entered their fancy carriage, and Eliza breathed a little easier as the threat of confrontation passed. But just as the heckler turned to take his seat, his eyes lit on Eliza through the open carriage window, and his look of icy calculation chilled her to the bone.

He did not look at all like the flippant dandy who'd ruined her presentation, and possibly her professional reputation to boot, with his boorish humor. In that unguarded moment, swift but unmistakable, his gaze had revealed both intelligence and malevolent speculation. Eliza wasn't sure which she found more troublesome.

THE LATCH ON the boiler's cover was stuck, and Eliza knew she was about to spoil a glove getting it open. She didn't care, as long as she made it to her cousin's party in time to wish him a happy birthday. That, at least, might end her day on a positive note. Nearly anything would be better than her experience at the lecture.

The India rubber gasket sucked at the lid, keeping it closed, resisting her tug. When it finally popped open, a spray of superheated droplets caught Eliza's forearm above the kid glove, prompting a curse she would never have uttered if she hadn't been alone.

Though she was standing in a relatively safe zone, Eliza still felt her hair and dress wilt in the steam. She waved the hand with the stained, crumpled glove to disperse the vapor and peered at the inner boiler casing and cooling tank gauge in dismay.

"Bloody hell!"

A gently cleared throat startled her and she jumped back from the velocimobile. A fresh puff of steam clouded the face of the intruder for a moment.

"Pardon. Can I be of any assistance?"

The voice was smooth, pleasant. The gloved hand that waved the steam away this time was elegant, the glove itself expensive and pristine. And the face . . .

"*You.*"

"Oh! Eliza, I had no idea you were back from school. Welcome home."

With a sigh, Eliza stepped back toward the velocimobile and faced the interloper over the hot boiler.

"Matthew, an unexpected pleasure. May I assume you're also on your way to my cousin's party?" She tucked the offending glove behind her back and hoped the rest of her appearance wasn't too unkempt. She'd paid little thought to her appearance when she'd changed out of her lecture suit. The snug driving helmet kept her plaited hair in place, and her lightweight coat and split skirt were sorely wrinkled and coated with road dust. It would have to do, she supposed. It was only Matthew, after all; he was used to seeing her streaked with engine grease, although it had certainly been awhile since he'd seen her at all. Nearly four years, she realized with a start.

"Indeed I am. Are you having trouble with your boiler? I know a little about engines, as you know, I might be able to help—"

"No!" Eliza bit her tongue and smiled sweetly. "No thank you, you mustn't trouble yourself. Please, proceed to the party. I have matters well in hand. I know more than a little about engines, as you may recall."

Hubris, her hindbrain warned. *That never ends well.* Eliza ignored the warning. She could handle things quite well alone. After that morning's set-down at the lecture hall, the last thing she wanted was the company of a man who assumed her less than competent merely because she was younger and female.

If Eliza had grown up with a big brother, Matthew would have given him a run for his money. He had never let her tag along when it came to working on the truly exciting projects. He found her interest in delicate clockwork devices charming and appropriate for a young lady, but not so her interest in things like locomotive engines and velocimobiles. And he always, always pointed out that she could lose a finger in the machinery, as if the mere prospect of such a hazard should be enough to dissuade any properly brought-up girl. As if he were not himself at the same risk. But if you didn't take that risk, how could you find out what made the thing *go*?

The early afternoon sun shone through the dark bronze of Matthew Pence's hair, lending him a halo that Eliza couldn't help but view as ironic.

"I'll put myself at your disposal," he insisted. She didn't remember him as being so obnoxiously chivalrous. "Consider me your minion. With two of us working, surely you'll be able to repair your vehicle more quickly?"

"It's just overheated," she explained. "Or nearly so. It ran close to dry but I caught it in time. There's really nothing to do but wait for it to cool enough to add more water. My own fault, I'm afraid. I've been stopping frequently to take photographs and letting the engine idle too long. This one builds up steam quickly, which is convenient, but it needs close minding because it's so small."

And it needed a thorough tune-up, something she hadn't been able to accomplish often enough while attending college. Poughkeepsie hadn't been much of a town for motoring, though had she needed to render a whale for blubber, she would have been in the perfect place.

The young man leaned his weight onto one foot, settling into a pose common among fashionable toffs of the day. It irritated Eliza, who knew it was just an affectation he adopted out in public, for polite society. A pretense that he was still a son of privilege rather than a machinery-loving apostate. He had always been good at blending in, though, becoming part of the prevalent social scenery. In some ways she envied him that skill. "Photographs? Flora or fauna?"

"Workers who claim their lost loved ones have 'gone west,' never to return again," she told him, daring him with her eyes to take her up on this topic. "I photograph them holding portraits of the missing. I was also conducting interviews and gathering anecdotal data. I've noticed some interesting correlations."

Matthew raised an eyebrow but didn't take the bait as he once might have. Back in the days when she had run into him frequently at Dexter Hardison's factory, Pence would have been the first to chide Eliza for taking such a risk, haring off on her own and talking to strangers.

Now it seemed he had lost some of that interest in her welfare, or perhaps simply developed more circumspection about stating it. In fact, Eliza thought, he seemed a bit distracted in general. Perhaps it was the problem of the engine. It was clear he still itched to get his fingers on it.

He wore a metal flower on his chest, a sleek, stylized

closed lily bud in some silver brushed metal. It was far more understated than her heckler's had been, but it reminded her of the man all the same. She wondered if Pence knew him.

"Hardison House is only twenty or so miles from here," Matthew pointed out. "I'd be more than happy to give you a lift, so you can make the party sooner. It wouldn't do to cross Charlotte by being late. She's inclined to be touchy these days."

"I suspect she has good reason."

Eliza thought she'd be touchy too if she were as tiny as Charlotte, Lady Hardison, but carrying the undoubtedly huge child of a man the size of her cousin Dexter. Because she was nearly as small as Charlotte, the very idea daunted Eliza. She had recently vowed only to look at slight, slender men as spousal prospects should she ever decide to marry. Preferably men with smallish heads and narrow shoulders. Pence's shoulders were rather broad, like most makesmiths', despite his fashionable slimness. It made her even more irked at him, though she knew she was being unreasonable because of the incident at the lecture. She couldn't help it; she resented those effortlessly capable-looking shoulders.

"I'll be fine," Eliza said firmly. "I don't require help, but I thank you for the offer." She procured a large bottle of water from under the seat of the vehicle, then used a funnel to add a slow trickle of liquid to the cooling unit. "In fact, you should start off again now or I'll beat you to the party."

In Pence's smug chuckle, Eliza heard the first hint of the younger version she remembered. "Not likely. You never could have before."

"Really? A dare? Would you care to wager on that? I'm more than old enough to gamble now, lest you be concerned for my morals." She was already tightening the fittings, closing up the boiler and securing the latch. A bet would make the last few miles to Dexter's party fly by.

Sadly, Pence declined to make it as interesting as he could have. "Certainly, Miss Hardison. If I win—and I don't mind saying I intend to—I'll claim the first waltz of the evening from you once the dancing starts."

"I . . . oh, fine then. Fair enough." Eliza was not inclined to waltz with anyone, least of all with Matthew Pence. But she didn't plan to lose, so it seemed a safe enough stake. No need to tell her competition about the Leyden jar battery cleverly concealed beneath the velocimobile's seat, and the boost its charge would give to her starting speed until the boiler reached full steam. "If I win, I'll claim fifty pounds and when my book is published you'll put an endorsement in the Times. Quarter-page at least."

The terms took him aback, it was clear, but he covered nicely. "All right. May I ask what this book is about? A novel, perhaps? I didn't know you had writing aspirations, those must be new."

With a final yank to the boiler cover's handle, Eliza cranked the engine until it kicked into life, then stalked back to the velocimobile's seat where she stowed the half-empty water jug and funnel before she strapped herself in. "It's a monograph on worker-landowner negotiation inequities and the impact of subliminal psychological manipulation by authority figures on common laborers."

Grinning at Pence's look of dismayed astonishment, she released the handbrake and engaged the gears simultaneously, triggering the start capacitor.

"Ready, steady, go, Matthew!" she called back to him, as he belatedly ran for his steam car.

Two

THE MINX HAD beaten him to Hardison House quite handily. Matthew allowed himself a brief sulk as he arrived in Hardison's forecourt to see Eliza's scruffy velocimobile already parked between a large steam coach and a venerable carriage.

Waving off the footman who approached to take his driving coat and goggles, Pence instead dumped his things on his vehicle's front seat before dusting off and heading in search of a drink to cool his parched throat. He found an underbutler with a tray of chilled champagne the moment he stepped through the parlor onto the terrace.

"Bless you," he murmured at the servant, knocking back one glass immediately, then taking another before the tray could be carried out of reach. Scanning the gardens, Matthew marveled at the changes the past few years had brought to the place, so much more noticeable here than in the house proper. Inside, the baroness had made some alterations, tidied things up, provided a woman's touch here and there, but the decor still showed strong signs of the Hardison mens' obsessions—the fantastical clockwork left visible through some of the wall panels, exposing the workings of the estate's elaborate chronometric communication system, and also more mundane items like a half-disassembled engine on an oilcloth, spread over the floor of a library that was probably meant to be closed to public view. In niches along the walls, where one might expect statuettes or other bibelot, polished specimen machines and masterfully tooled components were highlighted by tiny, carefully positioned lamps. Each piece was artwork in its way.

The perfect blend of elegance and industry: a house where one could entertain royalty or magnates of trade but still not worry overly much about getting grease spots on the Aubusson. And the people . . . Matthew knew he ought to find it vulgar, the way the adults indulged the children laughing and playing in the midst of the garden gathering. His family would find it horrifying, particularly his father, who was always so conscious of propriety. But Matthew didn't. They looked so *happy*, all of them. He wished he could have grown up one of those joyful, energetic children.

"Where's Hardison?" he asked the hovering underbutler, once sufficiently lubricated.

The young man frowned. "*The Baron* is in the rose pavilion, sir."

Matthew nodded and strode off, restraining another sigh at the servant's poorly hidden sneer. Another change wrought by the new Lady Hardison had been the addition of traditionally trained household staff to a manor that had done without them for years. None of the new servants had any truck with their master's preference to forego his title; a baron they worked for, and a baron they would call him, even if he was flagrantly involved in trade. Nor were they particularly thrilled at the dubious proclivities displayed by Sir Paul Pence's wayward son, who ought to know better than to dirty his hands tinkering about with the innards of motorcars and firearms and such.

"Matthew!" a flutelike soprano called. "You're here at last!"

Entering the delicately outlined framework of the so-called "rose pavilion," Matthew took the outstretched hands that Lady Hardison offered, placing a kiss on the back of each.

"Enough of that," stated her husband firmly.

Matthew gave up the lady's hands with a show of terror, then clasped Dexter Hardison's in friendship.

"Felicitations on your birthday, sir. Charlotte, you're looking even more radiant than usual."

"I'm all a-dew," Lady Hardison said wryly. She was noticeably pregnant, and this would likely be her last major social appearance before her confinement.

"Has Smith-Grenville found you yet?" Dexter asked. "He says he has a bone to pick with you."

Matthew shook his head. "I just arrived. I came in shortly after Eliza. Actually I tried to come to her aid on the roadside, but it seems—"

"She didn't require any assistance," the lady in question spoke up from behind him. "I'm so sorry to have thwarted your philanthropic effort, Matthew. Dexter, happy birthday!"

Eliza stepped around Matthew as she spoke, and while she stretched up to give her cousin a hug, Matthew tried to gather his scattered wits. This couldn't be the same girl. He'd just seen her, barely an hour ago. She'd looked the same as ever then, still the child he remembered, a skinny wisp of a thing in a ridiculously oversized driving coat, hair in a plait sticking out from the back of her helmet, bits of it escaping here and there, a light sweat on her brow from the steam of the engine and freckles all over the bridge of her nose. He'd been quite sure the freckles were still there an hour ago.

Stunning, he thought, as she pulled away from Dexter and embraced Charlotte, the older woman's rounded belly making it a bit awkward for them both.

Eliza Hardison had swept her inky hair into a loose bun arrangement and changed into a white, floating, garden-party sort of dress with a jade green satin bow just below her modest but remarkably well-formed—*when the hell did that happen?*—bosom. The fabric flowed down, the drape broken only by the sweet curve—*dear God, made for a man's hands*—of her hips. Her skin was almost as pale as the gauzy fabric, and nary a freckle in sight. Not that he managed to keep his gaze in the vicinity of her nose for long.

He pressed a finger to his upper lip, surprised to feel perspiration breaking out there. He couldn't decide whether to thank or curse the gods of fashion who had decided the bustle needed to make itself disappear again this season.

"Eliza, is the velocimobile giving you trouble again?" Dexter twitted her. "You know if you would only agree to a test drive, I'd give you such a pretty steam car, you can't imagine. And a wee airship to match."

"That's more than just a test drive, cousin. I'm sorry, I realize I'm the smallest person you know after Charlotte, but you'll simply have to find another replacement. Either that or convince the rally committee to postpone their race until Lady Hardison is out of confinement and back in flying form."

Dexter laughed, turning to bring Matthew back into the conversation. "While you were off in the city, I concocted a scheme to convince Eliza to take Charlotte's place in the Sky and Steam Rally. But she insists she's not the Hardison for the job. Her aspirations are too lofty, I think. Our little bluestocking social reformer, remember?"

Matthew smiled dutifully, trying to remember. Had Eliza been a bluestocking back then, even before she went away to pursue her studies at Vassar? He supposed so, but mostly he remembered his constant fear that she would lose a limb to some whirring fan blade or get her hair caught in a fly-wheel, and the attendant concern that Dexter would then kill Matthew for letting his cousin be maimed on his watch.

Or at the very least dismiss him from employment—with extreme prejudice and no character. He'd only been Dexter's assistant a year or so at that time, and hadn't known that he and the baron would become friends as well as colleagues.

Perhaps it was that old training kicking in, but Matthew's stomach clenched at the idea of Eliza haring off across the continent. Airships and steam cars still disappeared all the time going cross-country, particularly over the Sierra Nevada, and no gentleman in his right mind would encourage a vulnerable young woman to traverse such a hazardous route.

Strangely, Hardison seemed to be quite serious in his efforts to cajole Eliza into the scheme. "The airship doesn't have to match the steam car, you know. We can make it any color you like. Pence has an entire book of swatches now, he keeps it in the showroom for the ladies to choose from. And you'd get a healthy share of the prize money, of course."

"Dexter," Lady Hardison warned him, "you'll run her off. She's said no, leave it for a bit. Come with me, Eliza, we'll talk about things that would appall the men if we stayed."

"Feminine problems?" Eliza proposed sweetly.

"Millinery," Charlotte suggested.

"God help us," Dexter said, gesturing the ladies out of the pavilion before turning back to Matthew. "Ready to tell me about your mysterious errand in the city yet?"

"Not just yet." Matthew sipped at his champagne to cover his unease. That was a conversation for another time. "I trust you managed well enough in my absence? The place doesn't seem to have exploded."

"It was a near thing at times. A whole three days, anything might have happened. But no matter, I've simply left the worst messes in your office for you to handle at your leisure. Might want to arrive a little early Monday morning."

"I'll keep that in mind, sir. So you're actually hoping Eliza will take you up on this offer to replace Charlotte? Isn't she a bit . . ." he considered and discarded some words and phrases like *naïve*, *delicate* and *too young to be let off her leash* before finally settling on, "inexperienced?"

Dexter frowned. "I need her. Don't you go discouraging her, Pence. While Eliza may not be as tiny as Charlotte, she's not far off, and as far as I know, none of the other teams can sport anything like the range of our small dirigibles because of the weight and drag. The pilot of our entry must be petite or we lose that advantage. And Eliza drives as naturally as a fish swims. Sadly," he admitted, "she seems adamant in her refusal thus far."

Shaking his head, Matthew returned the frown. "But the risk? Yes, she's willowy, but surely there's a better option. There's always the possibility that portions of the Sierra Nevada truly are unnavigable, assuming she even made it to the airship leg without mishap. And never mind the physical dangers, think of the rough talk, the other racers and the crowds. Sending a gently born young woman like that into such company alone, unchaperoned, unprotected—"

"Oh, I wasn't intending her to be entirely alone, Pence."

"But the weight?" Matthew scanned his employer's frame and cocked an eyebrow. "You're not a bad driver, I'll give you that, but she'd leave you behind the first mile of the first airship leg."

"You misunderstand. I—"

"Pence!"

Matthew looked up and spotted his friend, Lord Barnabas Smith-Grenville, making his way down the garden path.

Dexter greeted the new arrival with a nod. "Smith-Grenville. I was just explaining to Matthew why I thought Miss Eliza Hardison should serve as my lady's replacement driver in the rally. He seems unreasonably resistant to the idea."

"Hardison, happiest of birthdays to you, and you already know I wish Hardison House the best of luck at the rally.

Though I might wish you better company than this turncoat here."

"Sorry?" Matthew looked at Barnabas, who was shooting an ostentatious glare at him. "Did you just call me a turncoat?"

Damn, he's found me out already.

"Indeed. It's no wonder you're opposed to Eliza driving and flying for Hardison House. She certainly has you beat for weight, Pence."

"What's this?" Dexter asked. He'd been looking like he might head off and mingle elsewhere, but now his attention was drawn sharply back to Matthew, who squirmed under the scrutiny. "Something to tell me, Mr. Pence?"

Matthew cleared his throat and squared his shoulders bravely. He might have to thrash Smith-Grenville for the whole business later, but for now it was time to come clean. "I'm participating in the Sky and Steam Rally myself, sir," he confessed. "It will be the first official professional venture of Pence Clock and Steamworks."

A heavy silence blanketed the three men for several awkward moments, broken only by Smith-Grenville's stifled throat clearing as he examined the nearest rosebush with sudden keen interest.

"Ah," Dexter finally responded.

"I was going to tell you, sir."

"But you didn't want to spoil my birthday?"

"There is that. It's a business matter, I had planned to discuss it at a more appropriate time." He shot Barnabas a glare.

"I didn't know about the last part, with the new company and so on," Barnabas said in his own defense. Dexter ignored him.

"Only a business matter? Matthew, you're my heir."

"Oh, I didn't know that part either. Right, if you gentlemen will excuse me, I'm off to find the hard liquor. Pence, Hardison."

"Thank you, Barnabas," Matthew growled at his friend's retreating figure. "Thank you so very much."

"Did you know he was entered as well?" Dexter asked. "Some business his family owns is sponsoring his car."

Nodding, Matthew returned his attention to his employer. "Yes. He didn't tell me, I saw his name in the ledger when they were taking my entrance fee. I don't think he has much interest in winning, it's just an excuse to go looking for his younger brother Phineas. Going west. Traveling across the Dominions alone is far too dangerous, and Barnabas could never afford a security detail. This way the expense is borne by the company as a promotional scheme, and Barnabas will have a car fast enough to outrun most of the dangers he may face on the trip."

"The Dominions are a long way from where I last saw Phineas Smith-Grenville. Barnabas really thinks he's come all that way from France? Rutherford Murcheson reported the lad missing and seemed to have no idea where he'd gone."

Matthew knew enough about Dexter and Charlotte's French honeymoon to know they'd done more than sightsee when they visited Honfleur. He also knew that Rutherford Murcheson did more than simply run Murcheson's Modern Wonderworks, the successful manufactory that was Europa's equivalent to Hardison House. Murcheson was a spymaster, and Dexter had been doing some sort of secret government work in France while posing as a honeymooning tourist. But the bulk of Dexter's activities were classified, so Matthew had never been quite sure why Dexter saw so many British naval officers on that trip. Phineas Smith-Grenville had been a lieutenant at the time, and had been part of some operation Dexter participated in while in France. Now, not even the navy seemed to know where Phineas might be found.

So many mysteries. Matthew shrugged, unsure what Barnabas really thought, not willing to say any hope was unreasonable at this point. "Opium is a cruel mistress, and not just to the addicts."

"He seemed so full of promise."

"I suspect you wouldn't think so if you saw him now."

"True. But we're off the subject. About your new enterprise?" The big man sighed, folding his arms across his chest. "You didn't want to inherit your family's fortune either, so I suppose I shouldn't be surprised you don't want mine."

"Father disinherited me because I told him my sister should be allowed to take control of the company after him. That's different."

"Not all that different. You stepped aside in her favor. And now you're doing the same, aren't you?"

They both spared a brief look down the path in the direction Charlotte had gone.

"Dexter, it was only a matter of time before you realized you needed to update your will. I was only ever a placeholder until a real heir came long." Matthew spoke without bitterness. Hardison was his mentor and over the past few years had become one of his closest friends as well, but everyone knew a man's own child took precedence.

"Charlotte wanted me to wait until after the baby was born. She thought it might be bad luck to change it beforehand."

"Oh. I see."

"I was going to tell you." They shared a chuckle, and the tension lightened. "Unfortunate timing aside, I wish you the best, of course, Matthew. And aside from staking you against my own driver, I'll offer you any other support you need. You'll train here, of course, and take full advantage of the facilities and staff. It's difficult enough when you're just starting out, even if you happen to be mind-bogglingly competent and steady. This is no time to be looking for a new team and organizing a new workshop, not when you should be focused on preparing for the rally."

Matthew shook the hand Dexter offered, relief coursing

through him. He hadn't realized how very worried he'd been about things. "I can't thank you enough for everything."

"Actions speak louder than words, Matthew. And you're not entirely off the hook, not yet." At Matthew's unspoken query, Dexter went on with a distinctly wicked grin. "As I said earlier, I have no intention of sending Eliza off into the wilderness entirely alone, if she does finally agree to drive for me. There are few enough people I'd trust with her welfare, and fewer of those I can feel certain will keep pace with her throughout most of the rally. At least until the airship leg. So really I ought to be thanking you. You've just spared me the expense of running a second car in the race so that you can keep an eye on Eliza."

THREE

CHARLOTTE HAD SET up a throne-like wicker chair under a pergola near a fountain, down the path from the rose pavilion. She held court there, surveying the tidy serving tables and well-appointed crowd with the elegance of a queen and the shrewdness of a general. Mostly, however, the crowd ignored her to allow her time to talk with her recently arrived friend.

"I like these new garden parties," Eliza commented from the stone bench adjacent Charlotte's throne. She idly watched a bee as it dallied in a nearby rose, thinking the scene was idyllic with a potential to sting and therefore a fitting symbol for a garden party. In her experience, there was always some social hazard hidden in the beauty, and all too often Eliza seemed to trigger the stinging response from some innocent partygoer. She'd never been much good at parties. "People seem more at ease, going where they will and playing games."

"We'll all be sunburned before the ball tonight, but I wanted something informal while everyone was here, and it was so wonderful that it was finally warm enough. And this way the children can participate." Her hostess passed an unconscious hand over her belly and smiled as she waved vaguely at the scene with the other hand. In the afternoon sun, most of the revelers had taken shelter in the shade of the lawn tents or under various pretty gazebos and pergolas placed strategically throughout the gardens. Others, more ambitious, engaged in casual sports, while small children dashed along the garden paths with sweets or cakes or cups of iced lemonade in hand. Though the foliage was still young, the new roses barely beginning to cover their supports, it was already taking on an informal lushness that lent itself perfectly to such gentle revelries. It was a far cry from the stuffy affairs they were all accustomed to, and Eliza approved thoroughly.

"Is that very uncomfortable?" she asked Charlotte, as she watched her cousin's wife shift in poorly hidden irritation on the thick cushion. Eliza thought it must be horrible, as it looked like the equivalent of carrying a large medicine ball tucked under one's rib cage. "I wonder you can breathe. It must be so unpleasant."

Charlotte shook her head. "Not precisely. It's . . . oh, how to put it? It was never explained very well to me, and now I see why. Difficult to put into words. It *can* be uncomfortable, but the real problem is you simply can't put the thing down when you get tired of it. There it is, darling creature, getting bigger every day. I fully expect to adore it, but good heavens, what I wouldn't give right now just to have a few minutes without it weighing on me. Especially in this heat. Even oxen get to shed the yoke at the end of the day."

Eliza giggled. "Charlotte, I don't think you're supposed to say that. And it's hardly hot yet. I may even go back in for a shawl."

"You're quite right," Charlotte agreed. "I'm always unbearably warm these days, though. And as for what I'm *supposed* to say, I think I'm supposed to either tell you it's all a miracle and I've never felt more like a woman, or terrify you half to death by telling you only the most gruesome bits, in the most repellent terms possible."

"Exactly. I'm usually more inclined to believe the latter. Miracles bore me. You may proceed with the horrors whenever you're ready," Eliza granted graciously. They shared a laugh, warm and easy in the dappled sunshine.

"There are some very interesting bits I would tell you if you were a married woman," Charlotte said apologetically.

Eliza sighed. "You could hint. You know I'm not *entirely* without experience in country matters. Not ruined," she hastened to reassure Charlotte, "but not utterly innocent."

She appreciated that Charlotte didn't condescend when she replied, "Your cousin would kill me if he found out. And he would, you know, because your mother would find out and she would tell him, so that he could kill me."

"That's all very true. I'm fond of you, don't risk your life on my account."

"I wish I could. I rather wish you'd hurry up and find some nice young man, Eliza, so that you could marry and I wouldn't have to bite my tongue all the time when we have these little chats. It makes me feel like an old biddy."

At twenty-three to Charlotte's twenty-nine, Eliza sometimes felt like Charlotte might indeed be an old biddy by the time Eliza actually found somebody to wed. Not that she was sure she had any inclination toward marriage. "Are you waiting for me to marry as such, or just to have carnal knowledge of some poor fellow? I don't know if the former is in the cards any time soon, but I'm sure I could arrange the latter."

Charlotte gave her a pointed look. "Be very careful joking that way, Eliza. I know you're in favor of equality, and your parents have quite given up on your becoming a society darling, but the fact remains you're part of the class that still cares about these things. Chaperones for grown women and forced marriages over innocent kisses may be things of the past, but there is still a bright line that unmarried women shouldn't cross without a great deal of thought and discretion. Hopelessly old-fashioned though it may be, that particular double standard will likely be with us as long as legitimacy and inheritance issues are with us. You wouldn't be happy with your options if you compromised yourself publicly, no matter what you'd like to think. Besides, men do seem to like the *idea* of virgin brides."

Eliza looked at her cousin's wife sharply, well aware that Charlotte had been a virgin bride once, but obviously not the second time when she married Dexter after five years as a widow. Glancing around to make sure they weren't overheard, she dared a question that had long plagued her.

"Charlotte, was it better being a virgin bride, or . . . the other kind?"

Charlotte blushed and bit her bottom lip, closing her eyes. It took her a few attempts to speak, and when she did Eliza was sure it wasn't her first thought on the matter but a much-tempered version of her original answer. "It's different with each man, but what really makes it worth doing is having a genuine affection for the other person. Trusting one another, and caring about one another's pleasure. Women can have pleasure too, you know," she digressed, with an earnest intensity. "Climaxes, I mean. Don't let anybody tell you differently. Insist on it."

"All right." Eliza already knew about climaxes and was uneasy with the notion that at some point Charlotte obviously hadn't. It was more than Eliza had wanted to know about her friend.

Perhaps society is right, and there are some questions we really shouldn't ask, she thought. *I do hope the one she's had the climaxes with is Dexter and not the dead one.*

Eliza winced at her own thoughts and changed the subject rapidly; Charlotte seemed as relieved as she to talk about anything else under the sun.

"Do you suppose you could still teach me to pilot one of those tiny airships? You did promise some time ago, long before all this rally nonsense came up. I know you couldn't demonstrate right now, of course, but if the controls aren't too different from a basket dirigible, I shouldn't need very much instruction."

"Naturally. Name the time. But about the rally . . . I do wish you'd reconsider, Eliza."

Humoring her very pregnant friend, Eliza said, "Since Dexter's failed to convince me, suppose you try. Why on earth should I want to participate in the rally? By all accounts the competition is brutal, it's dangerous, there are all sorts of dubious goings-on when the racers are parked for the night. And if I make it to the airship leg, there's always the possibility that those geologists are right and the air over the Sierra Nevada range is poisoned. It hardly sounds like the sort of undertaking a respectable woman like yourself would recommend to a naïve young thing like me."

Charlotte's snicker was hardly complimentary, but Eliza allowed it was well-deserved. And Charlotte didn't know the half of it. Vassar had offered many educational opportunities that did not appear on the curriculum, and Eliza had explored most of them.

"Eliza, how old are you now? Twenty-three?"

"Yes." It sounded hopelessly young and at the same time dangerously close to spinster territory, even in this enlightened day and age.

"That's young," Charlotte assured her. "I recommend the race for two reasons. It'll get you away from your family for a time, since you're always talking about wanting more independence. Second, and more importantly, I think you would have *fun*."

"Fun?" Eliza repeated the word as though Charlotte had suggested she kiss a toad. "It sounds positively uncivilized."

"Listen to yourself! You're an elitist snob, my darling. Time to go out and actually *do* some of the things you advocate, instead of trying so hard to become the new generation's Eliza Chen."

"I'm not," she insisted immediately, but a little bell rang

in Eliza's mind—because Charlotte had struck it hard. "I'm simply trying to focus on truly important issues. If some of them happened to be causes that my grandmother fought for as well, then isn't it all the more important people continue working to correct those ills?"

"Of course it is. But do you have to do it to the exclusion of all else? You're getting grim, Eliza. Oh, not all the time," Charlotte amended when Eliza started to protest, "but if you don't take steps soon it will only get worse from here. You need to get away from this place, these people. From academic life and charitable societies too. It might give you a chance to . . . oh, I don't know, explore other ways of thinking and living. Other things about which you're curious."

Eliza was sure she couldn't have heard that correctly. Was Charlotte implying she needed to sow wild oats? "I beg your pardon?"

"You say you want to be somebody whose opinion is respected. You want your voice to be heard. But right now, all you're doing with that voice is responding to the society you claim to want no part of."

"I never said *no* part."

"Near enough. You're letting those ideas shape you, and lately all you talk about is the things you don't want, the life you don't want to be trapped in. But what *do* you want, Eliza? Do you even know who you are, what sort of life you would lead, given the choice? What is your natural inclination? I don't think you can know that, because you've never seen anything but the safe little high society world and then academia, and I doubt you're destined for either of those."

Eliza bristled at the characterization. After that morning's fiasco at the lecture hall, she felt polite society and the academic world were anything but safe. It all felt like a wilderness, full of hidden perils and vicious beasts ready to attack. "You're hardly one to judge. Is your life so out of the ordinary?"

"My life," Charlotte asserted, "is exactly the life I chose

to live, *after* exploring other options about which you know nothing. A whole career, in fact, about which you know nothing. And I'm sorry if I sound impatient, Eliza, it's partly just this damned—this miracle of life within me."

"You're calling it a miracle of life and using profanity?" Dexter said, sounding concerned as he approached his wife. "Is it time to send the guests home? Are you going to start throwing vases? Do I need to procure any particular food for you?"

Charlotte chuckled wearily up at Dexter, who bent to kiss the top of her head. Eliza felt a pang of envy at their ease with one another, at the obvious affection between them.

He's definitely the one she's had the climaxes with, she thought, then had to look away from her cousin for a few moments and think about puppies to clear her mind.

"What has you looking so flustered, my delicate petit four?" Dexter asked Charlotte. Eliza couldn't help but smile at the endearment; he always seemed to have a new one.

"I'm worn out trying to convince Eliza to take my place. She's dead set against it."

"Just as well," Dexter replied. "Nobody would get a moment's peace at the rest stops with my cousin and poor Matthew at each other's throats."

Eliza's head snapped back toward Dexter. "Who?"

"Pence," Dexter repeated. "He's going to be driving for his own brand-new company, apparently, but I've offered him some non-financial support as well. I don't mind doing him a good turn to start him on his way. If I bet wisely enough, perhaps I'll profit from the whole business, even without an entry of my own in the race."

Charlotte scoffed at the idea of wagering, while Eliza tried to capture the thoughts flying wildly through her brain. She couldn't . . . could she? She knew if she agreed, she would be doing so for all the wrong reasons, not to explore the world for herself but to spite Matthew Pence. This was an old reflex, drawn from the days years ago when she'd been so frustrated by Matthew's attempts to restrict her actions. It was still strong, however, probably because she found that he still annoyed her. Made the hackles on her neck rise . . . sort of. Her reaction unsettled her, and she was inclined to go on the offense rather than wait passively and hope things would improve.

But if I win, it really would spite Pence so very, very well. It would show him he was wrong all along.

Then, clear as a bell, it occurred to Eliza that she didn't have to choose one reason. It could be both. Or rather, she could do it for herself, as a rare adventure per Charlotte's urging, and just accept wiping the smug look off Matthew's face as one more happy consequence of victory.

If Matthew was surprised to see Eliza Hardison approach him at the ball that night, he hid it well. At least he hoped he hid it well. He suspected he might have gaped, at first, at her overall appearance. She was breathtaking in a pale pink, shimmering gown that would have looked bland and insipid on most girls. On Eliza, it looked like she had blushed, and the seamstress had dyed the fabric to match that delicate glow. Her snowy skin was luminous, the contrast with her black hair astonishing.

Lovely as she was, however, he didn't quite trust the sweet smile she bestowed upon him. He hadn't completely forgotten the girl he'd known four years ago. In fact, in this light, he thought he could even make out a freckle or two. Though he'd have to look closer to know for sure.

"Miss Hardison, you look beautiful this evening," he said with a nod.

Demure as a girl in her first season, Eliza fluttered her eyelashes and gazed bashfully at the parquet floor. "Thank you, Mr. Pence."

"I'd still be honored to claim that first waltz if it's available."

She handed over her dance card with no complaint, and Matthew caught a whiff of jasmine as he bent to write his name on the flimsy page. He was just straightening when she spoke, stunning him to silence.

"Matthew, I know we've had our little disagreements in the past, and for my part I just wanted you to know that I don't bear you any ill will at all. I'm sure you only had my best interests at heart all those times you kept me out of the workshop. We should consider this a fresh start. Pax?" She offered him her hand, surprising him with the strength of her handshake. It was all business, in distinct contrast to her dainty appearance.

"Of course. We've both grown up a bit since then. I think we can let bygones be bygones." The strains of a waltz floated over to them and Matthew crooked his arm, leading Eliza to the dance floor with a growing sense of surreality. This beautiful creature on his arm, agreeing to dance with him, encouraging a new perspective on their relationship . . . was it possible this was the same girl he'd seen as a pesky little sister for so many years? He could barely reconcile this Eliza with the one he'd known four years ago, freckles or no freckles.

"You're right," she murmured once they had started their dance. She leaned in so he might hear her better over the music, and her perfume wafted toward him again, enticing. "We have both grown up since we saw each other last. It's funny, Lady Hardison and I were just talking about that earlier, in the garden. About how part of growing up is learning who we're meant to be."

"And who are you meant to be, do you think, Eliza?" Matthew could hardly feel his feet crossing the floor. This afternoon's confession to Dexter had gone better than he'd ever hoped, and Eliza's offer of a truce had stripped away another source of tension he hadn't recognized until its absence. Now the dance seemed charmed, the night itself seemed charmed. Everything in the world felt promising.

"That's just the thing," she said, flicking a glance at him then quickly looking away once more. He tightened his hold at her waist just a fraction, then reminded himself she was Dexter's cousin, and loosened his fingers again. "I don't quite know who I'm meant to be. Charlotte says it's time I found out."

"Lady Hardison is wise beyond her years, I've always thought. You should follow her advice." He thought that Charlotte would make an excellent role model for Eliza: beautiful, unassuming, ladylike and comfortable in the role of administering a large, if unconventional, estate. She'd always been lovely and gracious, even as a young widow, but since marrying Dexter she'd gained a whole new, vibrant energy. The glow of impending motherhood made her even more appealing. She was everything a woman should be.

"Oh, I intend to," Eliza assured him with a smile. "That's part of why I sought you out."

"It is? Did she suggest any particular course of action?" His brain misfired at the sudden influx of ideas about possible courses of action Eliza might take with him. None of them were appropriate for him to contemplate taking with Baron Hardison's maiden cousin. In fact, none of them were appropriate to think about in relationship to *any* maiden. He used the physics of the next turn to swing Eliza a little wider than necessary, putting another few inches of propriety between their swaying bodies.

Eliza shook her head. "It wasn't really that sort of talk. Well, she did, but that wasn't the important part. The main thing is she made me see that I've cast myself in a certain role for most of my life, but that role is still a product of the expectations placed on me. Charlotte said I should find a way to escape those preconceptions about myself. Allow my life to take its natural course."

"Lady Hardison is a perfect example of that right now, I dare say. I gather she did some sort of government work prior to marrying Dexter, but having seen her then and now,

I don't think anybody could argue with how well this more natural role agrees with her. She's clearly much happier."

Eliza looked taken aback for a moment, making Matthew wonder if he'd inadvertently said something offensive. Then she coughed, sounding almost as though she were choking, but waved him off with a satin-gloved hand when he asked if she'd like to sit down. In a moment, with a slightly strained expression, she spoke again.

"You know, you're absolutely right. It was so foolish of me to struggle against my nature all this time. All that talk of monographs and so forth. It's time I stepped forward and accepted the cards destiny so clearly wants to deal me. If I do, will you congratulate me, Matthew?"

"Con-congratulate you?" He could tell she was being oblique and had an uneasy feeling he ought to be aware of her meaning. How had he lost track of the conversation so quickly and thoroughly? "I suppose so. It's not every day a young woman reaches out to grasp her destiny, is it? Congratulations for . . . your new endeavor."

"Oh, I didn't mean now," Eliza said. She met his eyes at last, the triumphant gleam in her own setting off alarm bells in every corner of Matthew's psyche. "I meant in San Francisco, after I've beaten you out to win the Sky and Steam Rally."

FOUR

THE HARDISON STEAM car was a clear, bright crimson. As soon as Eliza had seen it, she'd declared she wanted a ball gown in exactly that shade.

"It's . . . pink," Matthew pronounced when he arrived, along with his vehicle, at the dirigible hangar being used as a pre-rally staging facility. Eliza waved him reluctantly past the security detail guarding the velvet rope that cordoned off their area of the hangar. Unlike Eliza, who was clad in a practical coverall over her walking dress, Matthew was cool and crisp in a finely cut spring suit of pale linen with an impeccable blue watered-silk waistcoat. Eliza thought he looked far too buttoned-up and proper to be loitering in a garage. Suddenly she felt frumpy, not dashing at all, in the shapeless coverall.

"It's a light shade of red," Dexter corrected Matthew sharply, peering out from behind the boiler.

"Amaranth," Eliza suggested, smiling a little too sweetly. "I think it's a beautiful color."

"Runs like a top," Dexter said, "and that's all that really matters."

Eliza ran a proprietary finger along the driver's side door. "It will get me where I'm going." She let a hint of skepticism color her expression as she glanced toward Matthew's steam car. A team was just unloading the sleek, gunmetal gray vehicle from a trailer, their job complicated by the fact that one of the tires had apparently gone flat during transport. A small thing, and irrelevant to the car's functionality, but Eliza couldn't resist a snicker when Matthew cursed.

"You'll need a realignment," Dexter remarked.

At least he was in the right place for such a thing. The vast hangar had been designed to accommodate several dozen luxury air yachts, and it could have housed a hundred steam cars with room left over. There was plenty of space for the eighteen rally cars and all the equipment it might possibly take to ready them, and the swarming attendants looked insignificant in the cavernous building.

Eliza took a deep breath and released it slowly, trying for the hundredth time to calm the nerves that had her stomach in knots. It was no use. Excitement filled the air she breathed, a buzz of anticipation that had greeted her on her arrival that morning had never ebbed. The press were not allowed into the hangar itself, and for that she was grateful; Dexter had warned her they would mob her whenever she left the hangar, and more would probably be waiting outside the hotel.

A barricade and a line of policemen secured the open hangar door, but Eliza could sense the crush just beyond them, the babble of reporters and flash of camera bulbs at the fore, the sea of spectators pressing in from behind. The "door" was really the whole end of the hangar, slid to the sides on tracks. It had to be that wide and tall to admit the largest of the dirigibles usually housed there, but the opening gave the space an oddly unprotected feeling.

"They're like sharks," Matthew said, following her gaze

to the wide wedge of light spilling in from outside. "Circling at the first scent of blood."

"Has there been blood already? We haven't even started off."

"Of course there's blood. Don't you know anything about your competition? Look over there," he said, nodding in the direction of a long cream-and-white steam car with an elaborately filigreed copper boiler housing. "Whitcombe and Sons, out of Manchester. That's the fourth or so son in the light gray. He's the driver."

"He's twice your size, and three times mine," Eliza whispered. "How can he hope to compete for speed in the dirigible leg?"

"The second smallest son is the one standing next to him. They're like a race of giants. But they didn't want to hire a driver. Rumor has it their company is close to going under. They need the win, and they need to keep the proceeds in the family." Matthew sounded more thoughtful than coldly speculative, but Eliza reminded herself that whatever information he had gathered on the others, he'd also sought for tidbits to use against her.

Eliza studied the even larger man next to the one in dove gray, then considered the whole Whitcombe family. They seemed to be assembled in force around the lovely rally car, apparently arguing the finer points of boiler maintenance, if their gestures were any indication. Not a happy crew, on the whole. And large, to a man.

"No women in the bunch, I see."

"Mother Whitcombe is dealing with the press outside. I passed her on my way in. Now, you see the white steam car behind me with the red and blue racing stripes? That's Moreau, the driver for the French consortium. All he has to do is show up to have reporters crawling over him, of course. But he's also brought an outrageous number of mysterious packages with him, and you can see his car is loaded to the gills. Rumors abound as to what might be in those boxes and hampers."

She stole a look around Matthew's shoulder at the steam car in question. The canvas top was down and the car was tightly packed, just as he'd said, with bundles and baskets galore. As she watched, the mechanics raised the roof, hiding the curious cargo. "It looks like he's going on a very extravagant picnic."

"Aye, perhaps. But I wouldn't put it past him to have something far more sinister in mind."

"You're just prejudiced against the French," she scoffed, turning back to her own vehicle. Dexter was fastening the boiler hatch with an air of satisfaction.

"Of course he's prejudiced against the French," Dexter told her. "He's also trying to scare you. She won't fall for it, Matthew. Charlotte and I have given her all the information she needs to win the race handily. And I've told her all she needs to know to keep this engine in tip-top condition, isn't that right, Eliza?"

She snorted. "I could teach you a thing or two about that engine, and you know it." But the truth was, if Matthew had been trying to worry her, he'd succeeded. This infuriated Eliza, but she couldn't help peering around at her adversaries, wondering what other secrets lay waiting to be discovered and exploited. And what had they learned about her in turn, that they might try to use against her? Matthew couldn't be the only one utilizing the psychological approach.

"You and Charlotte would have done better to spend the time finding another driver," Matthew said, reminding Eliza why she was so determined to beat him. "I still say this is insanity. You won't be safe, Eliza. Your parents are mad to let you participate in this."

"Matthew—" Dexter started in a warning tone.

"No, Dexter. Let Mr. Pence have his say." She turned to him. "You were expressing your concern, sir?"

He eyed her warily. "You're well aware of my concerns."

Eliza nodded. "You've certainly made no effort to keep them to yourself. Let me address them yet again. I'm past the age of majority, sir. My parents may not be thrilled, but there's no question of them 'letting' me do anything. I'll be exactly as safe as any of the other competitors, which is to say not very. And you do realize I'm not the only female driver? There are three others. Shouldn't you be making the rounds expressing your sentiments to them as well?"

"You're the only one I know. And besides, they're all older, and you're so . . ." He looked miserable but determined, and for a heartbeat Eliza felt pity for Matthew.

"So . . . ?"

He gestured toward her, then vaguely at the rest of the vast hangar. "So . . . well, dammit, you're the only one I know!"

Something stayed her automatic response, which would have been to snap at him. After a moment, Eliza said, "Part of me truly appreciates your obviously genuine feeling on this matter, Matthew. Truly."

"However . . ." Dexter murmured. Both of them glared at him, and he shrugged with an unrepentant look.

Eliza turned back to Matthew. "It is the same small part that will enable me to maintain a sportsmanlike demeanor when I accept your congratulations on my win a few weeks from now."

"If that should occur, Eliza, no one will be more relieved than I."

With a stiff little bow, Matthew turned and stalked away, leaving Eliza feeling slightly embarrassed.

"He's behaving as though I'd deliberately set out to hurt his feelings," she told Dexter with a frustrated sigh. "I can't even enjoy a little competitive banter."

"Don't let it spoil the win for you."

"Do you think I have a chance to win?" She knew Dexter would tell her the truth, which was probably why she had resisted asking him this question until now.

He leaned back against the fender, making no effort to hide his scrutiny of the other competitors. Seventeen steam cars, each as brilliantly turned out as the Hardison entry. Competitors from the American Dominions, England and Scotland, France and Germany and a handful of other countries. Eliza knew she was by far the youngest driver in the field.

"If it came down to skill at driving a steam car and dealing with any emergency maintenance that arises," Dexter finally said, "I'd give you an unqualified yes. Charlotte says you're a natural with the dirigible too. Nobody is a better judge of that than Charlotte, so I think your skills will serve you well in that leg of the race. And of course I wouldn't have asked you if I didn't think you had a chance. But there's more to the rally than driving and flying."

"True." She leaned next to him, echoing his posture, arms folded across her chest. "You don't think I rate as well at navigation and so on?" Her mind flew to the case of maps, the compass and other equipment she planned to rely on to get her safely across the continent.

"You're just fine at navigation. No, I'd say if you have a weakness, it's the intangible part. You're determined to win, but you're not interested in your competition. Well, not in *most* of your competition."

"What's that supposed to mean?"

He rolled his eyes. "Pence wasn't wrong. You have sixteen other people to outdrive *and* outsmart, Eliza. Not just Matthew. Most of these drivers won't even make it to San Francisco. They'll be lucky to reach Colorado Springs. Car problems, illness, exhaustion, those mythical poisonous gas clouds or snow monsters in the Sierras, any number of things might happen. But until they fall by the wayside, you still have an entire field to contend with. You might not have studied their weaknesses, but they've certainly studied yours. Psychology plays a large role in a race like this. You do have one advantage though."

She frowned at him. "What is that?"

Dexter tapped her nose, giving her an unusually impudent grin and suddenly looking like a young boy, for all his size. "You're an unknown quantity and they're almost certainly underestimating you, just like Matthew." He uncrossed his arms and fiddled with his socket wrench. "You know, your race against him really begins on the last day, assuming you each make it to the checkpoints within a reasonable range of one another. Until then, you ought to consider forming an alliance with Matthew. Help him if he needs it, let him help you. The others have already started making friends, aligning themselves together. Most of them know one another from previous races. This is an endurance test and they know that. They'll be pacing themselves, enjoying the event and sizing things up, not cutting throats right from the start."

Eliza could see he was right. Even as Dexter had spoken, the French consortium driver had wandered over to the vehicle of another Englishman, a man of exceedingly short stature whose virulent green steam car had been famously custom-modified to allow him to drive it. They were chatting like old friends while the shorter man patted the glossy enamel of his car's fender as though stroking a beloved pet. The consortium driver was opening a bottle of wine, which he apparently meant to share.

She was startled, when the diminutive Englishman looked her way, at the appealing brilliance of his sudden grin. She allowed herself a tentative smile back before averting her eyes, trying to look demure and unassuming. Easy to underestimate. Eliza suspected he banked on that quality himself.

"I suppose you're right. I don't know why I should trust Matthew, though, even for only part of the race. Not if he wants to win just as badly as I do."

"I never said anything about trust. You think Van der Grouten trusts the Watchmaker?" Dexter nodded toward the gruff German competitor, who was sitting in stony silence listening to the Watchmaker's chatter. The Watchmaker's spider-like vehicle, a gleaming brass contraption of gears and mysterious controls atop several pairs of articulated legs, loomed above the two men, and indeed above the other steam cars. Its inventor and driver, a famously eccentric maker of every type of clockwork *except* watches, would obviously have the advantage of height. But Eliza privately thought the unconventional vehicle looked unlikely to make it out of New York before falling apart.

"I think Van der Grouten knows the Watchmaker is insane," Eliza replied. "And I've never understood why he calls himself the Watchmaker."

"Nobody knows."

They observed the unlikely companions a moment longer. Then Dexter tossed the wrench into the air, catching it neatly and placing it in the proper slot in the enormous tool kit he'd wheeled over to the steam car's side. "Time to brave the press and win through to the hotel. You'll need a proper night's sleep before you set out."

Eliza didn't think she'd sleep a wink, but she shrugged off her coverall and obligingly followed Dexter from the hangar, passing Matthew's car along the way. He looked up as they walked by, and she caught a glimpse of something on his face that stopped her in her tracks. Concern, tension . . . and something that strongly resembled yearning. Eliza turned toward him for a moment, not sure what she planned to say, then covered her confusion by pulling her broad-brimmed hat on as if she'd meant to stop for that purpose all along. The moment flitted by, she waved with her fingertips and received a solemn nod from Matthew in return, then the open door loomed before them and she braced herself for the onslaught.

WHEN ELIZA TURNED toward him, the sun streaming into the hangar backlit her for a moment, transforming her slender figure into a silhouette of elegant curves. Her hair, which had seemed so securely battened down into its tidy chignon, revealed a nimbus of stray wisps that glowed a hot auburn in the afternoon light.

Then the clouds shifted, the illusion faded, and it was once again Eliza standing before his sun-dazzled eyes. She blinked at him, looking as though she was going to speak, then shook her head and put her hat on. He watched her fiddle with the ribbons, her nimble fingers fixing the bow just so. Then she waved and was gone, following Hardison into that damnable crowd.

He wanted to run after her, explain himself to her until she understood. He wasn't really so benighted in his views. He knew she was capable, even formidable. He knew there were other women in the race. But none of them were Eliza. None of them made him think of terms like "sylph" or "toothsome." He hadn't pulled his hair half out of his head and paced for hours trying not to think inappropriate thoughts about any of those other women. Only Eliza, maddening though she was.

Dexter hadn't needed to make looking out for her a condition of his support. Matthew would have been her watchdog anyway, whether she wanted him to be or not. For the first time in his life, he had a primal impulse to protect and possess another creature. And the creature in question was not remotely amenable. Nor should he be thinking this way about a Hardison, of all people. He was trying to make his *own* way, distinguish his *own* name, not become more attached to Hardison House. The last woman he should be daydreaming over was Dexter Hardison's cousin, a girl whom Dexter practically treated as a daughter.

"I think I'm going mad," he mumbled as he watched her go.

"At least you'll have somebody to talk to on the drive," remarked the mechanic who'd just approached him.

"I can think of better company," Matthew admitted, grinning ruefully. "Sorry, Toby. I'm short on sleep."

"Aren't we all, guv? But you make sure to get your rest

tonight. I've got a certain amount riding with you, as it were."

As the man filled Matthew in with last-minute particulars about the car, Matthew scanned the hangar, scouting out his competition. Over half of them were there, seeing to their vehicles or making an early start to packing up, and he recognized all but two. One Greek flag and one Dominion, two unfamiliar drivers. He had studied the racing roster and knew the names, but despite what he'd boasted to Eliza, he knew precious little else about the participants and their sponsors. Less than he should, he suspected.

One unpleasant presence was impossible to ignore. Not a driver, just a visitor, for which Matthew was thankful. Matthew had run across Lord Orm, the Californian cattle Baron, when the man visited one of Rutherford Murcheson's workshops in Le Havre the previous year. Matthew had been in France conducting some business with Murcheson on Dexter's behalf. Orm was there to perform some sort of efficiency study, officially, but all of them agreed he was more likely touring makesmith shops and other factories to steal ideas for a new enterprise of his own. Murcheson's bet was a dairy, as Orm had asked about glassmaking and bottling methods, and obviously was already in possession of a good many cows. He'd made sure to keep Orm away from the most cutting-edge projects, showing him only a curated selection of his multifaceted makesmithing operations.

Matthew had disliked the cut of the man's jib on sight then, and liked it no better now. He noted the fellow still wore that flashy lapel gadget, a gilded golden poppy. It was said to conceal a set of secret compartments under the lapel that could be revealed using a complex clockwork mechanism similar to one of Murcheson's famous curio boxes. All Matthew knew was that the thing was in exceedingly poor taste, and the weight utterly spoiled the drape of Orm's coat. It was also—and this was unforgiveable—so ornate that the decoration would obviously hinder, not enhance, whatever operations the device was meant to perform. Nothing like his own slim-lined, tasteful model, which converted with a flick of the hand into a set of light but useful tools.

Orm was deep in conference with one of the unknown drivers. Was the cattle Baron a silent benefactor, perhaps? His appearance worried Matthew, though he couldn't put his finger on any good reason why. Matthew was just making up his mind to approach the man when Orm left the building, disappearing past the press line into the thick crowd.

Well, he could find out about Orm and the unknown driver at his leisure. Of the rest of the field, he knew Whitcombe and Cantlebury from Oxford, and he had at least a passing social or business acquaintance with three or four others. Van der Grouten and the two French contestants he knew by reputation. Making up his mind to find out more about the mystery entrants once he returned to the hotel, Matthew let his thoughts drift back to the problem of Eliza and his embarrassingly sleepless nights of late.

He didn't ruminate for long before a new distraction arose.

"What's that smell?" One of the mechanics said, just as another of the men flicked something from the air in front of his face.

Looking up, his upper lip curling at the stench, Matthew saw the ceiling of the hangar many stories overhead. But the girders were obscured by a faint haze.

A shriek from the opposite side of the structure seemed to trigger a wave of reaction, and the crowd mobilized like a flight of starlings, pushing and pulling toward the wide-open door. The haze descended like something from a nightmare, a foul, hot rain that coated everything it fell upon with a slick, brown residue.

Matthew turned to see his mechanics throwing a tarpaulin over his car, and then his gaze continued to the bright crimson vehicle in the stall adjacent. The vivid color blurred as the noxious fumes began to make his eyes water. Cursing as he coughed and batted away the first heavy droplets of the disgusting spray, he sprinted and hurdled the velvet rope, reaching inside Eliza's car and rolling up the open window on the driver's side. He shouted for his team but they had already joined the crowd jostling in a panic at the exit.

Steer manure. There were cattle on the Pence estate, and as a boy Matthew had been taught the basics of their upkeep. He recognized the smell, though it had taken him a moment to place it, so far out of context. Liquified, possibly by the addition of some sort of alcohol from the stinging smell of it—and by the looks of it, sprayed through the dirigible hangar's vaunted, state-of-the-art fire control system.

"Help!" The voice from the far side of Eliza's steam car was nearly drowned out by the still-swelling commotion. "Mr. Pence!"

A pair of mechanics, apparently having the same idea as his own team, were struggling to pull an oilcloth from an overloaded supply box. Matthew hastened to their aid, and the three men were able to drag the heavy canvas over Eliza's vehicle just before the heaviest drenching of stinging filth began to fall. Looking across the garage, he noted with relief that Smith-Grenville's car was covered and protected as well.

"This way!" One of the men shouted, holding up a hand to shield his eyes. "There's a side door, sir!"

It wasn't locked, and Matthew gave a roar of pure relief when he half-fell from the opening into the unsullied air beyond the hangar wall. Hacking and swearing, he and his ad hoc companions pushed their way through the confused masses nearest the building, until they hit a clearing several yards off.

"Coated in . . . we're coated in horse shit!" The mechanic was so offended he forgot to beg Matthew's pardon.

"I believe it's cow shit," Matthew corrected him, staring at his own clothing in dismay. He had rather liked the crisp, pale linen suit and the waistcoat of robin's-egg blue figured silk he'd chosen to wear that morning. He would certainly never wear them again. Served him right for not donning a coverall the second he walked into the garage.

"Oh aye, cow," the second mechanic concurred in a Yorkshire burr. "Burnt enough of the stuff on t'fire back home to know."

Matthew frowned, trying to clear his head through the fug of stench and confusion. "That's right. Our gamekeeper used dung chips for his stove too. And from the sting and fumes, I think this has had some ethyl or other alcohol added to thin it out. One good spark in there now and . . ."

His eyes met the Yorkshireman's in a moment of perfect understanding and horror, and as one they bolted back toward the hangar.

"Water!" Matthew screamed to anyone who would listen. "We need water!"

A pair of policemen, evidently rerouted from the front entrance, blocked the way back in; Matthew nearly bounced off the larger one in his haste to get through the door.

"Nobody goes—eugh!" Large as he was, the man quailed before the mighty aroma of Matthew's ruined suit.

"It's flammable," Matthew said firmly, hoping like hell he seemed like a person in charge. "Flammable. One match could blow the place up, cars and all. We need water, now!"

"Flammable—holy mother of God!"

Within moments the swell of motion had turned, as pails materialized and onlookers rushed in to help the mechanics who dashed back in to save their cars from an even worse fate. Knowing both his own and Eliza's steam cars were fairly well-protected, Matthew threw his hand in where he could, helping throw soaked blankets over other steam cars and moving a barricade to allow the firemen access once they finally arrived.

"Fire!" The first cry went up from the back of the hangar, closest to the scaffold of catwalks and stairways that enclosed the offices.

The Yorkshire mechanic pulled something off the nearest wall and pelted for the rear of the building, Matthew hot on his heels. When the man passed him a cool glass orb, he stared at it in puzzlement, nearly tripping over a bundle of hoses in his blind rush. Smoke had started to curl off a pile of oil-stained rags along the wall, and licks of flame were already attempting to jump to the wall itself.

Just as the Yorkshireman flung his own orb at the floor next to the rags, Matthew realized what the glass ball must be. He aimed his a bit higher, toward the top of the rag pile where it met the wall, and shouted in triumph as the breaking glass released its powdery contents and the fire began to peter out.

An emergency chemical fire extinguisher, self-contained and at the ready. Now that he knew what they were, Matthew noticed the orbs in sconces at regular intervals along the walls.

"How did you know?" He asked the mechanic as they moved back, making room for the bucket brigade. "I thought those were some sort of lamps."

The man shrugged, bashful in the face of direct questioning. "Airship mechanic. A hangar this size, extinguishers are always to hand. I know a bit about steam cars as well. I suppose Mr. Hardison thought I'd be of use."

"And so you were," Matthew said, extending his hand. "Tell me your name."

"Roger Brearley, sir."

"Mr. Brearley, I'm going to sing your praises to Mr. Hardison. Without your quick thinking I believe this would've been a disaster."

Brearley grinned and lifted his arm, pointing to his sleeve which—like everything else in the hangar—was drenched with evilly pungent slime. "An even bigger disaster, you mean, sir."

Matthew frowned down at his own clothing, then surveyed the vast room where order was slowly beginning to win out over the chaos. With the immediate threat of fire averted, the sharp edge of panic dulled, but the dawning dismay at the magnitude of the damage was equally apparent. The smell would have been unimaginable . . . if he'd only been attempting to imagine it. He didn't see how things could possibly be set to rights in time for the scheduled start of the race in the morning.

"Bloody hell."

FIVE

ONE ENGLISH COMPETITOR, one French entrant and the sole driver from China were sitting on the sidelines at the race start, and Eliza was fervently thankful she was not among them. Their steam cars were irredeemably soiled, as they had all featured jaunty soft tops that happened to be open at the time of the sabotage. One Dominion driver had also been affected, but his sponsor had come through with a replacement vehicle just in time for the starting lineup. The rest of the steam cars had been cleaned up, though most of them had suffered cosmetic damage. The lineup was not nearly as bright and colorful as it should have been.

That it had been sabotage was clear. The liquefied manure solution was obviously calculated to do the most damage possible, even if the fire were thwarted. No culprit had been found, however, and the race's sponsors had agreed that the incident should not derail the event.

"You can say it, you know," Eliza said to Matthew as they waited with the other drivers to walk out to the starting line. The bank building off Tryon Square, where the race was set to start, was crowded with sponsors and luminaries. As cultured as the throng was, Eliza still had to raise her voice to be heard over the babble. Matthew leaned closer to listen and she caught a whiff of his shaving lotion, an unexpectedly warm and spicy note from a man she thought of as neither of those things. She scolded herself for liking the way he smelled.

"I can say what?" he half-shouted.

"That the sabotage means it's all too dangerous for a little thing like me."

He pulled back and shrugged. "It was already too dangerous for a little thing like you."

"I'm just surprised the incident didn't prompt further lectures." In truth, Eliza had almost looked forward to the challenge of arguing with Matthew about her continued right and qualifications to participate in the rally. Over the weeks they'd spent training in tandem at Hardison House, she'd grown accustomed to the regular infusion of righteous indignation those conversations afforded her. His failure to renew the battle in the face of these new circumstances had been vaguely disappointing.

Although she hadn't been there for the horrific spraying of flammable cow dung, Eliza had seen—and smelled—the aftermath, and assisted in the cleanup effort. She couldn't fail to notice that most of the other drivers eyed her and Matthew with a chilly suspicion, as their two vehicles had escaped relatively unscathed. Thanks largely to Matthew's efforts, Eliza's steam car gleamed as brightly as ever this morning, a rosy beacon against the field of scoured and hastily rewaxed competitors. Thanks to the color choice, the press had already labeled her "The Scarlet Woman," much to her mother's mortification. She'd received a number of telegrams from home, upon her arrival at the hotel, elaborating on that theme. Eliza's protests that the color was amaranth, not remotely scarlet, had thus far fallen on deaf ears. The reporters continued to use the epithet, and her mother continued to scold her from across the state and beg her to reconsider participating in her cousin's "mad scheme." At least the latter concern would become moot the moment the race began.

"It's not my job to lecture you now," Matthew said with a somewhat devious smile that Eliza hadn't seen before. "It's my job to win the race."

"It's your job to beat *me*, you mean. Fair enough."

"Do you think beating you would have any more effect than lecturing you? I suppose I could put you over my knee, in that case. It's unorthodox, but I'm certainly willing to give it a go if you are."

She started to respond, then gasped as his words and the attendant imagery registered. Matthew coughed into his gloved fist and looked away, but not before she saw the sparkle in his eye.

"You're strangely cheerful this morning."

"I'm excited," he demurred.

"I'm excited too. But aren't you worried about the saboteur?"

"Of course. Not as worried as I'll be if he starts targeting drivers instead of vehicles, however. There's always the chance the sabotage was meant to end with the . . . fertilizer. That was certainly bad enough to knock several cars out of the running. The fire might have been an unfortunate coincidence."

"You don't believe that."

He opened his mouth to reply and was cut off by the clanging bell that alerted the crowd it was time to meet the drivers. As the peals died down, Matthew turned toward Eliza and stepped closer, clasping her upper arms. "It's true, I don't believe that. I told myself I wouldn't say this again, but as it's my last opportunity, *please* don't do this. It's not worth the risk, Eliza."

She should have shrugged his hands off, or even slapped them away, but despite her anger she took comfort in the almost-embrace. Because she was anxious, doubly so since the sabotage, Pence's words may have grated but his hands were gentle and warm. His eyes were cool, however, and almost glittering. Flecks of pale green and icy blue muddled the crystalline gray and seemed to catch the light. Why had she never noticed before how odd Pence's eyes were? Not that it mattered in the slightest, she reminded herself firmly.

"Why is it not worth the risk for me, but worth it for you, Matthew?"

"Because you're—"

"Don't." Eliza lifted her chin, daring him to continue. He met her gaze with a stormy frown. "Think, really *think* about what you were going to say just then, Matthew. Think how if the roles were reversed, you would find it ridiculous, offensively ludicrous. And know that you sound every bit as ridiculous and offensive to me. I don't need your condescension. I'm not your little sister."

His frown deepened, along with his voice. "You have no idea how aware I am that you are not my sister, Eliza. I'm perfectly aware that you're—"

"Drivers to the start," a voice boomed over the loudspeakers outside, and Eliza yanked herself out of Matthew's grip. She marched out of the building before he could recover his poise.

"A WOMAN," MATTHEW finished as he watched Eliza walk out onto the red carpet that bisected the crowded square.

It was what he would have said, but not what he meant. Had he thought about it, *really* thought, as she'd exhorted him to? Of course he had, but he couldn't see any way around it. He wanted Eliza out of the race to protect her, not because she was a woman but because she was *the* woman.

Matthew had always considered himself an enlightened sort of fellow, supporting universal suffrage, women's property rights, equality in general. In theory, he believed in all those things. In practice, he now realized he believed them mostly with respect to theoretical women. Servants and millworkers and machinists, typists and cryptologists and doctors. Women other than Eliza, for whom he instead felt a protective urge so ferocious it alarmed him. His other urges toward her were at least an expected part of his physiology. He wanted to keep her safe so he could have her all to himself and do wicked things to her.

He hadn't recognized it four years ago, that instant and inappropriate reaction. He'd been too young and still too likely to react physically in the presence of any reasonably attractive female; all his other irrational responses to Eliza seemed only to stem from that root source. Those responses had bothered him, made him inclined to argue and fret, because he was normally easygoing, steady and reliable, and liked being so; he didn't know what to do with all those unpredictable sensations and the prickles of guilt that so often accompanied them.

She'd also been barely nineteen, his employer's cousin, a shrill harpy obviously headed for a future as a domineering virago and determined to drive him mad with her insistence on playing with dangerous equipment every time his back was turned. Wholly out of the running for anything resembling romantic consideration. And yet . . . Eliza was a shrew, but a lissome one, and debating her got his blood roiling. So of course his heart pounded whenever she hove into view.

Or so he'd reasoned back then. Now, with the perspective of a few more years and a bit more experience, he knew enough to be concerned that he still jumped like a green schoolboy when he caught a whiff of her perfume or spotted her across a room. He was mooning over the girl, and it just wouldn't do. Wouldn't do at all. She was not a woman over whom he could allow himself to moon.

"Best of luck, Mr. Pence," a smooth voice intoned at his shoulder as he finally made his way through the door.

Squinting against the sudden sunlight, Matthew turned and caught a glare of gold on a lapel, a hazy impression of dark hair beneath a tall hat and a face that was too long and too smug to sit comfortably on anyone.

"Lord Orm," Matthew replied with a nod, never slowing his pace. The prickling sensation of wrongness struck him again, and he recalled the unease he'd felt the previous day at spotting Orm with one of the drivers. That driver was still in the race—his sponsor had been the one to come up with a last-minute replacement—but Orm still felt like an ill portent there behind Matthew, watching him as he approached his car to take his post position. Matthew resisted the urge to turn and see if the man really was following him with his gaze.

The red carpet ended abruptly at the line of cars, two abreast, all stoked up and pointed west. Mechanics swarmed each vehicle, bristling with spanners and polishing cloths, a few with metallurgic lenses leaning close to boiler casings to assure themselves their precious steamers showed no signs of metal fatigue from previous adventures.

The morning was crisp, a late spring chill nipping at Matthew's face. But the cloud of heat from the double row of boilers surrounded him like a thick fog when he stepped between the cars and walked up the line. He passed Barnabas Smith-Grenville on the way and noted he looked slightly green around the gills. Nerves, probably. His shocking blue car had held up well to the previous night's vigorous scrubbing. Waving, Matthew continued past his friend's vehicle and toward his own. He had drawn a good position, third back on the right. He would be able to study the cars ahead to spot any adverse road conditions early, but still be ahead of the bulk of the field.

And ahead of Eliza Hardison's car by two ranks. At least he wouldn't be distracted by the sight of her in front of him.

This time he looked behind him to see if he was being watched, and he wasn't disappointed. Eliza's eyes met his for a long moment over the intervening vehicles before she gave him a solemn nod and turned away to consult with one of her mechanics—Brearley, the one who'd been so instrumental in stopping yesterday's fire. Eliza was in good hands, then, but he thought she looked pale. Tense. Not quite as bad as Barnabas. Matthew knew he probably looked the same.

And he probably hadn't helped Eliza's mood any, he realized, with his stubborn insistence on lecturing her. He'd known she was determined. He'd known she had the right, as any woman past the age of majority did these days, to choose her own course of action.

His task now wasn't to protect her, except in the sense that Dexter had charged him, to support her if she needed it and keep away any unwanted male attention. No, it was simply to defeat her. In order to prove himself in this brave new world of industry, to win enough capital to start his own enterprise and begin building his own future, he *must* defeat her. He must defeat them all, and Eliza was no exception.

HER HANDS COULDN'T tremble if she gripped the steering wheel hard enough. Eliza wound her fingers around the leather and hung on, forcing herself to breathe slowly. She hadn't laced very tightly that morning, knowing she'd be sitting all day, but the corset still prevented her from breathing as deeply as she had the urge to. It couldn't be helped; she needed the corset in order to wear the crisp white military-cut driving suit with the burgundy trim, the only possible choice for this morning's appearance. She would simply have to put up with the consequences of her fashion decision.

"No time to be dizzy," she admonished herself.

"Sorry, miss?" the mechanic piped up. Eliza had forgotten the window was open.

"Nothing, Mr. Brearley. Just starting-line jitters. Almost

time for you all to step back now, the countdown will begin any moment."

Her voice, at least, was strong. The experience of delivering lectures in the face of scorn had trained her not to let her nerves affect her speech.

"Copy of the ready checklist in the side pocket of yon balloon case, Miss Hardison."

"Yes, I remember." She gave the usually steady Yorkshireman a smile. "You sound more nervous than I do, Brearley. Things will go fine. The steam car is sound, and you know the airship is in tip-top shape."

The loudspeaker boomed, and Brearley took a step away from the steamer's door. "Aye, but I won't be there to assure myself of that. You'll keep the cases locked and the keys on your person until the air leg, miss?"

"As I've promised both you and Lord Hardison more than once. Wish me luck, sir."

"Luck, miss!"

The countdown had started, sixty seconds until the starter pistol would fire and the rally would begin. Mechanics scattered, clearing the raceway, and leaving the drivers alone with their thoughts as they waited out the final minute.

Eliza's thoughts ranged wildly, though she tried to keep them firmly on the day's driving route.

Pence meant well, for all he was a beast about it. He genuinely feared for her delicate self and spoke accordingly, seeming to forget that he hadn't any business doing so. Usually Eliza was able to dismiss him, but this morning her bravado was pure flummery. Outside she might be brash, but inside was all butterflies the size of bats, threatening the equilibrium of her stomach and mind. She imagined the fluttering as actual bats and stifled a hysterical snort at the thought. Her hands felt melded to the wheel, knuckles white and aching.

Thirty seconds to go. Eliza watched the hands on the enormous clock face that dominated the temporary arch through which the racers would drive. The arch and clock would remain for the rally's duration, with a daily posting of the leaders and their times, for the benefit of those New Yorkers who were following the news. The posting marquee was empty still, and Eliza made herself envision her own name there, in letters large enough to see from a block away.

Ten seconds. The crowd began to shout out the count-down, and Eliza readied her hand on the gear knob, her foot on the clutch. The car was warm, and it wouldn't do to set off with an embarrassing lurch. Slow and steady would win the race.

Five, four . . . well, perhaps not all *that* slow. But steady, at any rate.

Then the starting pistol, a jolt of adrenaline and the anti-climax of having to wait and listen to the crowd's wild roar as all the cars in front of her began to move. When she finally edged into motion, smooth as glass, she let herself exhale in relief. Her grip on the steering wheel loosened, her shoulders relaxed. The mechanics of driving were sec-ond nature to her, and she lost herself almost immediately in the delight of handling the finely made steam car and the joy of the beautifully clear road beneath her wheels.

Manhattan proper had come to a halt for the rally's start, and traffic was cleared from Tryon Square all the way across the Murray Bridge. Cheering crowds lined the streets, and policemen on horses and swift velocimobiles accompanied the racers to ensure security. Once over the bridge's impres-sive span, the crowd thinned and the racers sped forward, soon leaving the city and the police escort far behind.

PERFECT DAY FOR it.

That was Eliza's main thought entering the fourth hour of her drive. She couldn't have asked for better driving con-ditions. The sky was a clear, perfect, spring blue, with a few fluffy white clouds to the west for added interest. A recent spate of rainstorms had brightened the fresh green of the hedgerows and fields she drove past, but the road itself was dry and smooth. She knew not to take that for granted. The rally committee had paid for road repairs to the suggested route thoroughfares prior to the race, but only as far as St. Louis at the western edge of the Northern Dominion.

Once they crossed into the Victoria Dominion, things would likely turn rockier, literally. The end of broad, well-maintained roads, the end of the steamrails. The beginning of catch-as-catch-can byways, wagon tracks and the jealously guarded domains of the petty lords who essentially ruled the continent's interior. Eliza had heard that large swathes of Victoria and Louisiana might as well be medieval England, in terms of economics and the local methods of governance. She thought it sounded more like ancient Greece, and in her heart of hearts she'd feared Matthew Pence's dire predictions for her safety would come true.

But for now, sailing down the smooth stretch of road leading into Harrisburg, Pennsylvania, Eliza felt only optimism. The weather, the road, the fact that her car hadn't been sullied by steer manure—good omens, all. There were a few race fans along the streets of the charming city, but nothing like she'd seen leaving New York. If anything, the lack of excitement was anticlimactic, though Eliza was embarrassed to think such a thing when she was only a few hours into what was meant to be a great adventure. The city itself looked the opposite of adventure, its tidy streets and domed capitol building the very picture of order and respectability. It seemed unpopulated, as well. The racers were shunted through the center of town but their route had been cordoned off, and the mounted police escort made sure no spectators drew close enough to hinder their progress.

The crowds began again at the bridge over the Susquehanna, and Eliza heard the cheers as she geared down to join a short line of competitors creeping over the wide river while attempting to avoid hitting any careless pedestrians.

The Watchmaker's absurd spider-steamer was easy to spot, high above all the banners and placards. Eliza craned her neck and caught a glimpse of vivid green—Cantlebury's car was anything but subtle—and Barnabas Smith-Grenville's absurdly bullet-shaped royal blue vehicle. A black car she couldn't place was directly in front of her. Behind her, the crowd had closed in, suggesting no other cars were close at her heels.

No sign of gunmetal gray. Had Pence surged ahead or fallen behind along the way to this first stop, at the old Harrisburg Academy grounds? Not that it should matter, as Eliza was competing against the entire field of opponents, not Matthew alone. It was only a midday pause in the race, more a press opportunity than anything else, and of course all that really mattered was making it to Pittsburgh before midnight. But one of the race organizers was an alumnus of the Academy and had managed to leverage the opportunity for publicity to the school's benefit. The cars would gather on a field near the campus, there was to be a speech by the mayor and box lunches would be provided for the competitors to take along with them. It seemed a shame for Matthew to miss out, that was all.

Her boiler rattled, complaining about the stop-and-start pace along the bridge. Eliza frowned at the water and heat gauges, willing them to remain within safe parameters. She risked a quick tug at the pressure release handle, and chuckled as the crowd jumped at the sudden, sharp whistle blast.

Naïve, perhaps, but at first she blamed the startling whistle for the ugly expressions a few of the crowd members turned toward her. There were three of them glaring at her, all women about her mother's age, dark-clad and grim-faced. One of them looked her in the eye, giving a sort of enraged smirk as she called to the other two, who followed her lead while still keeping pace with the slowly moving mob. Manic fervor in their eyes, they neared the steam car, waving their placards and shouting something Eliza couldn't hear over the general hubbub.

Nonplussed, Eliza looked frantically ahead of her, focusing on the car she was trailing and noting with relief that they were almost across the bridge and the crowd had cleared from the main road ahead. As soon as she was off the bridge, she could speed up and shake the angry women off.

Mere feet before Eliza's car crossed onto the road proper, one of the women in black slammed a red-printed placard against her side window. Eliza shrieked, to her mortification, and accelerated sharply, almost slamming into the black car before she caught herself and braked. The heavy brown bulk of a police horse brushed by, the animal nickering as it literally jostled the car, and for a moment she had a perfect view of the mounted officer's polished black boot and blue-clad pants leg. A wide satin stripe ran down the outside of his leg. The boot left a squeak of black against the window.

And then he was gone, pushing her assailant along with him, and Eliza was on the relatively open road again.

Through her hind mirror, she saw two of the women rushing to the third's aid, and she saw the signs they were waving. It took her brain a moment to register the lettering, reading it backward and in quick glances as she was. That delay didn't lessen the impact one bit.

RALLY OF VICE, screamed one of the signs. The other, as best she could see as it faded from view behind her, proclaimed the drivers to be the DEVIL'S SPAWN IN DEVIL-STEAMERS.

The third placard seemed to have been broken in the fray, but Eliza already knew what it said. The sight of it was burned into her memory from that terrifying few seconds of it slapped against her window.

SCARLET DISGRACE TO WOMANKIND!

Harrisburg seemed much less charming than it had before she crossed the bridge.

Six

POLITE SMILES WERE the order of the day at the Harrisburg Academy grounds. A bunting-draped pavilion and bandstand had been set up, bright flags snapped in the breeze and the mayor was gladhanding the crowd with all the easy expertise of a veteran politician. Matthew conversed graciously with a group of beaming Ladies' Auxiliary members as he watched the mayor tickle another baby, but his real attention was on the gravel drive leading to the field on which the festivities were being held.

At last a flash of red eased his anxiety. There was no mistaking Eliza's steam car, coasting around the field behind a pack of other vehicles that included Smith-Grenville's flashy blue torpedo. Handlers jogged out to meet the racers, directing the cars to their various cordoned-off billets around the central green and the pavilion. Eliza pulled in between Barnabas's car and Cantlebury's green monster, three bright splashes of color among the field of mostly white, gray and black steamers. Beyond them, the Watchmaker's vehicle rattled to a hissing, screeching halt. The

Watchmaker pulled levers furiously, a final flurry of movement before the craft settled to the ground with a puff. A chuckle ran through the crowd at the display; it looked for all the world as if the strange steamer was sighing in relief at the chance to rest.

"And is your family from New York as well, Mr. Pence?" asked one of the ladies. Matthew turned back to them with a guilty conscience. He saw that a few daughters who looked of marriageable age had joined the group while his attention was elsewhere. One was clearly uninterested in the whole affair. The other, though pretty enough, looked a trifle manic. She seemed torn between simpering in Matthew's direction and glaring toward the latest group of racers to arrive.

The sun twinkled off a tiny pin in the girl's collar, and when the glare ended Matthew could see it was a delicate four-petaled flower, crafted in gold. Some of the older women were wearing them too. All the flower-wearers wore unpleasant expressions.

"Yes, they are. Well, they're divided between New York and Sussex, for the most part."

The flowers were ominous, but Matthew couldn't quite think why. As he mulled it over, attempting to back away from the effusive guild ladies, a group of mounted policemen cantered onto the green and pulled up a short distance from the cars. One of them dismounted on the fly and strode briskly to Eliza's car, handing her out and bending close to speak with her.

"*The* New York Pences?"

"Ah, well. Yes, I suppose so. If you'll excuse me, ladies, I must speak with one of the other drivers. An urgent question regarding a . . . a badly embractured fandangulator. I'm sure you understand."

"But don't go without your box lunch!" One of the matrons scooted forward, pressing a white, twine-secured box into Matthew's hands.

"Thank you, you're too kind. Good afternoon, madam.

Ladies." He tipped his hat and spun on his heel, fast-walking across the field to the lineup of the three brightest cars in the race.

Before he reached Eliza, however, Matthew's attention was diverted. Barnabas Smith-Grenville greeted him with the same glum, gray visage he'd worn earlier in the day. His voice matched his face as he rasped out, "Good afternoon, Pence."

"You sound ghastly."

"Bless you for a saint, Matthew, you always say the kindest things."

"No, really, you look ready for the doctor. They're coming to shove a boxed luncheon at you, shall I warn them all away?"

"They?" Barnabas looked past Matthew, bleary-eyed, and squinted at a fast-approaching gaggle of women.

"Ladies' Auxiliary or similar. With eligible daughters in tow."

"Daughters? Really?" Barnabas made a feeble attempt at straightening his sweat-soaked collar.

"You're not up to it. You hardly look fit to drive, man."

"He's quite right, Lord Smith-Grenville," Eliza agreed, appearing from the other side of Barnabas's car. "We could ask one of the ladies to help find a doctor for you."

"I'm perfectly well, thank you, Miss Hardison. Pence, what's in that box? Anything good?"

"Haven't opened it yet." Nor did he intend to in front of Barnabas, who looked as though the mere sight of food might trigger appalling consequences. "How are you faring, Miss Hardison?"

She looked lovely, of course, but rather shaken. Perhaps from the sight of Smith-Grenville, who truly did look like looming death. Eliza held herself stiffly, as though she had a pain.

"You just saw me four hours ago," she pointed out. "I'm

much the same now as I was then. Oh, I think it's our turn to be celebrities, look."

Along with the steadfast lunchbox ladies, the mayor of Harrisburg was bearing down on them. He was clearly recognizable as the mayor, labeled as such by means of a broad red and white satin sash across his substantial chest that read MAYOR.

"Welcome to Harrisburg. Welcome! Douglas Micklefield, mayor." He reached Matthew first, hand extended, and commenced a round of brisk hand-shaking while the trio of drivers introduced themselves. "We're proud to be your first stop. Anything we can do for you, anything at all, you have but to ask."

Eliza beat Matthew to it. "Sir, I believe our friend may require a doctor. He seems to have taken ill."

Indeed, even as she spoke, Barnabas swayed at an alarming pitch, reaching behind himself to his car for support. He'd gone paler still, except for his cheeks and forehead, which bore an ominous mottled flush.

"I don't need a doctor," he tried to insist. The force of his words was diminished by the fact that he said them while sliding down the car door.

"Barnabas!"

"Lord Smith-Grenville!"

"Doctor Adams!" one of the ladies called into the crowd. "Has anyone seen Doctor Adams?"

When Matthew stepped to Barnabas's side to keep him standing, he felt the heat radiating from his friend's body. He eased him to the ground instead, letting gravity finish its work, and limited himself to bracing Barnabas so he didn't topple over completely. The crowd, obviously sensing an event, began to murmur and gather in around the line of cars.

"You have a fever, idiot. You knew you were ill this morning, didn't you? You looked terrible then, but I thought it was just nerves. Why didn't you tell somebody?"

"Doesn't matter. I'll be fine. I have to find Phineas."

"Not with a fever, you don't."

"'Snot a fever," Barnabas insisted, but his words were beginning to slur and his eyes were glassy, unseeing. "Phineas . . ."

"I'll find him for you," Matthew reassured him.

"And I'll help," Eliza said.

He hadn't even noticed her joining them on the ground, she'd been so uncharacteristically quiet and reserved. She knelt opposite Matthew, and his concern was mirrored in her dark gray eyes.

Barnabas looked up at them, beseeching. "You have to find him. My baby brother . . . he took my hobbyhorse, you know, and I want it back. He never did take care of his things. Those flowers are beautiful, absolutely lovely. And they look so innocent. They use a special knife to cut the pods, did you know? Looks like cat claws, like . . ." He hooked two fingers, making a weak clawing gesture, then letting his arm drop into his lap.

"Coming through!" A voice rang clear over the babbling crowd. "Doctor coming through. Here you, step aside, make way."

The mayor greeted the doctor with a solemn handshake, then pointed out Barnabas slumped on the ground against his steam car. The doctor, a slim, bearded, elderly gentleman, wasted no time in joining his patient and beginning his examination.

"Fever, elevated pulse," he muttered as he worked. "Lymph nodes swollen. How long has he been like this?" He directed his question at Matthew but never stopped moving, deploying his stethoscope and exhorting a barely responsive Barnabas to breathe in.

"He didn't look well this morning. Seemed fine last night, though. At least, he didn't complain of not feeling well. We were all off our feed, I think, from nerves."

"I wasn't," Eliza volunteered. "I ate like no lady should.

But Mr. Pence is right about Lord Smith-Grenville, he barely touched his food at the pre-rally dinner."

The doctor spared her a glance, then did a double take, looking first at Eliza, then at her car and back again. "Lord, I hope you manage to avoid my wife, young lady. Now . . . his lungs sound clear. The fever is high, we need to bring that down immediately, but he seems fit enough to recover quickly if he receives the proper treatment. Where's Micklefield?"

The mayor harrumphed and took a small step closer, clearly wanting to stay clear of possible contagion.

"Micklefield, send a boy to fetch Horace and the ambulance. We'll need to move this young man to the hospital. Has he any family who ought to be notified? Or the rally authorities, perhaps?"

Arrangements were made, runners were sent, a whirl of activity that left Eliza and Matthew standing in the calm center next to Barnabas's car.

"You'll want something to eat," Matthew pointed out, spotting Eliza's lack of a boxed lunch. All the other drivers seemed to have received theirs. "They must have forgotten, in the excitement. Let me just—"

"I can ask for my own luncheon, thank you. Stay with Barnabas."

Eliza didn't need to go far. Several yards away, the lunch ladies still clumped near Mayor Micklefield, tutting and fretting in Barnabas's direction. As Eliza approached, most of them went silent, and their faces turned sour and disapproving. Matthew couldn't make out the conversation over the crowd, nor see Eliza's reactions, but none of it looked good.

The apparent leader of the Ladies' Auxiliary held a stack of three boxed lunches in her plump arms, but made no move to offer one. A few of the other ladies turned slowly and deliberately away from Eliza, their noses lifted. Eliza's shoulders squared, stiffened as if for battle. Matthew wanted to rush to her assistance, but was stuck holding Barnabas's head off the ground. All he could do was watch, heart in his throat.

After a brief exchange with the ladies, the mayor turned toward the one with the stacked boxes, his sharp tone carrying above the hubbub even if his words did not.

Matthew spotted the lapel pin glinting in the sun as the woman grudgingly handed Eliza a box, extending it as far from her body as possible, as though Eliza might bite or contaminate her. It was as dismissive as she could be without joining her companions in the cut direct.

Eliza took the box and inclined her head toward the woman, a polite nod the so-called lady hardly deserved, then turned to accept the mayor's outstretched hand. He sketched a quick bow, and she dropped a brief but elegant curtsy. Matthew could see her profile, the fierce spot of color on her cheek that gave the lie to the pretty smile she bestowed upon the town's leader. But she didn't rush, didn't lose her poise for even a moment. She bobbed her head toward the women again in farewell, then turned and made her regal way back toward the cars, her face as serene as if she were walking in an empty garden.

Matthew was strongly tempted to applaud. God only knew what had gotten into the women of Harrisburg, but Eliza had handled herself with an aplomb he never would have credited her with possessing. Not merely coping with things, she'd been something like magnificent.

ELIZA COMPLIMENTED HERSELF. Fulsomely, fervently, earnestly. Never had she cheered herself on so well, because never had she deserved it so well as when she took the words and actions of the Harrisburg Ladies' Auxiliary with a gracious smile and a thank-you for the box luncheon they had only provided her under duress.

Duress and shaming. She had rather enjoyed the shaming,

which the mayor had delivered in her defense. He did so only after she had an earful of "scarlet woman," "no smoke without fire," and "ought to be run out of the town on a rail like the harlot you are." Mayor Micklefield had put them in their place by countering with "glass houses" and "let he who is without sin" and something else that might have been from Marcus Aurelius. Then he had demanded the woman in charge hand over a lunch, and Eliza had managed not to burst into tears or cast up her breakfast on the lot of them.

Shock had helped. She still couldn't quite believe what she was hearing or seeing, despite the forceful lesson of the placard. That these apparently well-bred ladies would utter such words, would administer the cut to a gently born young woman who was quite possibly their social superior . . . Eliza knew what was written in the newspapers, had even heard some unpleasant shouts from the crowds, but facing it head-on was a different thing entirely. A wretched, terrifying thing. She could still feel the shame on her cheeks, and it infuriated her to have blushed at all because she had no reason to be ashamed. Her conduct, while unconventional, was irreproachable. What's more, she was paving the way for their own daughters to have more freedom, greater opportunities. And her car wasn't remotely scarlet. *Amaranth.*

They ought to be *thanking* her. Not refusing her a box of cold chicken and soggy bread.

When she returned to Matthew, Barnabas was still lying with his head on Matthew's lap, but he seemed to have regained some lucidity. He clutched Matthew's wrist and spoke to him in the gravest tones his hoarse voice would allow.

"I know you can't find him. Gone west, they never come back. But promise me, Matthew."

"I promise."

"Promise me you'll look."

"Everywhere I go, Barnabas," he reassured his friend,

clasping his arm. "If he's there to be found, I'll find him. At least news of him."

Eliza knew Lord Smith-Grenville was unlikely to die. He was young and strong, and would be given all the care he needed. His fever made him overwrought, though, and the delirium surely didn't help calm him. He seemed to think he was done for. Then she realized that, as least as far as the race and his current search for his brother were concerned, he *was* done for. She sent a grateful glance to Matthew, for his kind words to the sick man. Whether or not he found Phineas Smith-Grenville, he was at least attempting to ease his friend's concerns.

Pence looked up and met her gaze, catching Eliza off guard. His odd green gray eyes looked eldritch and wonderful in the sunlight, like uncut gemstones in some fairy palace. His brow was furrowed but he spared her a quick smile, and Eliza felt the flush deepen on her cheeks. Not shame this time.

A clanging bell and raised voices broke the spell. "Make way! Clear a path! Pardon, miss!"

She rushed to one side to avoid the men running in advance of the ambulance, an old-fashioned horse-drawn conveyance whose team of two were sweating already. Clearly they had wasted no time in getting to the fairground.

It seemed a matter of seconds for the attendants to scoop Barnabas onto a stretcher and load him into the vehicle. Then, with more clanging and rattling and shouts, the ambulance disappeared from the once-festive field and took any lingering air of celebration with it.

"Oh, dear!" One of the lunchbox ladies uttered into the ensuing horrible silence. "But now who will advise Mr. Pence about his poor fandangulator?"

No one had an answer for her.

Fifteen competitors had entered the field of the Harrisburg Academy. Fourteen would proceed out of it. That first day was supposed to be an easy drive, but Eliza couldn't help noticing that nearly a quarter of the racers were already out of the running before they'd even reached their first official checkpoint at Pittsburgh.

"Four gone already, out of eighteen. At this rate," she whispered to Matthew as Barnabas was driven away, "there won't be anyone left for the airship legs."

"I'm trying not to count those first three drivers." He slid the brushed metal flower from his pocket, gave it a deft flick and turned it into a knife to cut the string from his lunchbox. Eliza decided she wanted one of the gadgets for herself. "They never started, after all. Think of it as just one of fifteen gone. It doesn't seem nearly as bad then, even if it is poor Smith-Grenville."

"But why wouldn't you count them? It was sabotage aimed at the racers, surely the intent was to eliminate some of the competitors."

He examined the contents of the box, poking at a piece of fruit and lifting the paper from a cut of cold meat. At least the bread was also wrapped and didn't appear as soggy as Eliza had feared. "I don't count them because it doesn't seem nearly as bad then. I wonder if these boxes are all the same. Did you get an apricot as well?"

The racers were called to their cars, ending the conversation. As Eliza took to the long, curving drive that led on and off the field, she saw a tractor chugging over to Barnabas's car, a hitch being attached so they could haul it away.

"One gone, fourteen left," she whispered, finding Matthew was right. It didn't seem as bad when she thought of it that way. She told herself it was merely less competition to worry about.

And to her delight, she discovered her box lunch did not contain an apricot at all, but strawberries.

Seven

THE DRIVE TO Pittsburgh was more of the same bucolic loveliness, the odd distant fortress across fields interspersed with charming roadside villages and towns. The city itself welcomed them with more bunting, more speeches, in the floodlit central square. Armed guards were set to watch the vehicles while the competitors dined and slept in the best hotel, after being fêted by the cream of Pittsburgh society.

Nobody else took ill. No glaring women in odd lapel pins ruined the festive mood. The drivers rested, the cars were protected and all of them set off safely the next morning bound for the Northern Dominion and Meridian City. But Matthew was still edgy, unsettled. The whole enterprise felt wrong with Smith-Grenville gone, and even Eliza appeared oddly subdued.

As usual, though, driving relaxed him. Matthew relished the speed and freedom, and the stretch of unfamiliar road was a tonic. His steam car performed as flawlessly as it had in trials, efficient and enduring. It eased his mind further to see which vehicles and drivers were able to match his pace.

Van der Grouten's silver shark of a car, of course. He and Matthew swapped places for miles—the German always stony-faced when he swept ahead, Matthew grinning and waving cheekily when it was his turn.

Moreau, Whitcombe and Cantlebury formed the next wave, along with Miss Lavinia Speck, another British competitor. One of those four was ever within sight when Matthew looked back. Lazaris, the lone Greek competitor, and two of the other Dominion drivers made occasional appearances throughout the day.

But ahead, except when Van der Grouten pulled forward, the view was always the same. Amaranth red, gleaming in the sun. Matthew was tempted to give Dexter Hardison's engineering all the credit, and it was true Eliza's steamer was one of the best-built vehicles he'd ever had the pleasure to see. But it took skill, nerve and stamina to drive as hard as Eliza did to keep the lead, not to mention determination.

The weather was clear, the roads were still solid and Matthew arrived in Meridian, in the heart of the Northern Dominion, shortly before dusk. He found the city much like Pittsburgh—a somewhat larger version of Harrisburg, but all of them hamlets compared to New York City. A bit of a letdown.

Decent food at the hotel, though, he had to admit. And the press had been stopped outside the lobby for the drivers' privacy.

"The wine is more than acceptable too," Eliza pointed out to Matthew at dinner that evening. Then she looked to her right again, where one of the back-of-the-pack Dominion drivers was busy monopolizing her attention. Beau Parnell, a self-professed cowboy from the wilds of Victoria, did not let his lackluster driving impede his love for racing or his impression of himself as a master of the steam car. He clearly also fancied himself a playboy.

"But see, when you slide that coupling bracket onto that hose," he smarmed at Eliza, "that lard keeps the whole operation smooth and easy. Everything lasts longer too. You don't want that rubber to get all dry and neglected-like."

Matthew nearly snapped the stem off his wineglass watching the gestures with which Parnell illustrated his words. Did Eliza have any idea how inappropriate the man was being? She couldn't. Could she? Surely not.

Eliza sipped her wine and hummed with appreciation before responding. "Why, Mr. Parnell, what a . . . passion you seem to have for mechanical equipment." Then she turned her attention across the table to respond to a question from Lazaris, leaving Parnell to guess whether she'd understood him or not.

For Matthew, the question was not whether she'd understood Parnell, but whether she knew how precarious her position was. Too precarious to play the flirt or to lob double entendres back and forth with strangers who wanted to best her in the rally. Two stops ago, the good townswomen had somehow been primed to shun her. She was an innocent, still in need of guidance. In need of protection from men like Parnell, who might get the wrong impression entirely. Matthew frowned into his steak au poivre and pondered his best course of action. What would Dexter advise, were he here? Matthew could only guess, and hope his instincts were correct.

To the shock of the staff, the women stayed in the private dining room for port. Jeanette Barsteau, the French driver whose sleek forest green roadster still sported an old-fashioned tug-along for coal, even indulged in a cigar. When Parnell and his crony Johnston expressed their surprise—and obvious disapproval—she dismissed them with a toss of her fading ginger curls.

"I survived the war. I pioneered the Paris-Rouen rally. I have been driving since before some of you were born. I have earned the right to enjoy a cigar as well as any of you. Better than most," she added, with a pointed look at a few of the younger gentlemen. A smoke ring competition ensued, and the formidable lady seemed in line to win that too, with Eliza and several others cheering her on.

When Whitcombe and Cantlebury launched into a round of off-color jokes, however, Matthew decided enough was enough.

"Eliza, I think it's time you retired."

"Sorry, I didn't catch that? Oh, *bravissima*, Madame Barsteau!"

"*Eliza*. This isn't appropriate." He clasped her wrist, holding on firmly when she tried to shake him off. "It's time to take your leave."

The look she leveled at him could have boiled a frozen Alpine lake in midwinter. "I'm sure I can't have heard you correctly, Mr. Pence."

He glared right back, lowering his voice to a harsh whisper. "Parnell is looking down your dress. So is Madame Barsteau, by the way. And Cantlebury's next anecdote, if his repertoire hasn't changed since Oxford, involves nuns and a pony. No young woman should be in the room when he tells that one. Please come with me now."

"A pony? Really?" She made little attempt to lower her voice, and Cantlebury heard her clearly.

"Oh, I could tell you a tale about a pony," he volunteered to the general approbation of the group. "And some nuns!"

A cheer went up, and Matthew used the noise as cover for another fiercely whispered admonition. "Your cousin would skin me alive if he found out you'd been a party to this sort of thing and I did nothing to stop it."

Her expression turned sweet. Poisonously so. "Matthew, if you're not having any fun, I suggest you go elsewhere and find some. But you should know better than to try to spoil it for other people. I am staying." Distracting him with a condescending pat to his cheek, she twisted her other wrist sharply against his thumb to break his hold, then turned one slim shoulder to him, giving all her attention to the end of the table where Whitcombe was taking up Madame

Barsteau's challenge to another round of smoke rings, and Cantlebury was launching into the pony story with his usual gusto.

Worn out from the drive and his day's worth of worry over Barnabas, Matthew growled in frustration and rose abruptly from the table just as the waiter was passing by to pour another round of port. Physics and coincidence mated with spectacular results, and Eliza shrieked as half a bottle of port burbled down her cleavage.

"What in the—good *lord*, that's cold!" She stood, worsening matters. The port that had pooled in her lap began to soak all the way down her skirt, dripping to the floor.

"Begging your pardon! Begging your pardon, miss! I'll get—I'll fetch a—I'll—" The poor young waiter fled the room before finishing his utterance, leaving Matthew and the others to fling napkins Eliza's way to try to soak up the worst of it.

"Well, now I've completely lost my train of thought," quipped Cantlebury, who didn't seem terribly upset. He leaned forward, in fact, seeming to enjoy the unexpected entertainment.

"It was a lovely ensemble," Madame Barsteau lamented. "*Qu'elle dommage*."

"Perhaps it can be salvaged," Matthew offered dubiously. None of them had changed from their driving clothes before dining—it was the wild frontier, after all—and Eliza was still in a midnight blue skirt that could probably be cleaned. But she'd removed her smart bolero jacket to attend the meal, and the deep red wine had clearly ruined the delicate silk blouse she'd worn beneath.

Delicate, and now rather transparent. Her chemise and the lines of her corset were visible through the sodden fabric.

If Dexter would flay him for letting her hear the pony story, Matthew couldn't begin to imagine what the man would do for letting Eliza display her undergarments in public. "Let me help you to your room, Miss Hardison."

"Oh, you'd like that, wouldn't you?" She snapped over a sudden lull in the babble around the small room. Anyone whose attention hadn't already been riveted on the spectacle of the spilled port was now fully engaged in minding Miss Hardison's business. "That may have been an accident, but it was certainly a convenient one for you."

Matthew pulled his jacket off, mourning the potential loss of the fine linen even as he slung it around Eliza's shoulders. Settling it into place, he realized she was trembling. With rage, embarrassment or something else, he couldn't tell. It didn't matter.

"Please have a bath and a maid sent to Miss Hardison's room immediately," he instructed the flustered waiter, who had just dashed back into the dining room with the maître d' close behind. Matthew offered Eliza his arm and sighed with relief when she took it. They left to a chorus of apologies and "right away, sir" and so forth from the staff.

He'd stopped the pony story in its filthy tracks and gotten Eliza out of the room, all in one fell accidental swoop. As far as Matthew was concerned, the unfortunate incident with the port was a godsend. Eliza obviously held a different perspective on matters.

As soon as they'd entered the relative privacy of the elevator, Eliza flung Matthew's jacket off and slapped it into his chest. Her silent glare spoke volumes. The elderly lift attendant never so much as looked their way.

"Were you aware," Matthew said as calmly as he could manage, while trying not to look at the area in question, "that your shirt and chemise have been rendered somewhat transparent?"

She dropped her head to look, then gasped and snatched the jacket back, clutching it to her bosom. Her lips tightened, and he was treated to another few seconds of silence.

"Thank you," she finally blurted, as though it pained her. She shrugged the jacket back over her shoulders.

"You're most welcome." Matthew was in a different kind

of pain, himself. He hadn't been able to avoid looking entirely. He was only human after all, only a mortal man, scarcely able to control himself in the presence of the divine—which Eliza's figure was, even when not outlined in filmy port-soaked cloth. He'd caught a glimpse, just a fraction of a second of a peek, and seen that the cold had hardened her nipples. Now he felt light-headed and stupid with longing to look again.

Instead, he stared hard at the ancient lift attendant's bony shoulder blades under their dark red livery and tried not to let the color remind him of port.

ELIZA COULDN'T QUITE find the word to describe how she felt. *Mortified*, though apt enough, seemed somehow inadequate. *Frustrated*, certainly. *Aggravated* and *chagrined*. Highly displeased at the loss of her shirt and the permanent staining of what had been a favorite chemise and a nearly new set of stays.

She was also angry with Matthew, for being so condescending . . . and with herself, for her churlish behavior in the face of what had turned out to be his chivalry.

The elevator clattered to a halt at Eliza's floor, opening to an empty corridor with bland, tasteful wallpaper and thick carpeting. It was nice, but hardly what she was used to. And it might be their last night in anything like decent conditions before they reached Colorado Springs. Meridian City was relatively civilized, but certainly not New York. They would camp the next night, after they passed St. Louis and crossed into the vast Victoria Dominion. Assuming they made it farther, who knew what ramshackle amenities the frontier towns of Westport and Dodge City might offer? And between those two points was a two day span of driving, on wagon tracks if they were lucky, straight across the barely charted middle of Victoria.

It suddenly seemed so far, so alien and daunting. All that

distance, at breakneck speed, possibly risking her life and for what? To prove a point to herself, or to a man she didn't even like?

Fingering Matthew's jacket as they neared her door, Eliza realized that was no longer true. Not really. Her opinion of him . . . was in flux and had been for some time. She wasn't sure what she thought of him at the moment, but she liked the way his warmth conveyed itself via the jacket's lining. She found it rich that Matthew had bristled at Parnell looking down her dress when she'd caught him doing essentially the same thing several times himself. But if she was being honest with herself, she rather liked that too. It gave her an odd thrill to be observed that way, to know that at least in one respect he apparently no longer saw her as a child.

In other respects, unfortunately—

"Don't soak in that bath for too long. Remember we have an early start in the morning, and you need a good night's sleep."

She fingered her key, resisting the urge to poke him with it. "Thank you for the advice. I'll take it under the same consideration I take all your advice."

"Eliza . . . I'm sorry about your clothes being ruined and for any embarrassment you suffered, but I'm not sorry you had to leave before Cantlebury finished his story."

"The story's that bad, really?" She fitted the key in the lock, then put her back to the door and faced him. "What was the danger? That I would expire from girlish chagrin on the spot? Perhaps the shock of such lurid words would have caused my maiden ears to implode. Might not be so bad, of course. I could get those clever implants Charlotte has, become impervious to motion sickness and end up with better hearing than anyone. There is always a silver lining. And I would owe it all to Cantlebury and his wicked tale of the nuns and the donkey."

"Pony. It's always a pony."

Shrugging her shoulders reminded her that she still had

his jacket, but when she moved to take it off and return it Matthew pressed his fingertips to her shoulders to prevent her removing the garment the rest of the way. As a result it hung open, hiding nothing, framing the deep red stain. With his hands there, she couldn't pull it closed again either.

"Keep it. It's as doomed as your blouse and—and other things, anyway."

His words hardly registered. When he touched her, intervening fabric notwithstanding, all her attention had flown to those points of contact, and she'd lost her train of thought completely. Looking up to see if Matthew had noticed, she realized he was standing far too close for propriety. There in the corridor, where anyone might see.

She didn't care.

Matthew didn't meet her gaze. His stare was locked just below the level of his hands, as though the beam of his notice been caught in a snare there. Lips slightly parted, eyes dark and shadowed behind half-lowered lids. Eliza knew she was breathing too fast, that her heart was thumping at an alarming pace beneath her ruined shirt. Matthew seemed to have stopped breathing entirely.

She saw—felt—his every motion as though time had expanded, slowed down to let her capture each impression fully. His fingertips flexed once against her shoulders, then his palms flattened slowly against her, his thumbs grazing into the hollows over her clavicles. When he pressed gently, securing her against the door, Eliza's eyes fluttered shut and she forgot everything else in the world but his touch and the eager response of her nerve endings.

Even though she knew what came next, the brush of his lips over hers was startling. She gasped into his mouth, light-headed with want for things she couldn't articulate. Things she hadn't expected to want from Matthew Pence, but her body obviously felt otherwise. She wasn't inclined to argue with it at the moment.

His breath was hot, and tinted with port wine. When he pulled away, her mouth felt cold.

Opening her eyes, she watched as Matthew lifted his hands away, his expression as wide and astonished as a rabbit faced with the headlight of an oncoming steam carriage. For a moment he stood frozen, hands raised like a robbery victim, then he reached down beside her and turned the knob, opening the door before returning the key to her. He offered it dangling by two fingers, as though he were frightened to touch it, and dropped it into her palm when she reached to take it from him.

After a long moment they both drew breath at the same time, as if about to speak over one another. Eliza had not a coherent word in her head though, not one she could pin down long enough to utter. Matthew must have felt the same, because he remained as silent as she.

Finally, he nodded his head and strode away down the hall, never having said a word.

Eliza backed into her room and leaned against the door, closing herself in and pressing her cheek against the cool wood.

The first day of the rally was done, and what a long, strange day it had been.

EIGHT

IN THE MORNING, the dauntless ladies of the gold poppy lapel pins were assembled in force outside the Meridian Grand Hotel. Jostling for space with the press and the rest of the spectators, they wielded their elbows and bold placards with equal vigor.

"But who *are* they?" Eliza asked, sneaking peeks at the mob from the relative safety of the hotel dining room. She had pulled her chair out of place and was currently hidden from street view by one of the heavy red velvet curtains.

She was asking her table mates, the three other female drivers, but it was the waiter who answered as he poured Madame Barsteau a fresh cup of poisonously strong coffee.

"The ones with the signs and the flower pins, miss? They're the El Dorado Foundation Ladies' Society for Temperance and Moral Fortitude." The long name tripped off his tongue with the ease of long familiarity, but his expression suggested his acquaintance with the organization was not a pleasant one.

"I see."

"Do they really call themselves that?" asked Lavinia Speck, the one British woman in the race. She was a sweet-faced lady of thirty or so, but her shy smile concealed a sharp wit Eliza had already come to appreciate. Along with Madame Barsteau and Cecily Davis, the other Dominion woman, she had undertaken to debrief the newest member of their ranks on how best to handle the so-called "gentlemen" she would encounter if she pursued a racing career.

"They do, miss," the waiter confirmed. "And they mean every word of it."

"How unwieldy. There isn't even an acronym."

"The temperance part I understand," Eliza noted with a frown, "but what does the moral fortitude part refer to, exactly?"

Glancing about to make sure the maître d' didn't catch him lingering, the young man leaned closer, the gleam of gossip brightening his eyes. "It's about opium dens, miss. And human trafficking of a sort I can't discuss with ladies."

"I'm no lady," Madame Barsteau asserted. "You can tell me."

"If you insist, ma'am. The Foundation exists to fight the growing and nefarious presence of the illegal opium trade that's apparently sweeping east from the California coast. Dens of vice and iniquity, mysterious oriental rituals . . ." His eyes flicked to Eliza's face, and he bit his lip. "Begging your pardon, miss."

"Not necessary, I assure you. My ancestor didn't keep to the old ways." That was an understatement, but she hoped the boy would continue.

"The essence of it is that they think there's an opium house on every corner, and that one dose will render any poor fool an addict, doomed to fall into a spiral of sin. Eventually the opium eater will lose all touch with family, sell his body and soul for the next dose, and the next thing you know, he's gone west forever. Or, worse still, *she* has. They save their very finest moments of umbrage for ladies who demonstrate suspect morals, because we all know what happens when *they* fall into spirals of sin. It's not indentured service labor camps they wind up in, evidently."

"Good heavens." Miss Speck dabbed her mouth with her napkin, every inch the proper spinster, but Eliza could see the corner of her mouth and the smirk she was trying to hide. "What active imaginations those women must have."

Miss Davis, a native of the California Dominion herself, was less subtle. "What a load of claptrap. Haven't they got better things to do with their time?"

"Who is it?" Madame Barsteau asked, her piercing gaze never leaving the young man. "The one you know in this society? I can tell by the way you speak, someone close to you must be involved."

"My mother. My two aunts. And lately my sister, although I don't think it will take with her."

"You have my sympathy."

"Thank you, ma'am."

For Eliza, the boy's explanation had raised as many questions as it answered. "But are there actually any opium dens here? It seems so unlikely."

"Not that I know of," he admitted. "We've had a few folks go west, though. You don't need an opium house to fall into a life of vice and vanish forever."

"I suppose not. Liquor alone can kill, and I'm sure there are other narcotics that can besides opium."

"Oh, they don't die," he said firmly. "They go west."

"A euphemism—"

"No. Sometimes they even leave a note, explaining. Like I said, they sell themselves off. Or somebody takes them in lieu of payment, but it's all the same outcome."

"William!"

The sharp voice of the maître d' jolted the lad into swift action, and he scraped a crumb from the table and cleared an empty bread plate as if by reflex before he disappeared back into the kitchen.

In the silence that followed his departure, Eliza heard the muffled chanting from the street beyond the windows. Not the words but the rhythm, primal and hostile. She had thought them silly, but they were in deadly earnest. The incident on the bridge in Harrisburg took on a more sinister cast. To them, this was no euphemism, no theory. As far as they were concerned, people's lives were at stake. And Eliza, with her unconventional life choices and that suspicious hint of the orient in her eyes, must seem like the embodiment of the dangers they feared. The flashy red car was just fuel for the flame.

Charlotte's words came back to her, the challenge to see the world outside the privileged life she'd been born into. Now she began to see how many layers there were to that challenge. The provincial attitudes, so unlike those in the wealthier enclaves of the New York Dominion. The casual racism she had heard about but so rarely encountered near home, where so many Chinese merchants had established themselves and fully embraced Western ways. She'd been spoiled enough to think that spending four years in free-thinking Poughkeepsie was a horizon-broadening experience. But Meridian might as well be another world. Everything about Eliza must seem utterly alien and dissipated to these women.

She swirled the last of her tea in its bone china cup, studying the leaves, broody and unsettled. Charlotte had also discussed pleasure in that conversation. Another horizon she might broaden, though Eliza didn't think Charlotte meant her to combine that experience with the rally in quite such an explicit way.

Even after a night of sleep, a large breakfast and two cups of tea, Eliza could still feel the brush of Matthew's lips against hers. The mere memory sent a thrill through her, a sensuous thread of possibility that seemed to link all her most sensitive zones into one large, needy bundle. She knew exactly where he sat in the room—two tables behind her and to her right—and had felt his gaze on the back of her head throughout her meal. It was as if she'd become attuned to him, a compass to his lodestar, or perhaps the other kind of compass, bound to turn as he did. Then she realized she was borrowing imagery from John Donne, and rolled her eyes at her own mawkishness.

She had things to do, important things like running the gauntlet of reporters and angry temperance ladies, and ensuring her car hadn't been tampered with in the night. Taking an early lead. Establishing a pace the others couldn't hope to match. Remembering to check the only compass that mattered, the one in her car that would keep her heading in the right direction: toward St. Louis and the Victoria Dominion.

This was not a time for poetry. This was a time for action.

By THE TIME his breakfast was served, Matthew had nearly convinced himself it was all the fault of the port. Until, that is, Eliza strode into the room. She ignored him completely, too much so to be accidental. It was a very cold shoulder she showed him as she took a seat at another table, with her slender back to him. From the lively babble, she took eager part in conversing with the other ladies and seemed completely unaltered by the incident of the previous evening.

Matthew was altered. When he saw her again he resigned himself to it, because his reaction was unequivocal. His heart beat faster, his palms dampened and he *yearned*, damn it all. And as if those feelings weren't enough to manage, he also had to contend with the resentment, the sense of injustice, the sheer improbability of his situation.

He'd made it all the way through Oxford, through his whirlwind apprenticeship and journeyman tenure at Hardison House, fended off several seasons worth of eligible young ladies at balls his mother had forced him to attend, and come through it all unscathed. Heart intact, unencumbered. All that, only to succumb when he least expected it, from a quarter he had never bothered to guard because it was simply not a danger he could have foreseen or even imagined. Never in a million years.

Falling in love with Eliza Hardison. He wasn't sure when it had happened, but now that he'd admitted it to himself he felt like a fool for his previous willful blindness. Eliza, obviously. Eliza, *of course*. A hundred love poems danced through his brain, attempting to apply themselves despite his efforts to resist.

Eliza, the last woman on earth he needed to be chasing after, the last woman on earth who would want to be chased by him. *Or* . . .

He pushed the image down as soon as it popped up, but there it was, lurking in the back of his mind where the love poems frolicked. His moment of madness last night. That kiss, her face, his hands engulfing her shoulders, the way he'd seen and felt her breathing start to race, and that telltale *gasp* she'd let out.

It hit him hard, that one noise, caught and held on something in his soul. Or somewhere less noble, yet still undeniable.

Today she wore a blatantly unwise white walking suit, trimmed in black lace. The road dust would destroy it within minutes, but it looked marvelous at the moment. The coat, modeled in a hunting style, nipped in at her waist before falling in nearly a straight line from her hips to the floor, showing her figure to perfection from the back. But the front . . . might well give Matthew a heart attack. Because the skirt was a sham, the dress more a frock coat than anything else. It split at the waist, allowing her more freedom of movement and showing her long, black-clad legs from hip to toe.

Breeches were still on the cutting edge of fashion on the east coast, thanks in no small part to Charlotte's trendsetting efforts. Matthew had seen them on women, of course. They were all the rage in England and Europa. But he hadn't expected them here, in rural Meridian, on Eliza. And fitting like a glove.

She might as well wave a red flag in front of the bull that was the ladies' temperance group. He'd seen them picketing the hotel, recognized them by their signs and lapel pins, and finally inquired about them. The concierge, a circumspect gentleman who had clearly seen everything in his long tenure at the Grand Hotel, was not a fan of the El Dorado Foundation Ladies' Society for Temperance and Moral Fortitude. His daughter, he informed Matthew, had started taking him to task for keeping medicinal brandy in his home shortly after she'd joined the Temperance Society.

"As if her mother and I might fall into a moral decline from taking an occasional fortifying nip," he said in disgust. "At our age."

He hadn't been able to answer Matthew's other question. He had no idea what the golden poppy lapel pins signified. But he agreed with Matthew that they seemed an odd choice, given that opium was a primary focus of the Temperance Society's ire, and opium came from poppies.

"They might as well wear bunches of grapes," the concierge grumbled, before putting his professional face back on to handle the next guest to approach his desk.

When Matthew overheard the young waiter at breakfast discussing the Temperance Society with the ladies' table, he pricked up his ears and took the next chance to flag the young man down.

"Mum's told me," the waiter said of the pins, "but it didn't make much sense. Something to do with restoring the natural order of things and honoring God's creations, or some such. Mostly I think they wear them because a bundle of them come with the charter kit for the local chapters. My aunt has a jar of them just waiting for new members. She's the chapter president. I think the poppy is the foundation's symbol."

"The El Dorado Foundation?"

"I suppose so, yes."

The waiter knew nothing more about the foundation itself, however, leaving Matthew little more edified than before. The poppy motif still tickled something in his brain, though, and he suspected it wouldn't leave him alone until he'd figured out why. *Vexing.*

He didn't need more distractions. Getting Eliza through the mob would take all his attention, he thought. But to his surprise, when he reached the hotel lobby where the rally contestants were supervising the transfer of their luggage back to the vehicle holding area, Eliza had already secured protection. Parnell and Lazaris flanked her, looking full of ego and bravado as they proceeded with her out the hotel door and down the steps.

Matthew had to laugh when he followed them out. Their protection was hardly needed after all. The local police had cordoned off the walkway all the way to the holding area with sawhorses in a double row, and officers on foot and horseback patrolled the resulting corridor in a thick rank. The crowd could barely see the drivers, much less approach them.

It seemed excessive until he glanced back at the front of the hotel and saw the splatters of lurid red paint, the sloppily executed graffiti marring the white marble facade.

YOU WILL ALL BURN IN HELL, the primary one shouted. Others, less prominent, seemed to hint at whoredom and the evils of the steam engine. He couldn't see much in that quick glance, but what he saw was more than enough to make him wish they'd considered a third row of barricades. And perhaps a few officers with rifle harnesses, just to be on the safe side.

Parnell and Lazaris were both larger men than Matthew, more intimidating, and he was smart enough to be grateful for the added safety their escort provided Eliza. He still wanted to punch both of them in their leering, odious faces, but his logical mind allowed that such was probably uncalled for. It must have shown in his expression, however, as a wry voice beside him remarked that he must be either as ill as Smith-Grenville, or lovesick indeed.

Matthew glowered down at Cantlebury, who grinned even wider than usual in return.

"Lovesick, then. Oh, let me guess. Who, *who* could the young lady be?"

"Shut up, Cantlebury."

"She's really ensnared you, hasn't she? You're never snappish in the morning, Pence. Don't look them in the eye or kiss them on the lips, my boy, haven't I warned you before? Is all my instruction gone to waste?"

Cantlebury's instruction had been valuable indeed. Dwarf or no, when it came to debauchery and seduction the man had few equals in their class at Oxford, perhaps because he'd made such a study of it. Or perhaps, Matthew had to admit, it was simply that the women seemed to like him so damn much, and he got under their guard when they weren't looking. Despite his appalling taste in jokes and general lack of decorum he was never without a female companion, to Matthew's knowledge. Not even when racing, though people weren't meant to know about that.

"You're right, I suppose." Matthew forced himself to exhale, to adopt a cynical smile. "It's just a question of finding a distraction, really. Miss Speck is holding up rather well, don't you think, for a spinster of her age? Perhaps I ought to make a foray in that direction."

"Shut up, Pence."

Having scored even points, they shook hands like the gentlemen they were before parting ways to go to their separate cars.

Nine

It was a straight shot from Meridian to St. Louis, rolling hills providing little challenge to the cars. The paved road persisted in some stretches, and the continuing dry weather meant the rougher patches were at least firm and navigable.

Eliza spent the morning playing at follow-the-leader with Van der Grouten and Lazaris. The sleek silver monster and Lazaris's more understated black steamer were both fine machines, worthy competitors, and she found the game of stealing the front position strangely invigorating. For hours they dueled, Lazaris shooting her a wicked grin whenever she overtook or fell behind him, Van der Grouten awarding her a grave nod at each passing.

The wind whipped through her open window, trying to tug her hair loose from under her hat, and dust flew up behind the car in a giddy whirlwind, blinding whoever came directly after. This was the point, she realized for the first time. What they were here for, the reason the others came back to it. The thrill. The chase. The *fun*. She was in the middle of it, and almost didn't mind when she had to give up the lead again to pause in a stream to refill her water tank.

Matthew and the Watchmaker drove up as she primed the pump and saluted one another as they left their vehicles to perform the same duty as Eliza. It was a constant concern, the balance of water and fuel. Eliza felt fortunate that her multi-phased engine, with its hybrid mix of Stirling technology and Dexter's special blend of spirit fuel, ran cooler and more efficiently than almost any other car in the field. But steam was steam and power was power and physics meant that the relationship between the two had its limits. Ergo, driving into streams when the opportunity presented itself.

She was lucky too that she didn't need to leave her vehicle to fill the water tank this way. Matthew's pump primed near the boot of his steamer, and the Watchmaker's water intake seemed to snake up one of the "legs" of his peculiar spider-car.

They waited in companionable silence, all three seeming to appreciate the moment of respite under the warm sun. With the Watchmaker there, Matthew didn't dare approach Eliza for the more personal conversation she feared they must have soon. The water pumps chugged along, but quietly enough that Eliza could hear birds in the nearby trees, a cheerful accompaniment to the rustic idyll of the moment.

The birds flew up all at once, and Eliza had just enough time to register that their behavior seemed odd before the sound of the explosion reached her.

Not so much a sound, she though afterward, as a bone-shaking *whump*, something not just heard but felt. In the moment she knew only panic, the same primal fear that had sent the birds flying. She ducked by instinct, hiding herself below the level of her car windows as she tried to slow her breathing and think.

What in blue blazes just happened? Her mind threw possibilities at her, all of them awful, and she forced herself to sort things out one thing at a time. Matthew and the Watchmaker? Was it either of their cars? No, because they'd seen the birds when she had; they'd all looked up at once, and just before she ducked she'd seen Matthew shouting and running to his car.

Seen, but not heard, because all she could hear—still—was the reverberation of the blast. Her ears rang with it. But whatever it was, it hadn't happened close enough to injure her or Matthew. Or the Watchmaker. Her heartbeat began to slow to something like a reasonable pace, though her body still vibrated with the urge to run and hide.

She realized her ears were recovering when she heard another sound. Shouting, from close by.

"Eliza! *Eliza!*"

Matthew flung the car door open, nearly spilling her out, and stared down at her with a look of frantic relief.

"You're all right!"

"Yes, I think so. What was that?"

"No idea. It came from somewhere ahead. Were you still in front of the pack?"

"No." She pushed herself back to a seated position, her scattered wits slowly reassembling themselves. "No, Van der Grouten and Lazaris are both ahead of me. We've been passing the lead all morning. They overtook me when I stopped for water. Five minutes ahead, maybe ten? They'd been out of sight a few minutes when you arrived."

The Watchmaker's spectacled face appeared behind Matthew's shoulder.

"Van der Grouten was ahead of you?" When she nodded, he raised one skeletal hand to his mouth, visibly shaken. "Oh, Hans . . ."

"Let's get moving. We won't find out anything by staying here. Eliza, you should ride with me."

Just like that, her good will toward Matthew flew away like a startled bird. "And lose my chance at retaking the lead? I don't think so, thank you. We have no idea what happened, and this is still a race."

To his credit, he kept his thoughts to himself. With a curt nod, he stalked back to his steam car and began to close the pump mechanism, while the Watchmaker did the same. Eliza had only to pull a lever to ready her car, and as she'd left it idling she was able to beat both men out of the stream and back onto the dirt-and-gravel road.

Matthew would have never let me see this, was her first thought upon arriving at the scene of the blast. Her second was that she would have been happier not seeing it.

That it had been sabotage was clear. The Victoria Dominion was known for its sinkholes, its perforated limestone underpinnings and karst lands, but this new chasm bore obvious blast burns around the edges. Flames still flickered here and there among the chunks of rubble, creating a hellscape in the midst of the otherwise beautiful bucolic scene. Eliza left her car, barely feeling her feet, buzzing all over again with fear that grew worse as she approached the still-smoldering edge of the hole and peered down.

The air scorched her lungs, and the smell of cordite was fading beneath the growing stench of burning tires and another odor that was horribly familiar. She couldn't put a name to it; it was too far out of context. Then her mind identified it, and she ran for the nearest bush. By the time Matthew and the Watchmaker squealed to a halt behind her car, Eliza had already wiped her mouth clean and kicked some dirt and leaves over the evidence of her violent reaction.

"Don't look!" she called to them, but it was too late. They were already at the brink, already gaping at the horrors the chasm held.

The Watchmaker froze, but Matthew backed away from the edge, one hand pressed firmly to his lips.

"I told you not to look."

"It smells like—"

"I know."

Burnt pork. Neither of them said it, but neither of them would ever forget it.

It was so obviously too late to save Van der Grouten and Lazaris that Eliza didn't even raise the question. Not even for form. But what was obvious to one was not so clear to another, whose emotions might be more personally involved.

"Hans!" shouted the Watchmaker as he skittered over the edge, vanishing below the rim of the sinkhole in a flurry of dust and smoke.

"Jesus, it's still burning. He'll die down there!" Matthew tore after him, but stopped short of following him into the pit. "Watchmaker! Don't be a fool, man, it's too late!"

"No!" came the reply, the sound distorted by the cavern. And then a wail, piercing and anguished: *"Noooooo!"*

"He'll burn too if he doesn't get out of there," Matthew muttered.

"Then what are you waiting for?" Eliza stepped past him, testing the edge of the pit with a stamp of her toe. "The footing's firm enough here. Do you have a rope? I have one somewhere if you don't."

"Are you planning to lasso him?"

"Hardly. I was planning to go in after him."

"You were—are you stark staring mad, woman?" Matthew's face, already red from the heat of the blast site, grew redder still. Veins stood out at his temples. Eliza had never seen him so worked up.

"Well, one of us has to. While you're standing there trying to prove your masculinity, the Watchmaker's down there broiling!"

"If I wanted to prove my masculinity this is not how I would go about it."

Her body felt as taut and strained as his looked, angled in for the fight, but conflicted as to motive. The heat between them was not entirely anger, not entirely fear either, but a dangerous brew of those and other instincts.

The shuffle of rocks drew their attention down to the pit again. The Watchmaker was climbing back up, tears streaking the soot that covered his face. He slid on the loose surface, losing purchase more than once. Matthew lay down as far over the edge as he could and reached a hand down, helping the other man back to safety.

"You're on fire," Eliza pointed out, feeling unearthly calm because she was buzzing with adrenaline again and time was passing so slowly. She flipped up the long tail of the Watchmaker's black driving coat and used the fabric to pat out the flickering ember on his back.

"It would have gone out on its own," he told her. "The coat is fireproof."

He stumbled a few feet away from the pit and collapsed to the ground, pressing his head against his bony knees, and began to sob.

Still in shock, miserable that she had no help to offer the disconsolate man or the two who had died, Eliza turned away and found herself inches from Matthew's chest. It seemed inevitable, taking that final step toward him, leaning into him for support. His arms encircled her as if they had been waiting to do that very thing, one hand finding its way to her waist and the other cradling the back of her head.

"I'm sorry," he said after a moment. "I shouldn't have shouted. I was frightened for you."

"No, I was about to jump into a flaming pit. Feel free to shout at me any time I seem likely to do that again."

She felt his chuckle more than heard it, pressed as she was against his waistcoat. Felt too the hitch of a sob that broke it halfway through.

"I would have gone in after you, you know. Even without a fireproof coat."

Eliza squeezed him tighter, stroking his back to soothe him. "I know."

The crunch of tires on rough road alerted them, and they pulled apart as another car swung into line behind Matthew's and the Watchmaker's. It was Moreau, who approached the scene with baffled horror on his face and backed away with a string of French profanities that Eliza had to pretend not to understand.

Madame Barsteau, arriving moments later, reacted in much the same vein. Whitcombe was next; he heaved his bulk over to the lip of the crater and stared down at the wreckage, scanning its perimeter and not saying a word.

Miss Speck and Cantlebury, evidently driving in tandem, pulled up behind Eliza's steamer and joined the huddled group. Whitcombe soon pulled Cantlebury and Matthew away, however, leaving the women and Moreau standing over the still-weeping Watchmaker.

Moreau made the first move, crouching near the man and murmuring to him until he lifted his head enough to whisper a response. As they talked, Eliza explained what little she knew to the two other women. Mostly they all tried not to stare at the wreckage in the pit, and failed.

"Definitely a bomb," Whitcombe confirmed, returning after a few minutes of reconnaissance with his colleagues. "The tripwire's still attached to that tree over there, and there on the other side as well. The blast marks suggest the charge itself was buried, and I think the road surface may have been treated with an accelerant, based on the char. They may not have bargained on the sinkhole being triggered, but there's no way to know for certain at the moment."

"You seem to know an awful lot about it, monsieur," Madame Barsteau pointed out, her implication clear.

Whitcombe shrugged it off. "My family ran a munitions factory during the war and I came up there as an apprentice and journeyman. Then the war ended, we retooled to peacetime production and eventually I went off to read classics. But if there's one thing I know about besides the ancient Greeks, it's explosives. Which means if I wanted to get away with sabotage, they're the last thing I'd use. I'm not fatally stupid."

She nodded her concession, and Whitcombe continued.

"This was subtle, though. If I hadn't known what to look for, I probably would have thought this was just another sinkhole, with tragically coincidental timing. Most people would assume the fall made the cars explode, because they wouldn't realize the blast marks indicated the presence of other explosives. They'd have attributed this to accident, not sabotage."

"We need to reach the next town and alert somebody," said Cantlebury. "And send somebody to deal with . . . the remains."

"It would be faster to go back to that last city we drove through," suggested Miss Speck, to the disapproval of all the others.

"Perhaps that's what they're expecting!"

"Why give them what they want?"

"What if some of the others took a different road? We must go ahead to the checkpoint to warn them."

And so on, the arguments continued. Eliza let the words wash over her as she gazed across the newly opened chasm to the road beyond. At its edges, the gap encroached on the surrounding scrub and forest, but she could see a way around on the right-hand side. It would be harrowing, and she would simply have to hope that the ground didn't give way any further under her steam car's weight, but it was as good an option as any other. And this was still a race; the only way to go was forward.

"Eliza! Where are you going?" Matthew called after her, inevitably.

She had already started her car and backed up to turn off the road when he reached her window and gripped the frame.

"What the bloody hell do you think you're doing?" he demanded.

She threw the car into gear and revved it gently, allowing the boiler time to reheat. "The same thing all of you will decide to do when you're through discussing it. I'm driving on to St. Louis and then to the checkpoint. We can't help Lazaris or Van der Grouten, and we need to get to a town and let somebody in authority know what's happened to them. There's no point in lingering here. For all we know the saboteurs are out there in the woods, waiting for us all to assemble so they can wipe out the rest of us at one time."

"Or they could have set any number of these tripwires up ahead. You need to *think*, Eliza. This is the flaming pit all over again, *already*."

"Or they could have rigged an avalanche or set a dam to burst and flood the roadway somewhere past Dodge City, or perhaps they're behind that tree there with a bloody big shotgun. Perhaps they know the truth about the tainted air over the Sierra Nevada and they're already on the other side now, ready to have a good laugh when we start plummeting from the sky like so many downed geese. We can *think* all we like, but we can't *know*. In this case the flaming pit is the entire circumstance, Matthew, and you're in it too. It's either go on or stop the race. So I'm going on."

"Will you wait for me, at least? Let me follow you."

"You will be following me," she pointed out, "because I'll be ahead of you. I'll see you at the checkpoint, Matthew."

WHEN HE FINALLY caught sight of her car again, that reassuring blaze of red, they were already past St. Louis. He assumed she had stopped in the city to notify somebody of the accident, but the authorities must not have detained her for long. From the city limit they had another two hours' drive or so to the checkpoint where they would make camp for the night, but it seemed to take days. His mind was full of the horrors he'd seen earlier, the scorched and smoking remains in the charred hulks of steam cars, boilers twisted and skewed into shreds by the force of the explosion. The smell seemed to linger in his clothes.

How could she be so calm, so resolved? For the first time

it occurred to Matthew that Eliza had a strength he'd never fully appreciated, one that had nothing to do with physicality and everything to do with determination. Whatever she chose to do, she did with such singular focus and intensity that he wondered if she would ever have the attention to spare for another person in her life.

Dexter should have set Eliza to guard *him* instead of the other way around. If he had, she would have stuck by him with the same bullheadedness she was currently using to beat his time to the checkpoint. She'd been right, of course. They had all decided to continue, in the end, because there was really no other viable choice. Any decision to stop the race would have to be made by the rally committee, not by an assortment of frightened drivers at the side of the road. None of them were willing to backtrack and risk forfeiting the race. That meant proceeding to the checkpoint camp at the very least. All they'd lost by their discussion of what to do was time.

On the other hand, she'd turned to him at the most extreme moment and let him hold her. The simple truth of that gave him hope. But he knew he must borrow a page from Eliza's book, and take a risk if he wanted to advance. He needed to tell her how he felt.

He would tell her tonight. And pray that he survived to see the morning.

The decision made him feel steadier, more purposeful. It gave him another mission to think about, one other than the hopeless task of finding Phineas and the risky venture of attempting to win the rally. A shorter-term goal, but with the potential for longer-term gain.

The mood around the campfire that night was strained. There was laughter aplenty, but it was too shrill and held a frantic edge. The tents were pitched around the edges of the clearing, but most of the racers and the few officials in attendance huddled near the fire far into the night, reluctant to leave the group.

Moreau had taken the opportunity to spring his surprise, opening several of his hampers and boxes to reveal a startling array of portable cooking equipment and all the makings of a feast for the full company. He'd stopped in St. Louis for fresh bread, but he'd brought everything else with him. Camembert with a fricassee of nuts and wild mushrooms, to start.

Matthew joined Whitcombe on one of the logs laid out for seating near the fire. Moreau had already secured Eliza a seat near his portable kitchen and seemed nearly as concerned for her mental well-being as he was for the Watchmaker's. The food was clearly his way of offering comfort, and even in his foul humor Matthew had to admit the method wasn't all bad.

"*Je regrette*," Moreau announced to the group as they started on the creamy cheese and lightly warmed bread. "I intended a more festive occasion, and the wine I prefer with Camembert is champagne, so . . ." He uncorked the bottles with as little fanfare as possible, and from his seemingly bottomless hampers produced champagne glasses for all of them. It lent the already somber gathering an air of the surreal.

"Where has he been getting the ice?" Whitcombe wondered, studying the pale golden wine that glowed amber in the firelight. Condensation frosted the glass, testifying to the chill Moreau had somehow arranged.

"The hotels, I suppose. Or perhaps he's wired ahead for some things," Madame Barsteau said from the adjacent log. "He's done it before. Four years ago at the Paris-Dakar, he treated us all to *croquembouche* after a meal of *cailles en escabèche*. I have no idea how it's all managed, but I believe the consortium subsidizes his culinary flights of fancy to help cultivate his image as a suave madcap. And in this instance, I suppose to help him put weight on the competition."

Looking around at the gathering, Matthew noted the

dynamics revealing themselves under the increased tension. Cantlebury, who normally affected complete indifference to Lavinia Speck so as to avoid gossip, was sitting close to her and leaning in to talk quietly. It was just the two of them on their log.

Madame Barsteau and Miss Davis, who were normally quite companionable, sat together but looked wary of one another. Beyond them, Parnell and the other two Dominion drivers, Jensen and Jones, hunkered in a loose grouping that spoke more of isolation from the other clusters than camaraderie between themselves. Any other night, Jensen would be surreptitiously watching Parnell, copying his mannerisms. Parnell seemed to find the hero-worship amusing and occasionally threw out gestures that were obviously intended to gain Jensen's interest, like adjusting the brim of his hat with a certain flourish, or brushing his coat back on one side as though revealing a six-shooter on his hip. Not tonight, though. Tonight neither of them had the spirit for that.

Everyone looked equally shaken. Matthew gazed from face to face, trying to discern whether any one of them might be a plant, an agent of whoever had killed Van der Grouten and Lazaris. He agreed with Whitcombe that the explosion had been large enough even without the factor of the sinkhole to destroy any vehicle that tripped the wire. The bomber had either intended a driver to die, or not cared that death might result.

"Do you think Smith-Grenville really was ill? What if he was poisoned? Are we safe eating this French mess?"

Whitcombe had asked too quietly for anyone else to hear, and Matthew gave his question serious thought before answering. "I don't know too much about poisons, but an agent that slow, one that also caused a fever and other symptoms of influenza? It seems unlikely, and damned inefficient, especially since it's obvious whoever's behind this doesn't mind killing. No, I think it was just bad luck. I only hope none of the rest of us are incubating whatever Barnabas had.

And as for Moreau, I think he'd feel it was a mortal sin to taint good food that way. I also don't think he'd be stupid enough to try to poison us all at once if he wanted the win. Surely that would be grounds for disqualification."

"That's a relief." The big man swilled half his glass of champagne in one go, earning a frown across the campfire from Moreau. "I would have hated to miss the main course; apparently he's been cooking it up all day. Has a special pot rigged up in his boiler. It's quite ingenious."

The pot held a savory *boeuf bourguignon*, tender and rich, which Moreau served with a complex burgundy and a discussion of the merits of the pinot noir grape. He delivered that information primarily to Eliza, not to the group as a whole. But Matthew was listening. And watching Eliza, who smiled and nodded and seemed captivated far more than mere courtesy required. The Frenchman was a bit thick around the middle, and graying at the temples, but still exuded a smooth charm that ladies no doubt found appealing.

"He's too old for her," he muttered at one point, prompting a snort from Whitcombe.

"If you think she's remotely interested in the chef, you're more thick than I thought. And that's saying something, Pence."

Matthew socked Whitcombe on the arm in a friendly way and was surprised when the sudden motion sent them both swaying. He'd had too much wine, as they all had.

"Was that Phineas's picture you were showing around back in Meridian, by the way? Is Smith-Grenville really still bent on finding him?"

Matthew had the daguerrotype of Phineas in his naval uniform in a protective glassine envelope, and he'd been dutifully showing it to all and sundry whenever he stopped. Nobody had seen the young man, of course. He wondered if Phineas was even recognizable as the man in the picture any more. The last time Matthew had seen him, he'd dropped an alarming amount of weight, his hair was unkempt and his face unshaven. But it was the blank, uncaring stare that changed his aspect so much from the bright, enthusiastic young man he'd once been. Before the opium. The drug had stolen his soul, Matthew thought. Barnabas was convinced otherwise.

"It's only been a year since he lost touch. The last he heard, Phineas was headed for the Dominions. I think Barnabas didn't realize how *big* it is here, until he arrived. Back in London it didn't seem so hopeless. But if it were one of your brothers, would you give up looking?"

"Depends which brother we're talking about. I have several I wouldn't spare a piss for if they were on fire," Whitcombe quipped. "I take your point, however. If you have another copy of that thing I'll spend some time flashing it about, wherever I wind up when I'm through with the rally."

"San Francisco?"

"We all know I won't make it that far. It's not like I could pack a cargo dirigible, and that's what it would take to lug my arse over the mountains in any reasonable amount of time. I'll be lucky to make it to Salt Lake by the time the rest of you are boarding the cruise vessel for the ride home."

The season and circumstances making salad impracticable, Moreau had opted for lightly sautéed haricots verts with a hint of garlic, followed by more cheese. And more wine, so much wine. Matthew watched Eliza across the fire, the heat making an indistinct ripple of her face. She looked like something from a dream, hazy and unreachable. He passed the bottle along the next time one made its way around the company, sensing that he was already nearing the point of inevitable regret where alcohol was concerned. Eliza had been wiser, taking only a small splash of each offering, but she still looked affected.

She had earned a little forgetfulness. They all had, that day. But Matthew didn't think Moreau had earned the right to leer at Eliza's mouth as she forked in a dainty mouthful of vegetables with obvious enjoyment. He narrowed his eyes at the scene, catching Eliza's glare in return. She stabbed a single green bean with her utensil and, holding his attention, bared her pearly teeth. Then she bit the bean in two with a single neat snap.

Ten

Eliza couldn't help but snicker at Matthew's expression when she emasculated her bean at him. She'd been sorely tempted to stick out her tongue. Unkind perhaps, but she was tired of seeing him frown at her when she hadn't done anything to deserve censure. She'd had more than enough of that lately. Besides, the dinner was worth enjoying, and little else that day had been cause for happiness. Moreau had earned a smile or two at the very least.

It might have been the wine, but Eliza had a sense of well-being and belonging in the racers' camp that night and didn't want it spoiled. Mostly, she wanted to do something, *anything*, to put the day's events out of mind. Eating delicious food, drinking excellent wine, these things helped.

Dessert seemed likely to help as well.

"*Clafoutis*?" asked Madame Barsteau, eyeing the pans Moreau produced next. "*Comment confortable.*"

"I thought it appropriate," he replied.

Over the cherry-filled cake, Moreau served a heavy hazelnut cream. Eliza thought of her corset, her costume choices for the morrow, and ate a large helping anyway. Matthew glared at her again when she separated a piece of fruit from its pastry mortar and ate it by itself, dredging it first in cream. Tipsy, irritated, she repeated the act and watched, fascinated, as his eyes glazed over.

That was not entirely a look of disapproval.

Interesting as it was to toy with her food and Matthew at the same time, Eliza knew she should retire soon. She'd overindulged in both despair and alcohol, and her only hope of not being miserable tomorrow was to sleep off the wine and tears.

She wasn't surprised, however, when sleep evaded her. Even removing her constricting stays and donning a night rail gave her none of the usual pleasure and ease. Muscles tight, heart heavy, she lay on her cot and tried to clear her mind, but nothing would erase the picture of smoldering rubble, the smell, the glimpse into the hellish pit where two of her colleagues had died.

The only respite was no relief at all—those moments when her mind instead recalled the slap of the placard against her window, the cruel shunning by the ladies of the Temperance Society, even the way Barnabas Smith-Grenville had slumped to the ground.

The night was cooling, but the air in the tent was stagnant and stifling. Giving up on her attempt to sleep, Eliza decided on a walk instead. Perhaps the clear air would clear her mind as well. Donning her slippers and poking her head out of the tent flap, she scanned the campsite. The fire was nearly gone, down to embers that did nothing to illuminate the clearing. Across the encampment, Miss Davis sat in front of her tent, smoking a cigarette, staring into the night. None of the others appeared to be out and about.

Taking a chance, Eliza stepped out and slipped into the woods, treading carefully until she was certain she was far enough from the camp not to draw attention.

She knew the oaks and hickories, but couldn't begin to

name all the other trees she passed in the moonlight. Nor did she recognize the creatures making up that evening's symphony, only that the noises were similar to those she was used to at home but different enough to sound new at the same time. The drive, the meal, the tent, the rituals of bedtime, those were all experiences she'd had, to one extent or another. But this—the night air against her barely covered skin, the freedom of walking outside without the constrictions of her usual garments, the forest full of things neither she nor anyone in her family had seen or heard before—this was *new*, truly new to her. And it made *her* feel new, full of potential.

A world of possibility rose in her mind, taking the place of the day's horrors. Twigs and other forest debris crackled under the glove-soft kid of her slippers, and the smell of old wood, rich loam and spring leaves rose around her. Old, but also *new*. And this was only one forest, in one Dominion not so very far from home. What else might she find if she continued looking? Other forests, other landscapes, other people. Other *worlds*. How could she have planned to stay in New York when there was all this and more waiting for her to discover it?

Another sound registered, setting Eliza on alert. A heavy tread on the forest floor, somewhere close by.

"Who's there?" she whispered, cursing herself for her foolishness. It could be anything. A reporter hoping to find some sort of scoop on the racers. A local farmboy bent on mischief or worse. A wolf, a bear. And she had pranced forth into this wilderness to enjoy the night without so much as a good solid stick to swing in her own defense.

Easy enough to remedy. The woods were full of sticks. She grabbed the nearest fallen branch of appropriate size, hoping there were no spiders or other nasty crawlies on it.

"Who goes there?" she called, more confident now that she had her stick.

"It's only me."

"Oh, for—" Flinging the branch down, she brushed her

hands clean then braced them on her hips. "Honestly, this is ridiculous. You stare daggers at me all night for enjoying my food, then follow me out here? Why, to scold me or to rescue me? I don't want rescuing, Matthew. A girl simply needs a few moments of privacy on occasion."

"Who says I followed you out here to rescue you?" Matthew stepped closer, his eyes unreadable in the twilight gloom. Eliza could see his mouth curving up, a secret smile that made her want to touch his lips. Pushing the thought firmly aside, she folded her arms and stared him down.

"What then? Raccoon hunting? Planning a midnight swim? There are large predators in these woods, you know, you really ought to be more careful."

He took another step, bringing him within inches of her, and Eliza's plan to stand her ground fell apart. She backed up two steps, then a large tree stopped her retreat. Her heart raced as Matthew pressed the advantage, closing the distance and bracing his hands on either side of her shoulders.

"I'm the large predator."

A hot thrill swirled through her body, tingling its way through every forbidden zone.

"You've had too much wine."

"So have you. But it was good wine."

"I'm your prey, then, am I? Are you planning to devour me?"

He was close enough now for her to see the gleam of dark humor and heightened desire that altered his expression, to grasp that she'd said something inappropriate. Eliza felt a flush that had nothing to do with shame. She wondered what she'd said, to make him react that way.

"I might, at that. I'll bet you're delicious. My God, and you're all but naked. Eliza, tell me to go away."

Oh, inches now. She could feel his breath, warmer than the cooling night breeze against her face. Sweetened by wine and pastry, tempting beyond hope of reason. She didn't wish him away any more than he wanted to go.

He whispered it again. "Tell me to go away."

But his lips were already brushing hers, stealing away the last of her sense and replacing it with sensation. Soft breath, soft lips and the harsh counterpoint of his day's growth of stubble. Eliza shivered, and the heat inside her flared, unexpected and unsettling.

When Matthew's tongue swept between her lips, she gasped at the novel feeling, the sweetness of the invasion. It was gentle only for a moment, until she ventured to return the gesture. Something seemed to break inside him then and his kiss turned into an explicit assault, while he pinned her to the rough bark of the tree with his lean body.

Eliza knew how the sexual act was performed, the various parts that came into play, even the definitive feat of male hydraulics at the end. She'd seen a mare covered by a stallion, several incidents of cattle mating, and once—to her mother's eternal horror—an extended session between one of her father's foxhounds and a delicate spaniel bitch, on the lawn during a formal garden party. Neither those illuminating observations, nor her two previous kisses with bold young men at parties, nor her one experimental Sapphic interlude while away at University, had prepared Eliza for the swell of emotional and physical response to Matthew's attentions. She simply hadn't realized his tongue sweeping over hers would cause her heart to palpitate that way, or that his hands . . .

Oh. *Oh.* He pulled her closer with one hand at the small of her back, but with the other he drew a teasing line from her waist upward, coming to rest with his thumb and index finger bracketing one of her breasts. Her nipple swelled, knotting itself into a keen point of anticipation beneath the barely adequate covering of her night rail. Thin, impractical cotton lawn that might as well be transparent for all the good it did to conceal her response to him.

She didn't want to conceal it. This was a night for her to embrace new things, and this was the most wonderful new thing yet. She wanted Matthew to do more, more things she could react to, more magical conjuring of these fantastic urges from her body that had previously been so predictable to her. His touch seemed to turn her into a different creature, a wild and impetuous beast, and she wanted to rampage into the night and do every shameless thing she could with him.

He tasted of wine again tonight, still sweet but with a souring bite, and of hazelnut cream and of something that made her suspect she wouldn't care if he'd just eaten a handful of scallions—she'd still want to keep kissing him. Neither of the other boys nor the girl had tasted so good, felt so good, and now Matthew's hand was slipping up again, crumpling delicate fabric against skin.

Eliza arched into his touch, a moan escaping her lips for the first time since they'd started. Two fingers on her nipple, an exploratory tug, were apparently enough to turn Eliza into a wanton. She let her head fall back, *thunk*, against the tree, not caring about the flash of pain on her skull when it was followed so closely by a jolt of pleasure everywhere else.

"God, more," she whispered, and cried out again as Matthew lowered his head and pressed his lips to the tender crest of skin above the neckline of the gown. A neckline that was sliding lower, she realized with a start. He'd undone a few buttons and pulled the fabric down and away on one side, freeing one of her breasts. Before she could protest—not that she planned to—his lips captured her nipple. Kissing and, for the love of God, sucking the peak, which Eliza would swear was directly attached to that sweetly aching spot between her legs.

Seeking pressure, relief, Eliza hooked one leg around Matthew's, tucking her foot behind his knee and then his hip to bring them even closer. She recognized the hard ridge against her lower belly and instinctively angled herself to rub up against it, a firm touch against that needy, swollen place that seemed to demand all her attention. He helped, hitching her higher with strong hands that lingered afterward. His fingers curved, roamed, following the contours of her buttocks in a sensual sweep.

"I was only planning to talk to you," he murmured the next time his mouth pulled free, as though it made any difference now what he'd planned. The night air cooled the dampness on her skin, then his breath heated it again, keeping her focused on the warring sensations. When he spoke, his evening stubble rasped against her bosom. "I wanted to tell you I've grown very . . . fond of you."

"Fond?"

"*Very* fond."

"I see."

"I thought you should know. But this wasn't how I envisioned the conversation proceeding." He straightened up, eyes closed, breathing far too rapidly.

Eliza tried an experimental sway of her hips into him, increasing the pressure between them, and found Matthew's answering hiss and counter-push quite rewarding. He was no predator, but she thought she might turn him into one if she tried. For the moment, the power was hers. To frustrate or sate. To deny or to grant. Eliza was inclined to grant.

"The only problem I have with this conversation is that there's far too much conversing in it."

"It's normal to reach out after a shock, I suppose. After a death. A physical connection reminds us we're still alive. But I . . . I'm—what are—*ohhh*."

Fair was fair. He'd unbuttoned her, so she unbuttoned him. And sucked on his nipple, again in accordance with the principle of fairness. But in keeping with the evening's theme of novelty, she'd added a hint of biting, and he seemed to appreciate the innovation.

"Where did you learn to do that?"

"You just did it to me."

"Well yes, but not exact—*aaahhhh God yes but stop, better stop now, that's quite enough.*"

To Eliza's great indignation, he stiff-armed her, gently but implacably separating their bodies and keeping them apart by holding her away at the shoulders.

"Did I hurt you?"

"No," he squeaked.

"I just wanted to feel it. It was right there, I could hardly go on ignoring it." Even through the fabric of his trousers it had been firm and hot in her hand, a thick muscular length that seemed to pulse with a life of its own. She would have liked to investigate more closely.

"Mm-hmm." His eyes were squeezed shut, and so were his lips. He looked like he was trying to keep from exploding.

"Though one is always expected to," she allowed. "Ignore it, I mean. We all *know*, but young ladies are supposed to pretend they don't. Which is rather stupid, isn't it? Pretend we don't notice *that*, even when it's all . . . how it gets. And pretend we aren't in the least curious, when *of course* we are." She was prattling because she was flustered, and she knew that but still couldn't make herself stop. "I'm sure you are too. Not about *that*, I mean, about . . . although perhaps you're not still curious, because I'm sure you've taken the trouble to find out, as young men seem to have no shortage of opportunities to—"

"If I kiss you again will you stop talking about it?" He sounded quite desperate. No doubt this conversation too was failing to play out as he'd foreseen.

"I hope so. God, I hope so."

It was a kindness. Yes, a kindness he did her by covering her mouth with his and stealing her breath away with an exquisite, velvety roll of his tongue. That kiss was downright philanthropic. It deserved her honest effort in return, and she gave it, clutching Matthew's back to pull him close again and echoing everything he did with his mouth. In no time at all, he had her pressed against the tree again.

Her nightwear seemed to fascinate him. He couldn't keep his hands off the filmy stuff, couldn't seem to help sliding it over her skin and reminding her that she was wearing nothing under it. When he finally came up for air, he had most of her skirts bunched in his fists, exposing her legs up to mid-thigh.

Eliza's mind held only one thought: *Keep going, keep going, keep going.*

With obviously superhuman determination, Matthew stopped. When he let the fine fabric drop, Eliza wanted to pound something in frustration. His chest was closest, so she gave it a firm tap with her closed fist.

"Ouch, what was that for?"

"You're an awful tease, Matthew."

"Pardon?"

"Why did you stop?" It had just been getting interesting. Now Eliza felt all out of sorts, worked up and more tense than when she'd started her walk. The point of which had been to relax. Her gown had fallen back into place, more or less, but was sticking to her in various damp places, increasing her feeling of edginess. Sighing, she tugged the garment to rights and refastened a few buttons.

Matthew stepped back, grimacing at the evident discomfort of his currently too tight trousers. "If I hadn't stopped, I would have . . . kept going."

"And?" Was he honestly *that* thick? He seemed such a bright young man most of the time. Brilliant, even. And other good things, things she ought to admire but didn't at the moment, like honorable and trustworthy and decent.

"I'm hardly going to ravish you up against a tree, Eliza."

Ravishing. In a rush of confused emotion, Eliza realized he meant *actual* ravishing. By "kept going" he meant he would have *kept going*, and she might well have let him. Right there, in the forest, up against that tree. And she was a painfully naïve and inexperienced idiot, and Matthew was decent and honorable, and those were traits she did indeed admire in him. Most fervently.

She'd felt powerful, but in truth he'd been the only one

with any hint of control. Her sense of strength had been but a dangerous illusion, exactly the sort of thing her mother had always warned her about. And while Eliza had been caught up in the magic of the moment, now that the glow was fading she was horrified to think of the consequences she might have incurred if Matthew hadn't stopped.

He'd kissed her, touched her, and she'd completely lost her common sense. Fondness, hanky-panky in the woods, all this could only lead one place in the mind of a man like Matthew. The one place she didn't want to go. A marriage bed, from whence she could never again set forth to explore the world.

"It's not that I didn't *want* to. You're eminently ravishable."

And now the darling man was trying to make her feel better about things. Standing there in the moonlight, gazing at her earnestly with his strange eyes and his cheekbones so high and sharp they cast shadows, and generally looking like some sort of eldritch, beautiful creature of the night sent to tempt her into sin. He was lovely *and* he was exercising reasonable restraint, while being considerate of her feelings. It made her want to kiss him all over again.

That impulse terrified her.

Eleven

A RUMPLED, OUT-OF-SORTS Eliza had haunted Matthew's fleeting dreams during the few hours he'd managed to sleep after walking her back to her tent. She wandered, in her nearly transparent night rail, through a field of flowers that shimmered in the sunlight, almost blinding. He bent to pick one for her, and a thin petal of hammered gold sliced his palm. When he pulled back, instead of one line of blood he saw two, running parallel from his forefinger to his wrist.

"Cat claws," Barnabas explained, from his seat among the gleaming poppies. He held up a hooked double blade, but it wasn't a knife. It was his hand. "Beautiful, aren't they? They look so innocent."

Barnabas looked gray and skeletal, with the glazed, unseeing eyes of an opium eater. In the dream, Matthew understood that this was because he had turned into Phineas, and Phineas was dead. Rotting, in fact, there among the flowers, which were now real flowers instead of gold. They bobbed on the end of long stalks, looking soft and harmlessly sweet. But he knew they would still cut him if he tried to pick another one. Phineas harvested them one at a time, in dream-slow movements, swiping each stem with his claw but leaving the flowers to wilt on the ground. Matthew knew that wasn't how the tool was meant to be used. There was something about the blooms themselves, he was certain, some *other* thing Phineas was supposed to be doing there.

"You're wasting the flowers," he pointed out. It seemed a grave injustice for Phineas to spoil all those flowers when he was dead anyway. Matthew had only needed one, for Eliza, and he couldn't even get that.

"I'm sending them west," Phineas countered, becoming Barnabas again. "To find him."

Eliza drifted closer, holding a daguerreotype of Barnabas, who was holding up a portrait of Phineas. She gazed at the flowers, then at Matthew with an unreadable expression. "That isn't what I want," she said, then vanished.

Matthew had woken up in a cold sweat, reaching after Eliza but knowing it was too late. In the logic of the dream, he blamed dead Phineas. Once the nightmare left him and his brain was fully in the waking world, he decided he must feel guilty about leaving Barnabas behind. And about nearly ravishing Eliza in the woods, though she hadn't seemed to mind. Thankfully there were no reporters in the camp that night, nobody to broadcast a scandal about what had almost happened. As far as Matthew could tell, only one other person had seen him escorting Eliza back to her tent, and that was Cantlebury. Since he'd been in the process of sneaking from Miss Speck's tent himself at the time, Matthew was fairly confident of his discretion. They'd given one another the solemn nod of implied secrecy, and that was good enough for Matthew where Cantlebury was concerned.

His main concern now was simply staying awake. His

restless night took a toll, and Matthew had to snap himself from a doze more than once despite the increasingly jarring ride. It was mostly wagon trails now, and because of the rough conditions, the drivers had two days to make it to the next checkpoint in Dodge City. They would have to make camp wherever they could tonight, a prospect that didn't thrill Matthew. This was the territory of the frontier lords, who guarded their domains with the fervor of petty chieftains but did little to keep the peace beyond their walls and fields. Over the rolling, grassy hills with their picturesque scattering of wildflowers, Matthew caught occasional glimpses of armed outriders, and twice spotted castle keeps hulking in the distance.

Typically a traveler in this region ran the risk of highway robbery, or worse. Matthew kept an eye out for the telltale silhouette of wind balloons, the multi-sailed airships favored by wealthy adventurers and prairie pirates alike for their speed and maneuverability. Unlike the lords, the pirates had not been bribed to let the racers pass unmolested through these lands. Still, wind balloons were vulnerable when they approached the ground to launch an assault, and with any luck, the pirates wouldn't want to risk bothering with the racers. A single passenger in a steam car was unusual enough to draw attention, but also not as tempting a mark to a pirate as, say, a mail coach.

Eliza had passed him early in the day, along with a pack that included the Watchmaker, Jones, Moreau, and Madame Barsteau. A few of the others had been nipping at his heels all morning and half the afternoon, while Parnell and Jensen were too far behind to track. Nobody had stopped for lunch, as far as Matthew could tell, and none of them seemed eager to be the first to stop, even when it grew overcast in the late afternoon. Without markers, towns, waypoints to give a sense of distance traveled, it felt as though they had been driving forever along the rolling track, and would forever continue driving through the grasslands.

At least I'll sleep well tonight, he thought. He would be too tired for nightmares, surely, after this day.

The steam car strained going up the next incline, a slightly bigger hill among the others, and when Matthew got to the top he nearly lost control of the vehicle for staring at the vista before him. The darkening clouds hid most of the sky, but a thin strip of gold showed at the horizon, hinting at the sunset that might have been. Scattered across the landscape, rain showers slanted from clouds to ground.

Gold.

That shining gold line did it, brought all the pieces together in one moment of insight. Gold, like the poppies in his dreams, the poppies on the lapels of the horrible Temperance Society ladies. Gold, like the gilded frippery of Lord Orm's boutonniere tool, also shaped like a poppy. Poppies, opium harvesting, Phineas. And all the sabotage.

"He doesn't want us going west."

The next second he dismissed the notion of Orm as some sort of nightmarish mastermind, because Matthew's mind tended toward the practical. He didn't like Orm and he definitely didn't care for the man's taste in accessories, but that hardly qualified him as a villain. Motifs like stylized roses had come into fashion in times past, so why not a poppy? And he'd heard that an innocuous cousin of the opium poppy was a common wildflower in the California Dominion, so it made some sense for Orm to adopt it as his symbol. His cattle ranch was located somewhere near those allegedly poisonous mountains, after all.

El Dorado, he called the place. He'd boasted of the ranch's size and untapped mineral wealth when Matthew had seen him in France. Murcheson had spoken of the increasing need for gold in industrial applications, and Orm had claimed that the hills of his ranch were practically paved with it, but then added something odd. "All kinds of gold," he'd said, in a smug tone that spoke of secret knowledge.

Matthew's stomach clenched as his mind slipped sideways and ran up against another puzzle piece. The waiter at the hotel in St. Louis had said something, something about his aunt and a packet for the charter of the Temperance Society. Which had come from the *El Dorado Foundation*.

His car jounced over a particularly deep rut in the track. Matthew admonished himself and tried to focus on his driving again. He could have damaged the undercarriage of his steamer through his inattention; some of the ruts and dips in the track were easily deep enough to get him into real trouble. He would have to set aside the puzzle for now, but he knew he was missing some obvious connection and that he would have to think it through at some point.

When he reached the next rise, he saw a structure some way off the road, the first he'd seen in miles. Glancing at the sky, then at the nearest patch of rain, he weighed his options. It was not yet full dark. On the other hand, the wind was worsening and the rainy sections seemed to be converging and taking over more and more of the sky. The clouds had taken on an eerie greenish tint that didn't bode well, and whatever that structure was, it might be the only form of cover he could find for the night if he didn't fancy sleeping in his steam car.

Ahead of him, there were other drivers making choices of their own. Would one manage to take on a significant early lead through pressing into the rainy darkness for a few minutes more? Or would that driver bottom out in a rut that looked deceptively like a shallow puddle once filled with water?

Prudence won out in the end, and Matthew turned when he came to a narrow track through the high prairie grass. It led directly to the building he'd seen, which turned out to be a small complex of buildings sheltering in a grove. The biggest, a barn, had hidden the rest from his view. He headed for the farmhouse, wondering how in hell a lone farmer managed to survive this far out.

He had an answer within moments: heavy artillery. The sound of a mechanism drew his attention to the roof of the quaint building, where a turret gun had swiveled to point directly toward Matthew and his vehicle.

Throwing his empty hands in the air, he stopped cold.

"Please don't shoot! I'm not a pirate!"

It was the first thing that came to mind, but he felt stupid even as he said it. Of course he wasn't a pirate, and who was he talking to anyway?

"That's just what a pirate would say," a gruff voice pointed out from some hidden location. Cued by the sound, Matthew spotted a slot by the heavy-looking front door, just big enough for a firearm's muzzle. He knew it was big enough because a shotgun was pointed at him through it.

"It's also what somebody who wasn't a pirate would say," Matthew countered.

"We could argue that all night. Probably ought to shoot you just to be on the safe side."

"Matthew! What on earth?"

Eliza's was the last voice he expected to hear. She rounded the barn at a quick clip, racing to stand between him and the front door.

"Whatever he's done, please don't shoot him, Mr. Thayer!"

"I haven't done anything . . ."

"Oh, I beg your pardon, Miss Hardison." The door opened and out limped an elderly gentleman with a shotgun tucked under his arm. Not pointed at anyone, Matthew saw with relief. "I was just having some fun with the boy. Friend of yours, I take it?"

"Another of the racers. Mr. Thayer, this is Mr. Matthew Pence. Shake hands, Mr. Pence." She prodded him none too gently with her elbow as she stepped to one side, and

Matthew dutifully stuck out his hand. The old farmer took it with what looked suspiciously like a grin. It was difficult to tell behind the outrageous whiskers.

"Mr. Thayer is one of Lord Hasseltine's men. He runs this hay farm. He and his wife, that is. And his daughter Evangeline. She's the turret gunner."

A towheaded girl of twelve or thirteen peered up from a hatch by the roof gun and offered Matthew a tentative wave. From inside the house, he could hear a woman grumbling about something. Her voice grew louder as she neared the door, and he glimpsed a plump, busy shape for a moment before she disappeared again, her voice lingering behind.

"Still not givin' 'em any tea. Brazen scarlet hussy!"

"Beg your pardon again, miss," the farmer said to Eliza.

"Temperance Society?" guessed Matthew.

Eliza nodded. "They've been dropping leaflets, apparently. But Mr. Thayer has graciously agreed to let me wait out the storm in his barn. Which is just as well, because I don't think I could have made it any farther tonight. I scraped a hose on a rut a few miles back and now I'm losing pressure."

"The team is out to market so the barn's empty," Mr. Thayer explained, gesturing with the shotgun. "Should be plenty of room for your demon contraptions. That's what the missus calls 'em."

"Thank Mrs. Thayer again for her Christian charity in allowing this brazen hussy and her colleague shelter for the night," Eliza said, smiling graciously at the old man.

As if he weren't clearly charmed enough. Matthew thought she was laying it on thick, but since she'd secured them both a place to stay, he was not about to complain.

A sharp gust of wind plastered their clothing to their skin. The air tasted thick with impending rain. Eliza glanced from Matthew's car to the barn. "You should pull into the barn first, then you can help me push mine in after. Mr. Thayer says we may see hail, so it will be better to have the cars under cover."

The mostly empty barn usually held a large hay wain and housed a team of four oxen, in addition to storing the hay. Their large steamers fit with room to spare, to Matthew's relief. The rain struck just as Eliza's rear bumper cleared the large double doors, which he quickly closed.

"Warm, dry and snug as two bugs in a rug," he pronounced them. Eliza made a noncommittal sound and opened her back door to start rummaging for tools in one of the trunks. "Well done. You seem to have won Mr. Thayer over despite his wife's affiliations." He wondered whether to tell Eliza of his newly formed suspicions about the Temperance Society and its connection to Orm and the sabotage, but decided to wait rather than worry her. Mrs. Thayer hardly seemed like a saboteur, despite her grumbling and her refusal to provide them with tea.

"I did my best." She produced a jack and proceeded to raise the back end of her car, working hard to crank it as high as she wanted it. Matthew held his hands behind his back, forcibly restraining himself from helping. He was glad he wasn't standing next to her when she paused and removed her long, coatlike outer dress, leaving her in the fashionable black breeches and a frilly white shirt. If he'd been any closer he would have been unlikely to keep his hands to himself. The shock of seeing women wearing breeches had, generally, worn off. He'd seen them all over Europa, after all, and these days they were even de rigueur in New York City. That was entirely different from seeing them on Eliza. Or rather, from seeing as much of Eliza's shape as the breeches revealed.

They were more practical than the dress, however. She fetched a crawler and a tray of tools and slid herself under the steam car, disappearing from the knee up. Matthew knew he should be checking on his own vehicle, doing whatever maintenance needed doing. Instead he approached Eliza and nudged one of her boot soles with his toe.

"You seem out of sorts."

"I've lost pressure, I told you. If I don't find the leak I'll be stuck here, and I do not want to be stuck here."

"Nonsense, you won't be stuck." He couldn't resist teasing her. "I'd give you a lift to the next checkpoint."

She shot out from under the car, levering herself with her hands on the undercarriage, to glare at him. Then she wheeled herself back under without a word. Matthew heard her attack the car's underbelly with renewed vigor.

"It must be rather dark under there. I see a lantern here, would you like me to light it for you?"

One of her feet twitched in agitation and he could practically feel her exasperated sigh. "That would be very kind of you. Yes, please."

The lantern was an old kerosene model and did little to illuminate the deepening gloom under the vehicle. Matthew could hear Eliza cursing, not as sotto voce as she probably thought, as he went over his maintenance checklists. His own undercarriage seemed to have escaped harm, thankfully, and the car looked fine aside from a heavy coating of dirt. Even Eliza's amaranth beauty was dusted down to a shadow of its former glory. Perhaps Dodge City would have some sort of facility for them to clean their vehicles. Or at least for them to clean themselves. Matthew felt as filthy as his car looked.

Setting his tools back in their places, Matthew risked a peek under Eliza's steamer to see how she was progressing. Not well, from the sound of things or the look of the tube now dangling down where it surely should not be.

"Not a word," she warned him, before he could ask if she needed help. "Not. A. Single. Word."

"Eliza—"

"That is a word."

"I wasn't going to interfere. But you know, I did make a promise to Dexter before we left and I feel I haven't done very well in keeping it."

The tools stilled, her arms lowered and he could make out her profile through the loop formed by the drooping hose.

"A promise to Dexter? What did you promise him that you would need to tell me about now, Matthew?"

Her tone was ominously quiet and placid. He'd come to know that placidity spelled impending trouble with Eliza.

"Ah . . . that. About that." Perhaps if he said it quickly enough, it wouldn't draw as much ire. "He made me promise to look out for you as long as I was in the race. Make sure you got safely to Colorado Springs, at least. Frankly he thought you'd be too far ahead once the air leg started for me to keep up with you after that. Isn't that part a reassuring confirmation of his confidence in your abilities?"

After a long moment of utter silence, Eliza picked up a wrench and went back to work on her car.

Matthew scanned the barn and finally settled himself on a hay bale, one of a long double row that had apparently been left behind by the farmer's team on their trip to market. Perhaps as fodder for the farm's own beasts, perhaps simply excess once the wain was fully loaded. He thought they might make a better place to sleep, with the addition of a few blankets, than the back seat of his steamer.

Eliza cursed again, thumping something heavy and metal against the packed earthen floor. She kicked a heel to the ground, apparently for leverage, and growled at whatever she was struggling with in the bowels of the steam array. Dexter's design was brilliant, but for rough terrain it might need bolstering in the future to protect more of the workings that allowed the car to take on water so easily. Matthew was saddened for a moment to realize that suggestions like this were no longer his business to make at Hardison House. He cheered himself by thinking of how he might modify his *own* design to allow for both safe, easy intake of water and rugged durability against bumps.

"Bloody—ugh!"

He was like a moth to an open flame, utterly unable to help himself. "May I ask what it is you're doing under there, Eliza?"

Her answer was punctuated with more noises of effort and frustration. "There was a minuscule puncture in the intake hose but it was right by—*oof*—the coupling so I trimmed it and then all I had to do was refit the hose to the *damn* housing. But this *bloody* gasket fell off and now it won't reseat itself properly, so the housing won't seal back to the—*grrr*—main chamber."

"I don't suppose you'd accept any help—"

"*No.*"

"I thought not. Right, I'll just be over here on my hay bale then, enjoying the sound of the rain."

"It sounds more like gunfire than rain."

She was right, it did. Crossing to the door, Matthew ventured a peek out and saw the yard filling with dirty white hunks of ice. *Large* hunks.

"Hail. The size of billiard balls. Good lord."

Eliza only growled again in response.

"Perhaps I'll pass the time by reading. I have a volume of romantic poetry. Shall I read aloud to you?"

A hair-raising screech of metal on metal emerged from beneath the steam car's undercarriage, followed by what sounded like a deep sigh.

"Why on earth do you have a volume of romantic poetry with you?"

"For wooing women, of course."

She snickered. He heard it clearly, stifled though it was.

"And what would my cousin Dexter say if he knew his

appointed protector had come to the race armed with such a weapon of seduction?"

"Oh, he gave it to me. Not for the race, of course," Matthew admitted. "It was a long time ago. A birthday gift. A sort of gag gift, really, but it's become a bit of a good luck charm. Its usefulness for wooing women was an unforeseen benefit."

"I see. Do you have a favorite? Keats, or Byron? No, it must be someone more esoteric."

Matthew chuckled. "Not *the* Romantics. Just romantic, the adjective. The poems themselves are romantic, the poets are from various eras. I prefer to use the Cavalier poets for my wooing and my favorite is Robert Herrick, if you really want to know."

"I didn't before, but now I'm intrigued. You actually recite poetry? Does this ever win you any favors?"

"You'd be surprised what a well-timed verse can achieve." He approached the vehicle again and crouched near Eliza's legs.

"Oh, just go on and read it. You know you're dying to, and you probably won't stop talking about it until you do." Another round of clanging indicated Eliza was still attempting to improve the state of her vehicle's innards. The undertone of frustration in her voice told Matthew she was still not succeeding.

"I don't have to read this one, I know it by heart. It's 'To the Virgins, to Make Much of Time.'"

"You are joking."

"Nope. 'Gather ye rosebuds while ye may, Old Time is still a-flying. And this same flower that smiles today, tomorrow will be dying.'"

"The flower metaphor is a bit heavy-handed."

"With some women it doesn't pay to be subtle. 'Then be not coy, but use your time, And while ye may, go marry; For having lost but once your prime, You may for ever tarry.'"

"You skipped the middle two verses," Eliza protested.

Startled, Matthew coughed into his hand. "Well, most women I recite it to don't realize that. Or perhaps they're simply too overcome to mention it."

"You've never recited poetry to a woman in your life. Admit it."

She had him there, in truth. And he supposed he never would, if they all reacted to it the way Eliza had. "I admit nothing."

"You're not the type. Dexter wouldn't have *assigned* you to me if you were. That's why he gave you the book as a joke, not as an actual aid to seduction. You're straitlaced and predictable. And dull."

"Dull?"

"As dishwater," she confirmed.

"I can see now I should have lead with John Donne. That would have shown you."

"That," Eliza said, *"that* is your problem. Assuming it's your job to show me anything. You're not my mentor, Matthew. And after this I don't think Dexter will be either."

Mentoring her was the furthest thing from Matthew's mind, and he thought by now Eliza would have grasped that simple fact. He looked down at her legs again, so temptingly within reach, and looked away before the temptation could overwhelm his common sense. "So I take it you *don't* want to hear 'To His Coy Mistress'?

"That's not John Donne, it's Andrew Marvell. And no, I do *not.*"

She knew her Metaphysical poets. He added that to the list of things he admired about Eliza.

"Clearly I need to study my poets a little harder. I'll go read and let you finish your work here. Unless you've changed your mind about needing any help?"

The wrench skimmed out from beneath the steam car at

a brisk clip, knocking the side of Matthew's boot and ricocheting off to land a few feet away.

"Oops."

Matthew bent and picked up the tool, placing it within Eliza's reach before retreating to the safety of his volume of love poems.

Twelve

THE LIGHT HAD grown too dim to work by, and their one meager lantern was insufficient even for reading, much less performing any type of repair. There was no hope for it. She had actually considered braving the monstrous hail, just to put some distance between her and her unwanted protector, until she realized the steam array was simply beyond repair in the current circumstances. Even if the weather *had* permitted her to leave, she was truly stuck here for the night.

Eliza gave up with an exclamation of disgust and slid out from under the steamer. After stowing her tools, she stalked across the central corridor to fling herself down with more force than necessary on the hay bale Matthew offered.

"Morning will be soon enough. A good night's sleep and you'll wake with a fresh perspective."

She cut her eyes at him. "Matthew. Stop talking to me. Please. For both our sakes."

He returned her gaze evenly, shrugging. Eliza was infuriated to see a faint smile on his lips. He was disheveled and it was charming, and she hated that she found it charming. *Look out for her* indeed. *How dare they!*

"You sound like my old granny," she continued, "always spouting aphorisms and warnings. No wonder Dexter thought he could turn you into my race nursemaid."

Matthew considered that for a moment, then nodded his head, seeming to concede the point. He leaned back on his hands, legs stretched in front of him and crossed at the ankles, content to take his ease while he could. Eliza, still wound up from the events of the day, pushed off from the hay bale and paced back to her car to open one of her valises and hunt for food.

"I have some hard cheese and a little chocolate. I wish I'd thought to buy some of that cider while I had the chance, at the market just outside the city. Do you have anything?"

"Hmm."

Much more laconically, he rose and investigated his own vehicle for stray comestibles, managing a length of smoked sausage and a bottle of wine. He waggled the bottle at her inquisitively.

"Brilliant!"

"Mmm."

"Oh, for the love of—I didn't mean you had to stop talking *forever*, you dolt."

"I was taking no chances. It seemed unsafe to arouse your ire before spending the night with you."

Eliza blinked rapidly and coughed into her hand a few times. Matthew, catching his error, corrected fairly smoothly. "Spending the night trapped in a barn with you. Let's open this bottle, shall we? We'll have to share, I don't have any glasses."

"I have a cup. Just one, sorry."

He poured. They drank and ate, and after some time Eliza began to feel much more sanguine about their predicament.

"This could have been worse. A tornado, for instance."

"True. Or a brush fire."

A thunderclap rattled the rafters, and both of them flinched, laughing uneasily.

"I suppose we shouldn't rule out either of those possibilities quite yet," Matthew said, then swigged from the bottle. A week ago, she couldn't have imagined him doing such a thing. Even in the workshop he was always so tidy and fastidious, seeming to repel the dirt that naturally gathered on most makesmiths.

She found herself staring at his throat, the muscular column that moved as he swallowed. A very faint bristle shadowed his jaw, and Eliza noticed a smear of something—engine grease, or some other less identifiable grime from the road—on the side of his neck. Dirty at last, as she'd known he must eventually become. She wanted to wipe the spot clean, then run her thumb along that elegant line from his ear to his shoulder. Then, perhaps, to the little divot between his collarbones.

"Are you planning to sketch me or dissect me?" Matthew whispered.

Eliza gasped and lifted her eyes. He was smiling at her, bemused.

"Neither."

"What, then?"

Swallowing hard, she raised her hand to the smudge. "You have a spot of grease just here." She rubbed at it, accomplishing little in the way of cleaning. But she achieved a great deal else. Matthew's eyes closed and he caught his breath, holding himself still as a statue while her fingers traced the contours below his ear.

His skin was warm and damp, not quite slick with sweat. The pulse in his throat beat wildly, belying his outward control. Eliza loved that contrast, the tension she could feel, the way his breath shuddered when he finally released it. It gave her the same sense of power she'd felt when he'd kissed her the night before, heady and dangerous.

"All gone," she murmured after a moment, after she could no longer even pretend that her excuse for touching him was legitimate. When he clasped her wrist in his hand she shivered, her whole body lighting up from that simple point of contact.

"Eliza, what happened in the woods last night—"

"Failed to satisfy . . . my curiosity. On several points."

"Shouldn't have happened."

She'd felt the same way once they'd stopped. Somehow she forgot that though, now that she was close enough to touch him again. She wanted to kiss him, feel and be felt, more than she wanted whatever nebulous conceptual freedom she gained by avoiding him.

Society. Expectations. Having to choose between becoming a flagrantly ruined woman with no hope of being received in places I don't especially want to go, but with the freedom to go wherever else I choose . . . or becoming my mother, and dying inside.

Was that really the choice before her? She knew Matthew had no intention of ruining her. If they went further, no matter who did the enticing, he'd feel compelled to ask for her hand. He was also in cahoots with Dexter to chaperone her and had admitted as much. If his honor hadn't been enough on its own, his combined guilt and sense of duty would force him to marry her, or at least to try. And if she had so little resistance to him now, to yearn for his touch even when she was angry with him for patronizing her, how could she refuse him once he knew her inside and out?

Dexter's request and Matthew's promise didn't speak to her of trust in her abilities, but yet again of how little respect she'd earned from either of them. It wasn't even that they'd discussed her safety, but that they'd conspired about it and made decisions without her. As if she were a child.

And really, why wouldn't they see her that way? What

had she done with her life so far? *Who was she*? Eliza knew that seducing Matthew wouldn't make her any more a woman in his eyes, and that she shouldn't be making decisions now, when her anger at him was making her irrational. But the rebellious spark inside her, the side that simply wanted him and damn the consequences, insisted that it would prove something to him, somehow. Give her power over him. Her logical mind struggled valiantly, but her libido pummeled it to a fare-thee-well and stuffed it into a box somewhere the moment Matthew's hand started to travel from her wrist toward her shoulder. She could think about all those things later. Right now she was through thinking.

"It's not that I don't want to," he said, an echo of last night's assurance.

"We're not up against a tree," she pointed out. "Wasn't that your excuse last night, that you didn't want to ravish me against a tree? These are hay bales."

"Fine, then, perhaps I *don't* want to." He dropped his hand to his lap petulantly. "Perhaps I don't want you at all, and I was just trying to let you down easy."

"Liar."

He caught her wrist again before her grasping hand could reach its destination and prove him wrong definitively. It didn't matter. They both knew he wanted her as much as she wanted him.

"The truth, then. I don't want to do it *like this*. Parts of me have minds of their own, but that doesn't change the fact you're trying to make love and all the while staring daggers at me. Instead of feeling pleasant, it feels angry and spiteful. And also pleasant, but I can't help that."

"Pleasant?"

"*Very* pleasant. Are you angry because of what I said about giving Dexter my word I'd look after you?"

"No." She jerked her arm away from him, putting some

distance between them on the hay bales so her scowl could get the proper range for maximum effect. "I'm angry because you and Dexter didn't bother to *tell* me."

Matthew threw his hands in the air, clearly exasperated. "Because we thought you'd be angry about it."

"Of course I am, but not about the concern. I would have been miffed but ultimately not bothered by that, it's only what I'd expect. I'm angry about the patronizing secrecy. It makes me wonder what else you're hiding because you think it's for my own good. Anything else I ought to know, anything else you're trying to protect me from? How am I meant to trust you now?"

"And you thought seducing me would remedy that?"

"No," she said frankly, "I thought seducing you would take my mind off things for a while. And also be rather *pleasant*."

"Eliza . . . you don't make a *habit* of this, do you?"

She gasped in outrage and, before she could even think, slapped him hard. Then she gasped again, putting her hands to her mouth in shock at what she'd just done. "Oh, I beg your pardon!"

"I'll take that as a heartfelt no." He fingered his cheekbone lightly, grimacing. "I suppose I deserved it, however."

"I really am so sorry. I don't know what came over me." After a long pause that should have felt awkward but didn't, she sighed. "I always feel that way around you, never knowing what's come over me."

"But how can that be? I'm so straitlaced and predictable." He favored her with a droll look, then went back to wincing as he prodded his injured face.

"I know," she agreed, suppressing a smile. "It's a mystery to me too."

"Mysteries. That reminds me. I do have something else to tell you, though I wasn't keeping it from you for your own good, exactly. More because I think it might just be a product of my own delusions and lack of proper sleep."

"An actual mystery?"

"Here, let's get the blankets first. These bales are itchy and it's getting colder."

"At least the hail seems to have stopped." She'd noticed when she realized they didn't have to speak up to hear one another anymore. The hailstones had been almost deafening as they battered the roof of the barn. "If it had ended sooner I'd have kept working on my intake array and tried to move elsewhere for the night."

"You would have wound up mired in mud in the barn-yard, and I'd have been cruel and made you sleep in your steam car instead of letting you back in to the warm, dry barn. This is a competition, after all."

They retrieved their bedrolls and the extra quilt Eliza had packed on her mother's insistence, then spent some time dancing around one another before finally laying the quilt over the broad bales and rolling out their bedrolls head to toe across it. Side by side, but with at least a pretense at decency. Neither of them got inside their bedding, however. They sat on the blankets with their legs crossed like children. Eliza started taking pins from her hair, releasing the heavy braid from its wrapped coil and letting it dangle. It was always one of the best moments of her day.

Matthew dove in to tell her of his mystery, without preamble. "I think Lord Orm is somehow wrapped up in both the ladies' Temperance Society and the sabotage. Also, possibly, the illegal sale of opium. Stating it like that, I realize it sounds mad. Especially as part of this theory is based on a dream I had last night."

"We should have stuck to some safer topic, like the weather."

"I know, I know. But working backwards from my dream,

it all made sense. The poppy lapel pins that those temperance ladies wear are just like Orm's ridiculous boutonniere, in miniature. The Temperance Society is run and bankrolled by something called the El Dorado Foundation, and Orm's ranch in California is called El Dorado."

"That does seem like an awfully lot of coincidence." She'd been prepared to laugh off the theory until Matthew laid out his details. Now the possibility that he was right loomed like gathering storm clouds, heavy and impossible to ignore, changing the quality of the very air she breathed.

"In my dream, Phineas was harvesting poppies, in a giant field of them. It went on as far as the eye could see, and the poppies were golden. Not golden like yellow flowers, actual gold. He spoke of going west. Or rather, Barnabas did. He was there too."

"It's a myth—"

"But what if it isn't? What if Orm is somehow using the opium dens to press-gang workers, then literally taking them west to slave away on his ranch?"

"Now he controls the opium dens as well? They're nearly all owned by the Chinese, I thought. It doesn't make sense, Matthew, where would he get the opium?"

Matthew leaned forward, an earnest light in his eyes. He was convinced, and his certainty went a long way toward convincing Eliza. "Orm once said that the hills of his ranch were paved with gold, *all kinds* of gold. He added that part deliberately, *all kinds*. What if he was being clever and he really meant poppies? They grow wild in California, entire fields of them like in my dream. It would be easy enough to adapt that landscape for growing some form of opium poppy, I'm sure. And he wouldn't have to ship across the ocean, so he could almost certainly undersell the Chinese in both the legal and illegal markets here in the Dominions."

"But the sabotage? Murder? Why would he care about

the rally? Isn't he sponsoring one of the drivers? Jones, I think."

"It's only smart to have a man on the ground. I wouldn't be surprised if he had more than one driver or race official on his payroll. But I think his real goal is to stop as many of us as possible from getting to the last few airship legs. He doesn't *want* us going west over the Sierra Nevada. Think about it, if you had a giant illegal opium farm, would you want anyone flying over and discovering it? He's probably been shooting down airships for years. He might have even been behind that geological survey that found toxic fumes there. I think it was privately funded."

Eliza mulled all these ideas over, worrying at them in her mind until she thought she had them in some sort of order. "This would be an interesting twist on my premise." At Matthew's blank look, she explained further, falling naturally into her lecturing rhythm. "This is what I studied at Vassar. I told you, I'm writing a book about it. Myths and common legends come from someplace, they always have some origin point and often even a grain of fact at their heart. I've long argued that the ruling classes have used the power of certain myths, encouraged their growth or even deliberately propagated them, to keep their workers in line. Not only in antiquity, but here and now. The inland lords and eastern manufacturers know there are freeholds and land for the taking in the west, and they don't want their farmers or laborers sneaking off in the night to find their own stakes. What better way to keep them at home than by making the whole idea of going west synonymous with never being seen again, even turning it into a metaphor for death?"

"Not to mention the poisonous gases."

"Each additional tale like that only serves to bolster the fear surrounding the central myth. But in this case, if you're right, perhaps the entire thing is more fact than legend. Only it isn't poisonous gases and mysteriously disappearing addicts, it's anti-airship guns and a complicated scheme to conscript a labor force."

Matthew frowned, apparently thinking of additional pieces. "I'll bet one of the last legs is routed directly over his land. He couldn't demand a change in the race route without arousing suspicion, and he couldn't shoot us all out of the sky at once on that last sprint over the Sierras. That would also cause a huge fuss and there would almost certainly be a search party. He needed to eliminate as many as possible before the last day, and in enough different ways to make sabotage seem improbable."

"Not needed. *Needs.* And what real proof do we have? I don't see how we can stop him."

"It's true, they'll laugh us out of the rally if we bring my crackbrained theory to the officials in Dodge City. But Eliza, what if he really does have Phineas?"

She took his hands, squeezing in reassurance. "Consider that this is the first real lead you've had about where he might actually be. Before, you had no hope of finding him, did you?"

He shook his head, clearly not liking the admission, but too honest to deny it. His fingers played over hers, twining and untwining.

"So at least now you have hope. Will you tell the race officials your theory tomorrow night?"

"I'm not sure yet. I'll have to sleep on it." Matthew seemed distracted, staring at their still-joined hands. "You think I'm a prude, don't you?"

"Come again?"

"For not letting you take advantage of me."

"Are we back to that?"

"I'm not sure you even like me. And as I've said, I'm very fond of you."

She sighed, trying to think of a way to respond that wouldn't start another argument. As much as she sometimes enjoyed arguing with Matthew, she'd had quite enough of it for one evening. "I like you. I'd like to know you better. But I don't think you respect me very much, which is hard to take."

He grinned, and she couldn't help returning it. "You're beating me pretty soundly for time in this rally, and I assure you I have a healthy respect for that. And for your conviction, which I admire enormously. I had no idea you were so educated about this myth business. Not sure why, really; I knew you'd been away studying. You must have been studying *something*. But I knew you as a child, and I think I needed time for my mind to catch up with . . . the rest of me in recognizing that you weren't a child anymore."

"I'll choose to be flattered by that."

"I hoped you might. Believe me when I say I don't see a little girl when I look at you."

"But you still won't let me take advantage of you."

It was Matthew's turn to sigh, in obvious frustration. He freed one hand to push his hair back, raking it away from a furrowed brow. "If I asked you to marry me, what would you say? Hypothetically?"

"Hypothetically or otherwise, I would say no. I don't want to marry, I want to have a life of my own." The whole idea of marriage stuck in her craw. Wives might no longer be the chattel of their husbands, but in the marriages she'd seen it didn't seem to matter. They still fell into the patterns of matronhood, motherhood, a host of expectations that held no appeal for her. Running a household, caring for children, losing the chance to do *so many things*. It wasn't that she never wanted a home or family. But not now, not yet, when she had so much else to do first. "I don't see why the two must be connected."

Nearly tearing his hair out, Matthew growled in exasperation. "Neither do I. I'd love to be taken advantage of. But you don't want to marry, and I . . . oh, I can't believe I'm saying this. I don't have a French letter, and I don't think withdrawal works worth a damn. If you were to get pregnant

I'd never forgive myself and neither would you. You'd have to marry me then, and it would be forcing you into something you don't want."

"Oh."

ELIZA'S EYES WERE wide, startled. Matthew cursed himself for laying out the truth so bluntly, but he simply hadn't known what else to say. He wanted her desperately, of course he did, but he *couldn't*. His honor might be overridden by desire at the moment but it wasn't gone completely.

"Oh," she said again, after a little pause. "By French letter, I take it you're referring to some sort of, um . . ." She made a gesture with her free hand that drove Matthew several feet closer to the edge of insanity. He grabbed her fingers and wound his through them again, to stop her before he could visualize any more.

"It's a lambskin sheath. To catch the—"

"I understand the mechanism. I know what it is and what it's for, I just didn't know they were called that."

"Ah."

He'd half expected her to be horrified, but to Matthew's slightly apprehensive surprise, Eliza now merely looked speculative. He wasn't sure that boded well for his self-restraint, as her ideas in the past had led him quite far astray from paths of strictly virtuous behavior.

"That's very practical of you, Matthew. Very considerate." She seemed to be more interested in filling the silence and giving herself more time to consider than actually complimenting him.

"Sweetheart, what are you thinking about?"

"Sweetheart?" She lifted her eyebrows at him. "I like that. I'm thinking of a friend at Vassar."

"I see." It seemed an odd time for reminiscence, and he knew there was more to it by the look in her eye as she tilted toward him over their hands.

"If you saw what I was thinking, you wouldn't look nearly so calm or collected. I'm thinking terrible things for which I will surely go to the devil. Probably the very sorts of things those temperance ladies suspect me of."

"Eliza, I've explained, I really can't."

"You can't do *that*. You do realize there are other things we might do, yes?"

Thirteen

Matthew swallowed and tried to will his heart to beat at a normal pace. He wondered if Eliza cared that his palms were sweating all over hers. "Hypothetically?" *The cracking voice is stellar. You're a born Lothario, Pence.*

Her grin was evil, pure delightful evil. For all the world, though he would never say it, like a wicked child bent on mischief. Adorable. "Where would be the fun in that?"

It was the same look she used to get when she thought she'd successfully slipped by him, just before he thwarted her by pulling her away from the giant turbine, the molten metal, the thousand and one hazards the workshop presented. She'd given the same enthralled, hungry look to the machinery that she now bestowed upon him. As if she were itching to get her hands on it. What little blood remained in his brain simply couldn't support thoughts of denying her. He wanted to be the engine she took apart to see how it ran. It was a new world out here on the frontier, and if she wasn't bothered by the muddy morality of it all, why should he be? It wasn't as though anyone would know but the two of them.

"As long as we don't do *that*," he said, scarcely believing he was in such a position.

Her grin widened and she bent closer still, then seemed stricken with a moment of uncertainty. "I don't actually know what most of the other things are," she confessed.

He freed his hands and cupped her face, stroking his thumbs over her high, sharp cheekbones. This, at least, he was reasonably confident about. "I do."

At least he knew enough to start with. Matthew was certain he'd come up with more ideas as he went along. And so might Eliza, he thought, his cock twitching at the possibilities as he kissed her until they were both mad for more.

She was trickier to undress today. Her shirt seemed to have an endless amount of tiny buttons, and beneath that he was faced with a set of stays and a chemise. Eliza batted his hands from the back laces of her stays, never taking her mouth from his, but the fastenings on the front of the garment baffled him and he finally gave up.

She leaned away long enough to mumble, "They're like hooks." Then she gripped the placket on either side, exhaled mightily and squeezed, somehow popping the whole thing open at once. "If you'd messed with the lacing it would have taken you hours and you'd have needed to lace me in again in the morning."

"I would have been happy to, but I like your way better. Curse this lantern, though, I can barely see you."

"Will this help?"

To his utter shock and delight, she pulled her chemise off over her head. His brave, defiant, beautiful girl. "Immensely. Thank you."

"You're welcome. Now you."

Matthew shrugged his suspenders off, popped a few shirt buttons open, then gave up and took it off over his head as Eliza had, tossing it off the bales with a flourish.

"That'll be a nest for mice by morning."

"Don't care."

"You're quite lovely, you know," she murmured, raising her hands to his shoulders. Following the contours, she worked her way to his chest, learning him muscle by muscle. He itched to do the same to her, but forced himself to be patient, to let her set the pace.

HE FELT ESSENTIAL under her hands. Like a part of herself she hadn't known was missing until she found it. She'd known a fraction of this sensation in the woods, but to face him this way, uncovering themselves to one another as a conscious decision, was unfathomably better. Eliza liked all of him, everything she touched, from the rounded muscles of his shoulders and arms to the firm, flat planes of his chest. She brushed the divot between his collarbones with her thumb, then with her tongue, and found it salty but wonderful. He tasted necessary.

When she got down to the rippled muscles of his abdomen, Matthew finally reached across the narrow divide between them and mirrored her movement, teasing his fingers across her belly. He was bolder, dipping below the waist of her breeches.

"These need to come off next."

"Boots first," she reminded him. He slipped from the bales with a cheeky grin, positioning himself on the floor beyond her toes.

"Your foot, madam?"

She offered one leg up and he pulled, levering the tall boot off in one practiced motion. Then the other and, to her chagrin, her socks, which had to be the worse for wear. Eliza expected him to climb back up, but he didn't. He coaxed her to stand, then set to work on her breeches, quickly discovering the side buttons and the silky, specially designed short drawers. He slid both down at once, slipping his hands beneath the fabric and caressing her legs from thigh to heel until the clothing was gone.

And that was it. Standing naked in front of a man. Not so difficult after all, so why was she shaking? People did it every day. But Eliza felt stripped of more than clothes. Matthew's sparkling eyes seemed to notice every facet of her being, not just her appearance.

"We can stop if you want to," he offered. She shook her head fervently.

"Why on earth would I want to stop?"

"In that case, lie back down."

She'd planned to be more active, but when it came down to it, Eliza found herself lying back and simply *feeling*. Matthew traced her from toe to neck and back again, caressing each part of her with seemingly infinite care. Then he started another round with his mouth, licking and nibbling everywhere he'd stroked. Everywhere except the place she wanted him most urgently. When he finally brought his fingers there, sliding up from her thigh to run them gently over her folds as he kissed her mouth sweetly, Eliza was embarrassed to realize she was whimpering, shamelessly pushing into his touch.

"You're wet," he whispered, as though it were a miraculous discovery to have made. "I have to investigate more thoroughly."

He slipped down her body, kissing his way, and in her ignorance she didn't realize what he meant to do until he replaced his fingers with his tongue. His hot, velvety, muscular, absolutely astounding tongue.

"*Oh*. I never want you to stop doing that," she informed him.

"What if I did *this* instead?" His tongue of wonders swiped over her clitoris, and she realized if he kept going, she would climax. Would he want that? Was she supposed to like this? Then he did it again and she didn't care whether she was supposed to or not. When he used his fingers *and* his tongue, well, that was just cheating and she was no match for it. It felt too good to resist, too good all over but especially in that center of hot anticipation, the furnace he was stoking so patiently. She couldn't help but burst into flame, wailing his name as the orgasm burned through her.

When the heat finally eased and he lifted his head, she felt cleansed but embarrassed. For all her brave talk, she hadn't known a thing, not really. *Mouths*, that simply hadn't occurred to her, though after the fact it seemed obvious and brilliant. Why not mouths? Of course. So much better than fingers alone.

"You taste wonderful," he mumbled against her inner thigh. His chin was wet. Looking down her body, she saw him resting his head on her leg, eyes closed as he nuzzled about. His arms still cradled her hips, and he was petting her in gentle, soothing, aimless strokes along her flanks. He looked absolutely content and like he belonged there.

"I can't see how I would. I need a bath more than life itself."

"No. You taste like life itself. And I need a bath too, so what does it matter?"

He slipped one finger back inside her, then worked another in more slowly. It tugged, stretching her, but didn't quite hurt. She already wanted more, wanted to *learn* more.

Matthew shifted again, crawling up to hover over her on all fours, pressing kisses here and there as he went. He lingered over each of her breasts before finally reaching her mouth and settling in, lowering himself between her legs. It was slow and dreamy, perfect. But his trousers were scratchy against her still-tingling thighs, and his erection pressed against her pelvic bone insistently every time he moved.

"Is there a quid pro quo I ought to know about?" she asked at last, between languorous kisses.

Matthew opened his mouth, but nothing came out. He bit his lip, shifty-eyed, looking embarrassed and aroused and generally worthy of affection. After a moment he seemed to come to a decision. "There *is*, yes, in theory. Or so I've heard. Nobody's ever . . . I've only ever done the one thing, the primary activity that we agreed *not* to do. And I wouldn't ask you to try that other thing. I don't think it's the sort of thing nice gentlemen ask ladies to do."

"Oh. You mean you've never done that thing you just did? You seemed quite good at it."

"How would you know?" he pointed out.

Eliza shrugged. "If I ever gain a basis for comparison perhaps I'll report back. In the meantime, carry on as you did, it was splendid. Aren't we long past the part where we worry about what nice gentlemen and ladies do?"

"I suppose we are."

"If we're debauching one another, we might as well do the thing properly. Why are your trousers still on?"

"No good reason springs to mind."

He practically leapt up, shucking his trousers and drawers so quickly Eliza didn't have time to prepare herself mentally. Suddenly there it was, the piece of his body whose existence she wasn't supposed to acknowledge, standing out at a stiff angle and bobbing gently as he leaned over to toss his garments on an adjacent hay bale.

Words ran through her head in a rush, and she just as quickly discarded them. *Penis, male member, manhood, willy, that thing . . .*

"What do you call it?"

"Fred."

"I beg your pardon?"

"I call it Fred," he repeated, apparently quite serious, and just as apparently quite comfortable and cheerful standing naked in front of her with Fred drawing all the attention. Eliza made no effort not to stare, though she could feel herself blushing madly. *Want* coursed through her all over again as she watched Matthew grasp it in one hand. He slid his fist down its length and back again, firmer than Eliza would have expected, then set it free.

"You've *named* it?" She wasn't sure whether she found that appalling or hilarious.

"Well, you're the one who asked." The light finally dawned, and he snickered at himself. "Oh. I think the word you're looking for is *cock*. Some prefer *prick*, but it's always been *cock* in my mind."

"Except when it's *Fred*."

"Correct."

She reached out tentatively, then drew her hand back. "May I touch it?" It seemed the sort of thing a man might have strong feelings about. If he went and named the thing and all. As though it were a pet. She wanted very much to pet it. She was fairly sure it wouldn't bite.

He edged close enough to lean his knees against the bale, offering himself up. "Eliza. *Sweetheart*. Henceforth, whenever we are naked and alone you have my blanket permission to play with Fred as much as you like. *God*, this is madness."

He said *God* again when she touched him, running her fingers over the surprisingly soft skin of his cock. She liked that word. It was cheerful and blunt, just like Matthew's manner now that he'd given himself over to lewdness. A good solid word for a good solid thing. *Very* solid, when she tried gripping it as Matthew had, and found the muscular core beneath the deceptively velvety surface. The skin slipped over it as she moved her hand, revealing and concealing different things. Matthew's breathing grew heavy, serious, and Eliza glanced up to see his lids had drifted down to half-mast. But not closed, oh no. He was watching her, watching everything she did with avid interest. The veiled ferocity of his gaze raked Eliza's skin, charging the moment with even more tension.

She wanted too much, was thinking too much. Her

response disconcerted her; it was so uncontrolled, so extreme. Surely people did this every day without going mad. Eliza decided she needed some detachment. To treat the whole thing as a learning experience, not the mess of hot emotions it was rapidly becoming.

Trying to think objectively, she experimented with her hands to see which actions produced the best noises from Matthew. The underside of his erection seemed more sensitive than the top, and when she stroked hard enough to move the loose skin around the bit that peeked out at the end, he groaned in a most gratifying way.

"I won't last much longer if you keep doing that." He seemed to be warning her of this, for some reason.

"Do I want you to last longer? Isn't that defeating the purpose?" Her fingertips brushed against Matthew's testicles, eliciting another delicious sound from him. *Oh, Fred's cohorts are sensitive too.* She wasn't supposed to be filing that knowledge away for later, but she couldn't help it. Eliza was already anticipating a next time.

"It's nice to be able . . . oh, do that again. Again and again, just like that. No, harder." He wrapped his fingers around hers and tightened both their hands, moving so hard and fast that Eliza thought it *must* hurt him. But it didn't seem to. Quite the opposite. Instead, he shuddered and stopped, started again, pumped his cock a few times more in no discernible rhythm and then spent himself in a glorious mess.

The edge of the hay bale, the blanket, Eliza's knee, their joined hands. The thick white fluid seemed to be everywhere, though there was less of it than she'd been led to expect. The girls at college really hadn't known much, she decided, even the ones who claimed to know much more than they ought to. She felt spent herself, for no good reason . . . and like she'd accomplished something miraculous and strange.

Matthew sagged onto the bedrolls and flopped to his back, still breathing hard. After a second he pulled Eliza down with him, rolling half on top of her and kissing her like his life depended on it.

"I can't believe we just did that," he said after an indefinite period of time. Eliza was half-drugged by the lazy sensuality that had overtaken her. She hummed in response and tried to catch his lips with hers again, but he evaded her and stood, finding his discarded shirt and attempting to clean up with it. "You're quite sure you won't marry me?"

"Positive," she murmured, feeling somewhat less positive than she had an hour earlier. "I'll marry someday, for love. Once I've done all the things I want to do."

"Tell me some of them." He flicked the ruined shirt away, then crawled back onto the hay bale bed, tugged a bedroll open and flung it over both of them as she considered.

Under the blankets, snuggled against Matthew, Eliza felt nearly giddy with happiness. It was illusory, she reminded herself, a side effect of their no-doubt-foolish activities and the overall heat of moment. But for the moment, in the drowsy dark as their sated bodies relaxed and melted together, it was almost too perfect to bear.

"I want to see Europa, especially France. And Italy. Oh, and Switzerland, I want to see the Swiss Alps. Climb as high as I can."

"I'd love to go back to France. I never made it to Paris, I was too busy in Le Havre when I was there. You should add England to your list, by the way. If only for form."

"England is a given," she assured him, as if he ought to have known.

"Good girl."

"Yes. But even the good girls rarely get grand tours. Let's see, what else?" Matthew rolled to his side, getting more comfortable, one arm around her shoulders. She nestled against his chest, toying with the sparse dusting of soft hair.

"Finish my monograph, of course. I suppose I'll have to adapt my premise if your theory about Orm turns out to be correct. All my fiddling about with staged photographs of the missing, and discussing myth creation mechanisms, seems pointless if there's been an actual conspiracy to abduct people and spirit them away. I'll have to throw out most of my work and start fresh, and a revision that drastic will take some time, obviously.

"And after that I'd like to spend some time in the workshop. I think Dexter's intake array is a good start, but I had an idea about modifying and reinforcing it to protect against incidents like this afternoon, with the rut. I can do the designing on my own, but I'll need the equipment at Hardison House to mill the parts for a prototype."

"I had the same thought, about fortifying the array. We'll have to compare notes. You never finished letting down your hair, I just realized. Wouldn't you like to?" His restless fingers had found a stray hairpin, which she accepted from him and added to the small pile on top of her shirt. "I know I'd like to see it."

"You just want to make me lose time in the morning, brushing and rebraiding it," she accused him, then yawned mightily.

"Speaking of morning, have you set an alarm? Just in case mine doesn't go, it's always good to have a backup."

"Mmm hmm." The chronometer in her car was set to go off at five o'clock in the morning. It would honk the horn, which ought to wake them, the farmer's family and possibly the local roosters.

Matthew echoed her yawn, apologizing reflexively. "I would have liked to do more things, you know. I'm just too damn tired."

She was too sleepy to muster a response, other than a contented sigh.

A few minutes later, nearly lost to slumber, she felt Matthew press a kiss to the top of her head. He whispered something then, and she pretended not to hear it. She was so close to sleeping it could have been a dream, anyway, and it would be better if it were because it wasn't something she could hear from him. Nor something he ought to be saying.

It had sounded suspiciously like, "I love you."

FOURTEEN

JENSEN HAD DECIDED to continue despite the dark and rain, and he wasn't the only one who paid for that choice dearly. When the hail had begun, he'd run off the road toward what he thought was a crofthold in the distance. The small, square light he'd seen turned out to be a storm lantern hung under a tree branch at the hastily erected encampment of the Watchmaker and Mr. Jones.

Jensen cut a swath through the sodden wild grass, and plowed straight into the delicate structure of the Watchmaker's vehicle, which in turn had flipped over onto Jones's steamer, taking out the canvas roof and most of the windows before rolling off again.

When Eliza and Matthew pulled up, the Watchmaker's folly lay on its back, extendible wheel struts collapsed over its undercarriage, looking for all the world like a giant dead spider.

Fortunately, aside from the bump on the head Jensen had taken, nobody was hurt. The Watchmaker and Jones had used their two tents to construct one large shelter against the storm, and the three men seemed to have spent the night in relative comfort despite the obvious ill feelings over the wreck.

"The two Frenchies are ahead of you," Jensen volunteered. "They'll get word to the rally authorities in Dodge City that we need rescuing. But if one of you were to get there first and take the lead back for the Dominions, I'm sure we'd all appreciate it."

"Not I," the Watchmaker grumbled. "I don't care who wins."

"Not the Watchmaker. But Jones and I would appreciate it."

Matthew eyed Jones, wondering if he were in line for praise or punishment for the night's events. Surely if he were working for Orm, he'd have been meant to stay in the race as long as possible, to be the last man standing no matter what was required to achieve that goal. On the other hand, this crash was certainly no fault of his, and had eliminated two other competitors. Yet Jones himself showed no particular emotion other than regret at the empty bottle by his bedroll.

He let Eliza take the lead as they set out again, not out of chivalry but because the wagon track had narrowed somewhat and somebody had to go first. The landscape was more of the same: rolling grasslands and occasional cultivated fields, small outlying holdings guarded against pirates and endless sky that had cleared overnight to a pristine robin's-egg blue. Lovely, but hostile. It grew less lovely as the road widened in late afternoon, signaling they were nearing Dodge City.

Still, Matthew was glad for the drive, and for the time to think. He had let Eliza set the pace even before they were on the road, taking his cues from her when she woke that morning. He'd been up for some time, working on a new modification for his vehicle, culling makeshift parts from his own supplies and from a rack of tools in the corner of the barn. He was just leaving some coins in their place when he heard her stirring.

She was quiet and pensive. Not sorry about what they'd done, and not shy with him, but definitely not ebullient as he himself was. But then he'd wanted her longer. Did she really want him at all, or was he simply convenient and willing? Would she change her mind if they ever did do *that*? If Dexter found out what had happened, would he kill Matthew quickly or roast him alive on a spit over a smelting pot? All very important questions for which Matthew had no answers.

Then he nearly ran himself off the track, remembering random moments from the previous evening. Eliza's hip by his cheek, the sweet taste and sound of her pleasure. Her hand, so fragile but so strong, moving under his as he came. Her inky braid slipping off her shoulder to coil on the bedroll, a line of finest black silk against the rough wool. Her face, always her face, and the light in her eyes he'd never seen before last night. He would have gladly given up the race to remain in that enchanted barn with Eliza forever. Instead, he could only gaze ahead at the rear of her car, remembering and trying not to let the memories stir him to the point of discomfort.

Still running in single file, Matthew and Eliza passed Madame Barsteau at a point he reckoned was a few miles from town. She was overheated, but waved them on without concern. They arrived in the heart of Dodge City just in time to see Moreau emerge from his muddy once-white steamer, wave weakly to the cheering crowd and crumple to the ground in a dead faint.

"HE'LL LIVE," THE doctor pronounced after examining Moreau at the hotel where they'd been installed for the night. "It's that influenza. Don't appreciate you folks bringing it to town."

He spoke to the assembled group of drivers in the common dining hall, but made a particular point to glare at Eliza, who felt like a child being reprimanded in school. Moral censure was the last thing she'd expected in a town that evidently boasted seventeen saloons, but the place was rife with temperance ladies. Boasting their poppy pins and sporting their placards—she wondered if placard-making instructions were some part of their organizational documents, as the signs were all remarkably uniform—they marched along the raised wooden sidewalks of the main road through Dodge City, using the last of the daylight to illuminate their righteous indignation. The sheriff of the town, upon Eliza's arrival, had apologized in advance. His men were keeping the women away from the hotel where the racers were housed and guarding the cars overnight, but he didn't have the manpower to do much more.

The doctor didn't look any more approving than the ladies of the Temperance Society. *Imagine if he knew what I'd been up to last night.*

Eliza shrugged, feeling the others starting to follow his gaze. "I, for one, feel quite well."

"He also has signs of chronic dyspepsia. All that foreign nonsense he eats, no doubt."

The man sported a sizable paunch beneath his waistcoat, and evidence of the supper he'd been summoned from still clung to his shaggy gray mustache and beard, so Eliza thought he shouldn't cast stones.

"Moreau does love a good meal," confirmed Matthew. "Thank you for seeing to him, doctor."

"Had to. It's my job, keeping a body well. All you should know there's two kinds of folks here in Dodge, the righteous and the sinners. When night falls it's the sinners' town. You leave the hotel at your own peril, body *and* soul. Some a'you I don't suppose care much about that. But you been warned, and I don't want a midnight call to tend to any a'you who choose to risk it and end up with a bullet or stab wound for your trouble. I'll come, but I won't like it. Good evening to you all." He shot another sidelong glance at Eliza, then spoke as though he couldn't help himself. "So shall righteousness hate iniquity, when she decketh herself, and shall accuse her to her face. My good wife and her ladies see through you, *miss*."

She didn't know from what pocket of schoolroom knowledge, from which of her governesses or tutors, the response came, but she had one for him. "The Lord knoweth how to deliver the godly out of temptations, and to reserve the unjust *unto the day of judgment* to be punished. It is not for you or your wife to make that judgment, sir. Nor is it for me. Only for the Lord."

She assumed her most demure face, her very best posture, and stared him down with all the earnest innocence she could muster until he turned on his heel and stalked out of the hall.

A lull followed his exit, punctuated by the clink of dinnerware as a serving girl began to clear the table. Finally Madame Barsteau broke the silence.

"I am intrigued by this notion of a town that goes to the sinners at nightfall. Who will join me?"

"Always up for a bit of sinning, ma'am." Parnell offered her his arm.

"Cecily?"

Miss Davis stood and brushed her skirts down briskly. "If the good doctor was the representative of the righteous, I suspect I'll much prefer the wicked."

"Anyone else?"

"I don't think it would be wise," Eliza said with false regret. She wanted wickedness that night, but would have preferred it in the form of sneaking into Matthew's room. Or sneaking him into hers, she wasn't particular as long as they got to continue their . . . conversation of the previous evening. She wanted, *needed*, to touch him again. Sadly, however, sneaking was far too risky in the current setting. "There are probably still temperance ladies at large. I'll stay in the hotel and go up early, and then I'm for a bath and a good night's sleep."

Matthew and Whitcombe shared a glance, and the large man nodded, then followed his three colleagues out into the night.

When the others were gone, Cantlebury drummed his fingers on the table impatiently. "All right, enough with the suspense. What's this about, Pence?

MATTHEW LAID OUT his theory and evidence to a skeptical Cantlebury and a thoughtful-looking Miss Speck.

"I spoke to Whitcombe earlier. He's keeping an eye on the others. Him, I trust. You two as well."

"And Miss Hardison," Miss Speck pointed out. "I gather you trust her."

He'd honestly forgotten that didn't go without saying now. He could scarcely think about anything other than Eliza; of course he trusted her. Clearing his throat, he looked at the beautiful lady in question and caught her covering a smirk with her hand. He couldn't kiss the smirk off her lips tonight, to his extreme woe.

"I trust her completely. The other three, I don't know. But one of them could well be Orm's man. Or woman. Statistically I suppose it would be more likely a woman at this point, but if Orm is involved with these Temperance Society types it seems unlikely he'd sponsor a female driver."

Cantlebury pursed his lips, pondering. "Assuming, of course, that your theory about Orm is correct—and I grant you, I'm inclined to think it may be—why tell us and not the rally authorities? Or *somebody* in authority?"

"Tell them some women were wearing floral jewelry and I had a dream about my friend's little brother harvesting poppies, therefore they should risk angering a wealthy, powerful baron? You only believe me because you know me. Besides, aside from the local constabulary, who would I report this to? There are a few army outposts in this part of Victoria, but there isn't even a proper garrison until we reach Salt Lake City. As for the rally committee, all they can do is stop the race, and then where are we? I can't stop now, I made a promise to Smith-Grenville. True, at the time I thought it was a promise that wouldn't come to much. But if Orm does have slave labor taken from opium dens, if he really is as implicated as I think in all this, I owe it to Smith-Grenville to investigate. To at least *look* for Phineas at El Dorado. What's more, I feel I may owe it to Phineas. I sometimes wonder if we haven't all misjudged him. This drug business, it seems so wrong, so out of character for him."

"Opium can change a person's character," Miss Speck reminded him.

"True. And I realize that my quest is not everyone's. I'm going on, race or no race. Perhaps others would prefer to stop. I wanted to give you two and Whitcombe the information and let us all come to a decision together about whether to take it to the rally representatives."

"Did Whitcombe give his proxy vote?" asked Cantlebury.

"He says he'll go on if there's a rally to race in. The longer he stays in this thing, the longer he's away from home and his mother's wrath over him losing. You've met the widow Whitcombe, I believe?"

"Indeed I have, and I'd fear her wrath too. Well, that's two of you."

"Three," Eliza volunteered. "I'm going forward."

Matthew knew she'd feel that way, but he still clenched his teeth when he heard her say it.

"Lavinia? What say you, my love?"

Miss Speck smiled at Cantlebury, her soft brown eyes shining. "Whither thou goest."

He was caught off guard, struck dumb by her for a second or two.

Cantlebury cleared his throat before replying. "Who would have thought we'd have so much scripture in one evening? You know I'm staying in the rally too, right?"

She laughed. "Of course, darling."

"Just wanted to be sure. So we're at least five. Madame Barsteau is in 'til the end, I'd be willing to wager. I don't know Parnell or Miss Davis well enough to guess."

The serving girl returned to finish clearing. Once she'd gone, Cantlebury hopped from his chair and offered a hand to Miss Speck.

"Perhaps if any of us make it as far as Salt Lake, we can contact the garrison. But for now, it sounds as though we race tomorrow. Time for us to retire for the evening. Darling?"

"That's a bit forward, don't you think?" Matthew nodded at the couple's joined hands.

Cantlebury looked supremely amused. "Not at all. I signed the registry as Mister and Missus. Nobody knows us from Adam here, Pence. We common folk don't quite draw the attention you socialites do."

"Oldest trick in the book. Good one, Cantlebury."

"Will you wait a moment before you go?" Eliza asked, reaching for Matthew's hand under the table and speaking low so only he could hear. "I should go up with them. I can't be the last one here in the dining hall with you, it would only give the temperance ladies more grist for the mill."

He turned her hand in his, rubbing a thumb across her palm and whispering back, "Does this mean I can't even kiss you?"

"It would be begging for trouble. And don't try sneaking into my room later either."

"I would, you know. As the doctor said, the town belongs to the sinners after nightfall. When in Rome, and all that."

"I wish you could, I'm not averse to further sinning with you. But you won't. You mustn't, Matthew."

"I won't. Sleep well and dream of me, sweetheart."

Eliza suppressed a delicious shiver at the lewd things his fingers were doing to hers, then pulled her hand away reluctantly and spoke to Miss Speck and Cantlebury again. "Since you two are a respectable married couple, I'll walk up with you, if you don't mind chaperoning me as far as my room. Good night, Mr. Pence."

"Good night, Miss Hardison. *Cantleburys.*"

SHOUTS AND SHRILL cries roused Matthew, instead of the gentle ring of his chronometer. Rubbing the sleep from his eyes, he stumbled to the window and pushed the sash up, raising the volume abruptly on the ruckus.

The sidewalks near the hotel, even the packed earth road, were crawling with Temperance Society members bearing their telltale signs. More townsfolk arrived as he watched, joining the fringes of the crowd and craning their necks to see into the hotel's wide bay windows.

Dragging yesterday's trousers, shirt and shoes on as he went, Matthew ran from his room. At the gallery overlooking the hotel's common hall, however, he skidded to a halt and gaped at the spectacle below. The shrillest of the temperance ladies stood on one of the sturdy trestle tables, facing off against Eliza, who struggled to fend off a battering with a placard. Eliza wore breeches and a short jacket with a longer flounce in the back, and she appeared to be dripping wet from head to toe.

He shouted to her, but couldn't make himself heard over the commotion. He had to worm his way down through layers of society ladies and others to descend the stairs and get to the table, where he could finally hear what they were shouting about.

"Shameless scofflaw!" screeched the woman, raising her sign to swat Eliza over the head with it.

"You're mad as an inbred hatter, and stop *hitting* me with that ridiculous placard."

The placard in question was a worse-for-the-wear white, and bore one word in large red letters. HARLOT.

"You've made your final mistake, Jezebel, and you'll find out you've gotten too big for those britches when my husband arrives." Her eyes held the manic gleam of the zealot.

"That doesn't even make *sense*."

Eliza made a fair point. Sidling past the last few ranks of crowd members, Matthew gained the side of the table at last and tapped on Eliza's boot to get her attention.

"Good morning, Miss Hardison."

"Matthew, do you have any idea what—*ouch, stop that*!" She raised her arm to block further cracks on the head with the placard, which fortunately seemed too light to do much more than annoy. "I woke early to give my steam car a quick rinse, went for a fresh bucket of water and found myself pushed into the trough. *Pushed*. And then this woman here— *lunatic*, rather—started screaming about having me arrested for wearing trousers."

"They're breeches," he noted.

"*Thank you*. I said the same thing and she insisted it was still against the law for a woman to wear them within the city limits."

"Law-breaking hussy!" the woman confirmed. Her friends in the crowd babbled their support for this accusation, while the less temperate onlookers began to question one another about the law. If it were on the books, it didn't seem the public in general knew of it.

"When I tried to return to my hotel room for dry clothes, there was this horde of temperance ladies barring my way. It's outrageous."

"I agree. Madam, I believe we need to rouse the gentlemen from the rally commission, and—"

"Mr. Hoover!" The woman shouted over him. "Arrest this woman!"

The sheriff, a tall, lean man with a handlebar mustache and one of the largest hats Matthew had ever seen, strode across the suddenly silent room, his spurs chinking against the dusty floor. He halted at the head of the table, forcing his wife to turn her back on Eliza in order to speak with him.

"Edith," he drawled, then leaned to one side and doffed his hat with a nod at Eliza. "Miss."

"Good morning, Sheriff Hoover." She waved her fingertips at him with one hand, the other still keeping a wary guard against placard attacks.

"We're all up a mite earlier than usual, wife. Seems to be some excitement."

Mrs. Hoover drew herself up to her full height and stabbed a finger in Eliza's direction. "Look at that, Mr. Hoover. Would you just look at that shameless display!"

The sheriff leaned over again and scanned Eliza's wardrobe, raising his eyebrows slightly as he saw the shameless trousers in question.

"The young lady appears to be wearing britches. She also appears to have taken a swim. Or was it a dunking?"

"A dunking," Eliza volunteered.

The sheriff nodded, rubbing his bristled chin thoughtfully. "And you're standing on a table."

"She ran up here to escape justice," his wife explained huffily. "I followed her to secure her for you."

"For me to do what, offer her a towel and a dry pair of britches?"

Even some of the temperance ladies laughed at that, Matthew noticed.

"To arrest her, you fool! For breaking the law!" She produced a folded piece of foolscap from her jacket pocket, brandishing it in her husband's face. "Copied from the law books in your own office, Mr. Hoover."

He ducked to avoid taking a blow from the paper, then snatched it and read the writing quickly.

"Edith, did you know it's illegal to have a pigsty in front of a house in Dodge?"

"And what of it?"

"Do you know how many people in this town have pigsties in front of their houses? It's also illegal for a man to relieve himself on the street here, by the way. He can use the side of a building, but not the street itself. That's the law. Also illegal to perform a wedding ceremony for your goat, even if it's to another goat. I can only assume there's one hell of a story behind that one."

For a moment the woman looked ready to back down, but a murmur from a few of her backers bolstered her indignation back to full steam. "This is a question of moral terpitude, husband. Turpitude!"

"Does anyone here actually know what turpitude is?" the sheriff asked the room at large, not seeming to expect an answer. "'Cause I don't, and I figure maybe I'm missing out on something really interesting."

Matthew snickered and caught a wink from the droll lawman. Then the crowd muttered and parted again to allow the two hastily summoned rally officials, a pair of timid-looking gentlemen who had assumed their assignment would end once they'd clocked the racers' arrival and departure times. They'd deliver their results to the express rider who would begin a relay back to the last telegraph office in Meridian City, then take a slow coach back to New York City.

Neither man looked pleased to be awakened before it was even properly morning yet. And neither of them had any help to offer Eliza. The taller of the two, in fact, took one look at the developing situation and began to disclaim the rally committee's legal responsibility for any and all actions performed by race participants in violation of local ordinance or royal decree, and so forth. He stopped only when Whitcombe, stepping up behind him, clapped a huge hand over his shoulder and met his frightened glance with a dead-level stare.

The sheriff raised his hands, quieting the hubbub. "Now, the law my wife has copied down here dates back to 1865. Probably should've been struck from the books a long time ago, along with the one about the goat-marrying. But the fact remains, it's the law, and I'm sworn to uphold it. However—" He scowled and raised his voice above the crowd's response. "*However*, the law Mrs. Hoover is referring to clearly states that it is unlawful for a woman to *dress as a man* by wearing *trousers*. Unless she's holding the reins of a horse at the time, which doesn't seem to apply here. So let's think about that."

"There is nothing to *think* about," his wife interjected.

"Well, now, Edith, you've been running all over town with these other fine ladies, calling Miss Hardison all manner of names that suggest you don't think much of her virtue. Up until yesterday I was ready to give you the benefit of the doubt, but having met the young woman now she seems to be quite a well-brought up young lady. Polite, pleasant, modest. I hear she wouldn't even stay in this dining hall alone with Mr. Pence, there, lest somebody get the wrong impression. But all that aside, I have to ask you all, is there anyone in this room who thinks Miss Hardison's getup there counts as dressing like a man?"

Everyone shifted, looking around one another for a better perspective. Matthew saw one man take a sharp elbow jab from the woman beside him, apparently for appreciating the view too much. Eliza's breeches, tailored to fit her form perfectly when not sodden, were a dark aquamarine blue. Her short boots were hidden under navy brocade spatter-dashes that rose nearly to her knees. Her jacket, which was clearly ruined now, had once been a delicate confection of ruffles in subtle gradations of blue, trimming a tight bodice of cream colored *peau de soie*. She looked more blatantly feminine than any other woman in the room.

"Perhaps if the man were an eighteenth century French

courtier," suggested a hidden voice Matthew recognized as Cantlebury's. A ripple of amusement swept the room, and the mood relaxed a fraction.

"As this is not eighteenth century France, I think we can all agree the lady is not dressed like a man. Especially not a man from around these parts," the sheriff added. "Furthermore, and correct me if I'm wrong, but those aren't trousers she has on. They're britches."

"Breeches," Eliza corrected, stressing the regional difference.

"All right then. Not dressed like a man and not wearing trousers. Edith, honey, I can't arrest this young woman. Now let's everyone go back outside and wait for the race gentlemen to send the drivers off."

He lifted his still-protesting wife down from the table, and Matthew automatically offered Eliza a hand, then panicked, fearing she might rebuff him. To his relief, she simply took his hand and stepped down via a chair. To his delight, she kept her fingers clasped around his far longer than propriety called for. It wasn't enough to make up for his lonely night, but it was something.

Though she smiled at the crowd around her, many of whom leaned in to offer words of encouragement, Matthew could see the strain she was hiding. When most of the spectators had dispersed, he bent close enough to whisper, "You were magnificent up there. And very brave."

"What I am is very tired of this," she replied. "I wish I were home. I don't quite wish I'd never come in the first place, but I'm beginning to think you were right. This was no place for me."

He shook his head. "No. I was wrong, Eliza. You've come alive doing this. You're more than strong enough. Anyone can see that, and I was a fool not to. You're like a force of nature, and I think you're the popular favorite to win this rally now. Otherwise Orm wouldn't be wasting so much effort to target you."

Sighing, she withdrew her hand and gave him a weak smile. "I'd better go get dressed. Again."

He plucked at one of the ruffles near her neck, drawing away a soaked piece of dirty straw. Even bedraggled, she was beautiful. Still, she was *very* bedraggled. "Good idea."

Fifteen

THE UPROAR OVER trousers delayed the day's start by only fifteen minutes, when all was said and done. The sunrise glow had nearly faded from the clouds when the eight drivers set off toward Colorado Springs on their last road leg. Whitcombe, Parnell and Miss Davis took an early lead, taking off hell bent for leather as soon as they cleared the last buildings on the outskirts of town. Eliza led the other five in a loose file, spanning a mile or so along the almost invisible trail through the vast plains of the western Victoria Dominion.

That loose formation probably saved them.

The pirates struck from nowhere, hard and fast. Eliza saw their airships, two giant wind balloons with black sails, against the horizon ahead. She slowed, looking behind her for the others, then ahead in an attempt to spot the leaders. Blossoming fire made it all too easy. Something was exploding, and she only hoped it wasn't one of her competitors' steam cars.

At least it wasn't as loud as the sinkhole had been.

Braking more sharply, she rolled down her window as Cantlebury came abreast of her vehicle.

"Any idea?" he called, eyes on the explosions.

"I can only assume it's the pirates. Do you have any weapons, Mr. Cantlebury? I have a small pistol, but I fear that wouldn't do much good in this case. I'm not even sure where to aim." The pirate ships' balloons were not simple air-filled bags, or even the type with an internal honeycomb structure, but lumpy conglomerations of countless smaller ballonets. Unless one knew which were the critical spots, shooting might not even send the ship off its course.

"Ugly sons of bitches, aren't they? If you can't make it elegant, it isn't an impressive engineering feat in my book. I have a fowling piece, and I recommend aiming for the engines. Avoid the turbines in the rear, however. Wouldn't want a ricochet. Let's move to just behind the top of this next rise. From there perhaps we can see what they've done to the steam cars. Or otherwise. I mean, for all we know it's some newfangled mode of crop dusting, not sabotage at all."

He waved airily at her and sped off, stopping a half mile or so away on the hill in question and exiting his vehicle, fowling piece in hand. Eliza was right behind him with her pistol, and the others followed within a few minutes.

"Whitcombe's car looks like it took a bad hit. He may be inside, I couldn't see him." Cantlebury said to the other three as they all crouched behind the ridiculously meager cover of some scrub oak. "Miss Davis's is obliterated, but she's sitting off to one side of the wreckage so perhaps she's not badly hurt. No sign of Parnell unless he's still in his car. Does anyone have any better anti-aircraft weaponry handy? So far we've a fowling gun and a ladies' pistol. Meaning no offense, Miss Hardison, I refer primarily to the floral mother-of-pearl inlay in the grip, which is lovely work by the way."

"No offense taken, sir. And thank you."

Miss Speck displayed a revolver of her own, a somewhat

more impressive sidearm than Eliza's. Madame Barsteau had no weapons.

"I have something," Matthew offered. "It hasn't been tested in action, I only came up with it the night of the storm, but it's better than nothing."

He quickly laid out his plan, considered Eliza's vehement objection once she heard the particulars and pressed on anyway. The pirates circled over the wreckage, and Matthew was concerned they would soon shift their attention to the second cluster of cars. They were screened in their position over the hill, but not well enough to remain hidden for long.

"Right, so . . . Madame Barsteau, you'll drive my car for me. Cantlebury, Eliza and Miss Speck, you three will follow to the halfway mark in Cantlebury's vehicle, then stop there, get out and cover me with your firearms."

The whole thing moved so quickly Eliza didn't know what to think. She and Lavinia crammed into Cantlebury's narrow steamer, with its single bench seat, and barreled down the hill after Matthew. Stopping halfway per his instructions, they separated and looked for some form of cover. Eliza chose a thinly leafed scrub tree, behind which she cowered, shaking and sick to her stomach. Madame Barsteau drove on, straight into the heart of the trouble. One of the airships clearly spotted the newcomer, coming about to meet the onslaught. The car looked tiny on the ground with the massive ship looming over it.

His solution wasn't a conventional firearm. Instead he had fashioned a crude grappling hook from the tines of a rake and attached it to a launching device that strongly resembled a harpoon gun. A long cord—Matthew said he always carried it, just in case—trailed from the end. When the car was almost beneath the ship, Matthew emerged from the passenger window, sat on the sill and fired his makeshift grapnel over the wooden side of the vessel's oversized wooden "basket."

He'd told them he would only have one shot, and for a

moment it looked as though his efforts would be in vain. *Too high, you aimed too high*, Eliza thought, her heart skipping a beat at the realization that Matthew would be directly in the crosshairs of any gunmen on the ship. The pirates could fire, or drop more explosives, and he would never have time to evade them. But she crossed her fingers as the hook sailed in an arc over the bow and down again to snag on the opposite side. Matthew must have told Madame Barsteau to make haste because the car spun dust up in its wake as she drove straight for the ground below the other ship.

It would have been spectacular if it hadn't happened so slowly. The snared ship's crew had no time to respond to the change in direction before they found themselves tugged along, soaring serenely through the sky and broadside into their companions in crime. If they'd been at full running power with momentum enough to resist the car's pull, the trick never would have worked. But hovering rendered the ships uniquely vulnerable, and Matthew had used that weakness brilliantly.

More grenades flew from the pirates' decks, exploding in puffs of dirt and grass in Matthew and Madame Barsteau's wake. It was too late; the heroes had already loosed their line and were heading back up the hill when the ships' sails and balloons billowed into one another, bringing their basket hulls together in a collision that looked gentle from the ground but must have been anything but for those on board.

And then the flame, and the explosion, a flash of fiery helium that almost scorched the onlookers, even at a quarter mile away. Eliza ducked behind her tree, acting on instinct though some part of her knew it was wholly inadequate protection. Another instinct compelled her to confirm, through the brush, that the car was still moving, that Matthew was still on his way back to her.

They were all recovering from that shock when Parnell came dashing across the plain toward them, with Whitcombe in hot pursuit.

"Bastard!" the big man shouted as the leggier Parnell gained distance from him. "Don't let him get away!"

Fool that he was, Parnell seemed to judge Cantlebury the weakest link in the chain of people blocking his path and aimed straight for him. It was a simple enough matter for Cantlebury to stick his fowling piece out at the critical moment and trip Parnell. The lanky cowboy flew face-first into an especially prickly scrub oak, his hat soaring in the opposite direction.

Cantlebury nodded in the tree's direction as Whitcombe wheezed up to the hilltop. "Got him."

"Thank you." Whitcombe pounced on Parnell while he was still trying to disentangle himself from the branches and began digging in the other man's pockets. "Where is it, you sly son of a bitch?"

"I don't . . . know what you're . . . talking about . . ." Parnell gasped. He was bleeding in several places, from the tree and apparently from the earlier blast, and from the way he was clutching his side Eliza thought he might have a broken rib or some other injury.

"The telegraphic device. Where the bloody hell did you hide it? I know you didn't drop it, I was watching for that. You must have . . . *a-hah!*"

He yanked a small metal box from Parnell's trouser pocket, ignoring the man's yelp of pain.

Eliza had seen an almost identical device before. On many occasions, actually, as it rested in a carefully lit alcove in the gallery of specimen machines at Hardison Hall. A miniature radiotelegraphic transmitter. Dexter and Charlotte's had a dent in it the shape of a bullet, and though they'd never given the full story, Eliza gathered the metal had stopped the bullet from injuring Charlotte. The inner working was mangled, but Parnell's tiny machine was clearly the same sort of thing.

"Who were you contacting?" she demanded, striding

forward to join Whitcombe by the stunted, shrub-sized oak from which Parnell still struggled to free himself.

"I'll never tell!" he screamed, as though he were being tortured.

"No need for melodrama, Mr. Parnell," she scolded.

"He was tapping out a message to the pirates on one of those ships. And from what I could see, they laughed at him and threw him to the wolves. Which is what you deserve, you smarmy, conniving bastard!" Whitcombe finished his speech with a well-aimed prod to Parnell's side and seemed satisfied with the whimper he got in return. "Jesus. Did we just kill them all, Pence?"

Matthew and Madame Barsteau had returned in uneasy triumph. Matthew looked pale, and Eliza wanted nothing more than to rush to him with open arms and thank him for his heroism. She couldn't, not with everyone there, but she vowed to find the opportunity before the day was through. Her heart was still pounding, but her mind soared clear and calm above everything else. He had saved them, with a bent rake and some thin rope. All because he'd seen a girl in a gun turret and had a brilliant idea, then implemented it without a thought for his own safety. And even if he hadn't done those things, she would *still* be madly in love with him. Those things had just brought it to her attention.

Matthew clapped Whitcombe on the shoulder. "I appreciate your saying 'we,' but at the moment I feel entirely to blame. And I think . . . I beg everyone's pardon."

Then Eliza's hero and true love walked his pale, trembling self over to the next pathetic little bush where he bent over and was overtly, unheroically sick. When he was done he fell back, sitting abruptly with his head down, hands wrapped around his knees. Eliza's heart broke. She scanned the group, completely at a loss as to how to proceed.

Miss Speck reached out to Eliza, touching her arm. "Go to him. We all know, Miss Hardison. Nobody cares right now. Just go."

She went, and he leaned into her when she knelt next to him and put one arm around his shoulders.

"Some of them jumped off," he whispered through silent tears. "I saw them fall. They didn't want to burn. My God, I've never even seen a dead body before except at a funeral, Eliza. Much less killed . . . how many men? How many?"

"Shhh." She couldn't say how many because she didn't know, and she didn't want to. She couldn't tell him it would be all right or that he was justified, because she didn't know that either.

"Eliza, when you said you shouldn't have come, that the rally wasn't the place for you . . . I understand now. I understand how you felt."

"Matthew—"

"I thought I might go home covered in glory and start my business as a champion for the Dominions, but how can I? How can any of us think we've *won* after this?"

"Matthew, *listen to me*." She pressed his chin with her fingers, turning his head so he had to look her way. "You are a hero. You are the finest man I know. Not because of what you did to those men in the airships, but because you *care* about what you did. They didn't care. They were throwing grenades even at the end. You're ill to think of it, because you're so very *good* you can't stomach a world where you have to do such a thing to save your friends. But you *did* save us, my love. You charged in and did what you had to do, and saved us all."

He gazed at her for a long moment, his face drawn as her words sank in. Then he nodded once, slowly, as if it pained him. "I'm no hero. But I can live with the part where I saved you. And the others."

"I'm absurdly in awe of you right now," she confessed. "Your facility for using your engineering knowledge in practical applications with whatever materials you find at hand is . . . quite thrilling."

"Temptress." He wiped his mouth with the back of one

shaky hand. "I'd kiss the dickens out of you right now, but you wouldn't thank me for it."

"My Matthew, always so considerate."

"I wish I were your Matthew."

"Don't. I'm sorry, I shouldn't have said—"

"I know."

Gathering himself, he rose to his feet and rejoined the group. Eliza stayed on her knees, trying to think through all that had just transpired, all she had just said, the thoughts that ran through her mind when she was in danger. No, when *Matthew* was in danger. Lavinia Speck had said that the rest of them knew, and didn't care, about Eliza's closer-than-appropriate relationship with Matthew. Eliza had cared. She had been holding back, until she heard that kind voice granting her permission to do what she had so badly wanted to do.

But wasn't part of her goal in leaving New York, her safe society home, to find out what life was like when the only permission she needed was her own? Why was she still waiting on those outside voices, that external approval? Was even the threat of death not enough to jolt her from her old limitations?

Matthew and his two friends were deep in conference over Parnell, who had been freed from the scrub now and was kneeling in the center of the group with head bowed. Somebody had bound his hands. Their voices murmured over the soft prairie wind, a strange counterpoint to the scene of devastation in the valley below. Fires dotted the grassy plain, flitting like the playful children of the great blaze that still burned where the two airships had gone to ground. The land was still too damp from recent rain for a wildfire, or they would have all been in greater danger than the airships could have ever posed. If Eliza hadn't seen the sinkhole so recently, she might have called this a hellscape. She didn't like having that framework for comparison.

Closer to the hill, the steam cars of the three race leaders provided a focal point for some of the child fires. Miss

Davis's car was still burning hot, and the lady herself appeared to be reeling as she attempted to climb the hill.

"Miss Davis!" cried Eliza, leaping to her feet and down the slope as fast as her feet could take her.

"Sweet Mother of God!" one of the men yelled. "We forgot about Cecily!"

"I thought she was dead," Madame Barsteau replied.

A rustle behind Eliza suggested the others were in pursuit, and they soon caught her up. Together, they swarmed the dizzy Miss Davis and helped her ascend. She fainted at the top of the crest, and Whitcombe was just in time to catch her before she hit the dirt.

An ominous bruise bloomed on one of the lady's temples, and even with limited medical knowledge, Eliza had seen at a glance that her eyes looked wrong somehow. As none of them were quite sure what to do, and they didn't want to linger where other pirates might soon descend in search of their missing cohorts, they finally agreed they should all press on to Colorado Springs.

Sixteen

"Call that driving? What'd we just run over, a damn boulder? My old aunt Tillie steers better'n you!"

Matthew should have insisted on gagging Parnell when they trussed him up.

"Shut up," he told his unwilling passenger for what must have been the twentieth time since leaving the site of the pirates' attack.

"None of y'all will live to see the end of this thing. My boss will spring me from whatever pissant sheriff you're taking me to, and you idiots will all be *dead*. I'll be drinking his best liquor and laughing about it when you're in the cold ground, son."

But Matthew heard a note of something else in Parnell's sneering tone, and rather than stop and throw the accused into the increasingly rocky countryside to fend for himself, he decided to take a different tack.

"Is that what Orm told you and Jones? That you would be laughing at the end, rewarded for your service, after we were all taken care of?" He put all the amused skepticism he could muster into the question.

"Beyond our wildest dreams," the man assured him. Then he repeated it, suggesting less than complete assurance. "Beyond our wildest dreams, that's what he said."

Matthew snorted. "So you finally admit it's Orm."

"Aw, goddammit, you little piece of—he's the Lord of Gold, that's all. And he'll send you all west."

"Excellent. I've always wanted to see the Pacific Ocean. But tell me this, does your Lord of Gold like his money?"

He could almost hear Parnell's brain working, even from all the way back there on the floor space behind his seat. It was a silence that spoke volumes.

"'Course he does," the villain answered at last.

"Does he take extreme measures to guard his property and his involvement in the illegal opium trade? Have you ever seen him shrink from any measure, even murder, to keep himself and his wealth secure?"

"That's just what any rich man does."

Matthew tsked, shaking his head. "Those pirates were Orm's men, and they left you on the ground. Laughed at you. He'd given you equipment to signal them. Do you think they'd ignore that signal if he hadn't ordered them to? They were never going to rescue you. You were set up. Your Lord of Gold abandoned you. Was it because you hadn't managed to round enough of us up into a cluster, and so many escaped the ambush? Or was that his plan all along, perhaps, regardless of how the attack went . . . yes, that makes more sense. Why even risk leaving you alive? If Madame Barsteau and I hadn't done away with the pirates, I strongly suspect they had a grenade in reserve with your name on it. And with you out of the way, who would have ever known that it was anything other than a tragic attack by prairie pirates, one of so many that happen in the Western Dominions?"

"You figured it out."

"Your employer suffers from hubris. He's left his marks all over this business, for anyone who knew what they were looking at. Almost as though he signed it, certain he would never be caught or face reprisals."

"No one can touch him," Parnell said. Matthew would have expected bravado, but instead Parnell's obvious awe of Orm seemed to verge on fear. "You have no idea who you're dealing with."

"Orm? Middling height, unprepossessing looks, seems to like wearing gaudy trinkets? Likes to hear himself talk?"

"Joke now if you want. It doesn't change the fact that if you keep going toward those mountains, you'll be dead before you ever see the Pacific Ocean. All y'all will be dead."

"But *why*? Why the elaborate schemes, the expense, why go to all this *trouble*?"

"I ain't saying no more."

Matthew sighed. "Well, at least I've accomplished *that*."

MISS DAVIS HADN'T spoken for almost an hour, and Eliza was growing concerned. Well, *more* concerned, as she'd been worried about Cecily since spotting her on that field. Her stumbling gait and eerie, uneven pupils. She'd vomited *before* getting in the steam car, at least, and so far had not done so again.

Madame Barsteau's trim rally steamer was a single-seater, with no room for a passenger. Miss Speck's car was also too small for a second rider. Eliza didn't mind taking on Miss Davis for the drive, but feared the woman would need medical care she was helpless to provide. As Madame Barsteau had helped her colleague into Eliza's vehicle, she'd warned Eliza to make sure Miss Davis remained awake and talking as much as possible.

"She has a . . . I haven't the word. *Une commotion cérébrale*."

"Concussion," supplied Whitcombe.

"*Oui, exactement.* Concussion. Cecily, you must stay awake if you can, at least until we reach a doctor."

Miss Davis nodded, listless and gray. "I know, Mother, stop telling me."

Frowning, Whitcombe leaned into the car, blocking most of the doorway as he peered into the injured lady's eyes. "Miss Davis, do you know what year this is?"

It was as if the answer danced just out of her mind's grasp. Her pain and frustration were evident. "I . . . do. I know I do. Just forgotten. So tired. And it *hurts.*"

"I know, it happened to me once. For two whole days all I wanted to do was sleep, and they kept waking me every few hours. Yours is worse, though."

"Hurts."

Cantlebury trotted up with a pair of dark spectacles. "Here, she needs them more than I do. We need to move now. The longer we stay here the less I like it. Whitcombe, you're riding with me, yes?"

"Yes, I suppose. *Dammit.*"

"You drove well."

"I was never in the running after Colorado Springs anyway. But I'd have liked to make it to that point on my own, at least."

They'd resumed their long file for the journey. Eliza was second to last, with Cantlebury and Whitcombe bringing up the rear. Matthew had taken the lead, with Parnell tucked into his cargo area, and Eliza had to wonder if he'd drawn the livelier companion.

"Miss Davis. Cecily, are you awake?" She nudged her passenger's shoulder and was relieved when Miss Davis mumbled something. "What was that?"

"What happened? Where am I?"

"You were driving in the Sky and Steam Rally, and some saboteurs bombed your steam car. You have a concussion. I'm driving you to the next stop in Colorado Springs."

Eliza had the answer down pat now, because it was the

same thing poor Cecily had asked every time she woke up enough to speak.

"What time is it?"

"Four o'clock in the afternoon. We should be there in another few hours."

"Hurts."

"I know, Cecily. Just a few more hours and we'll get you to a doctor. Try to drink some more water if you can."

The woman licked her dry lips and accepted the water flask Eliza handed her, but as she lifted it to her mouth she shuddered violently and lowered her hand again. "Can't."

"Please try. Just a sip. You're parched."

Though the shaded spectacles made it difficult to tell for sure, it appeared as though her eyes were closed again already. Eliza rescued the flask before it could fall from her fingers and put the cap back on tightly.

The bruise on Miss Davis's temple had darkened to a truly frightening purple black. Her periods of wakefulness were growing shorter and, to Eliza's mind, less lucid. Her speech slurred, and even when she slept the pain seemed to be unbearable. She alternated between fitful whimpering and, more worrisome, periods of deathlike stillness.

One of those frightening, too-quiet stretches had begun as Eliza drew close enough to the distant mountains to make out some details. After some rough patches of travel through craggy hills and valleys, the land had leveled out around them, a great flat plain stretching out to the foothills of the true mountain range. Eliza felt as if she were an insect crawling along an enormous plate, vulnerable to whatever unfeeling hand from the heavens cared to flick her away or squash her into oblivion. On the other hand, the range of visibility was far too great to make it a likely ambush point for the sky pirates. Her existential anxiety heightened, but her fear of actual attack by the hand of man eased for the first time in hours.

There had been a few simple bridges and raised fords

along the way, but for the first time since leaving Westport, Eliza began to see signs of actual human maintenance in the roadway. It wasn't paved, but it was smoother and flatter than it had been, the larger ruts filled with gravel or sand. There was a small, sturdy bridge at one point, and then a larger trestled one of metal and heavy timbers, spanning a gorge they could have never crossed otherwise. The smattering of single cabins near the road swelled to hamlet size here and there. And then at last a sign, hand-painted and rough, but reassuring, with an arrow pointing west, COL. SPRINGS 5 M.

Eliza chuckled, wondering who had put the sign up, and how often it was read by people who didn't already know the distance to town. "Cecily, wake up. Look, we're nearly there." She shook Miss Davis gently by the shoulder, but the lady slept on. "Come on. Time to wake up. Cecily. *Cecily!*"

She took her eyes from the road for a quick glance, then jerked them front again, trying to breathe slowly and carefully and not think of anything in particular. She especially could not think of what she'd just seen, the thin trickle of blood from Cecily's ear.

"Puppies. I'll think of puppies and keeping the car on the road and that is *all* I shall think of until we reach the checkpoint. Happy, fluffy puppies gamboling in a field of grass. Cecily, wouldn't that be adorable? *Cecily.* Puppies, tumbling and playing, picture that." She reached for Cecily's shoulder again but drew back, unwilling to investigate more closely until she had to. At this point it no longer mattered; there was nothing more she could do.

By the time she reached the checkpoint, she had passed through that point of being overwhelmed by hysteria and entered a state of unearthly calm. She parked the steamer carefully, narrating each point of action meticulously to her silent companion.

"I'm venting down the boiler. Turning off the spirit flame now. And double-checking the brake to make sure it's fully engaged. You should always do that, Cecily, even on the flat. It's quite hilly here, though, of course. All the more need for caution."

The first rally official to reach her car looked grim enough at first. After one glance at Eliza's face and another to take in her passenger's condition, the man turned chalk white himself. A furor broke out, the crowd's noise turning to panic and frantic activity, as somebody opened the door and Miss Davis tumbled out. Eliza never saw who caught her, only knew she didn't hit the ground.

Eliza was not so fortunate.

She came to from an application of smelling salts, and after a moment's disorientation felt a keen sympathy for Cecily Davis. The first thought in her mind was *What happened? How much time has passed?* The sky over her head was a lurid blend of reds, pinks and purples. It was either the most spectacular sunset she'd ever witnessed or she had hit her head like Cecily and was hallucinating the whole thing.

"No, we're old friends from childhood. I'll do it once we're sure she's all right."

"Matthew?"

Getting her bearings slowly, she realized she was lying on her back on the street, her head pillowed on something softer than packed earth. Matthew knelt at her side. She blinked when he bent close, inspecting her eyes in the quickly dimming light.

"You do *not* appear to have a concussion. Do you know where you are? Do you know *who* you are?"

"Colorado Springs, Eliza Hardison. Oh, mercy, did I *faint*? Tell me I didn't." *Mortifying.* She'd never fainted in her life.

"I think I would have too, under the circumstances. Also, your lips are dry and it was warm in the steamers. Did you remember to drink?"

"Oh. No, I suppose I didn't think to. I was so busy trying

to get Cecily to . . . oh, Matthew. Oh no." She struggled to sit up, looking frantically around her. All the cars had arrived, and most of the crowd seemed to have moved down half a block or so to a grassy area in front of a bandstand.

"Miss Hardison, if I may?"

The new voice startled her. It was a woman with a kindly face and iron gray hair, who had evidently been standing near her head. She carried a small torchlight in one hand, and now she knelt down by Eliza and lifted a hand to her forehead. With the skill of many years of experience, she positioned Eliza's head and raised first one eyelid, then another, shining the light in each eye and then holding it back to observe them both at once.

"I'm Doctor Miller, by the way. Are you in any pain? Headache?"

"No, I'm quite well," Eliza assured her. She didn't think she'd fallen very hard, but they seemed to be taking extra precautions with her.

"How is your stomach? Any queasiness?"

"None at all."

"Grip my fingers, please. Now with the other hand. Good. What's my name?"

"Doctor Miller."

"Excellent. I believe your 'old childhood friend' here is correct, you don't appear to have a concussion, but you are probably suffering from dehydration. Water, a meal and some sleep should set you right. He was quite concerned for you."

Matthew didn't look concerned so much as miserable. Eliza took his hand impulsively, sensing there was more to his worry than her silly fainting spell. He squeezed back, still trying to give comfort rather than take it.

"Matthew, what is it? Tell me, please."

But as soon as he drew a breath and steeled himself to begin, she realized. She'd known already, in her heart.

"Cecily? Miss Davis?"

Slowly, he met her eyes and shook his head. Such a small, subtle movement to tell such a grave piece of news.

The doctor stood, taking her time to brush the dust from her skirts. "Mr. Pence, perhaps you would escort Miss Hardison to the hotel now. The sheriff's men won't be able to hold back the crowd much longer anyway, and she really does need fluids and rest. No alcohol, Miss Hardison. You may take lemon or barley water, or lemonade if you must, but fresh spring water would be best."

THE EL DORADO Foundation Ladies' Society for Temperance and Moral Fortitude was out in full force in Colorado Springs. They'd retreated to regroup when Matthew arrived with Parnell and his tale of the pirate attack. But by the time Eliza had been shown to her room and brought a dinner tray, she could hear them in the street. Chanting, though she couldn't make out the words.

She drank a glass of the ice water that accompanied the meal, then undressed down to her chemise, moaning with relief as she unfastened her corset. Thus released, with a dressing gown on to ward against the night's chill, she was able to eat in relative comfort. Or would have been able to, if her mind didn't keep taking her back to that moment, the passenger door opening, Cecily falling out. Miss Davis was already dead, Matthew had told her. Only for a few minutes, Doctor Miller thought, but it had been too late to revive her.

A soft knock at the door interrupted her unwanted reverie, and she was grateful for the excuse to stop staring at her stew and bread without eating more of it. Although she hadn't dared to hope, when she saw who it was she felt an easing as palpable as when she'd removed her stays.

"You can't be here, Matthew."

"Nobody saw me come down this hallway. Let me in before anyone does and we'll be fine."

She did, closing and locking the door behind him. "You can't stay long."

"I know."

They spent several minutes just holding one another. No words, because there was nothing they could say to make things better. For Eliza, it was enough just to cling to Matthew for a brief time, reassuring herself that he had made it through another day alive. She'd been missing something, and apparently it was his hand on her neck, cradling her head against his chest. Once she had that, she felt things might one day be all right.

Time was short, though, and Matthew had come with news. "Parnell is dead."

"What? How?"

"He hanged himself." Matthew sat down on the small straight-backed desk chair, passing a hand over his weary face. "The sheriff left him writing what looked like a letter, and went out to conduct some other business. The next time he returned to check on him, Parnell was dead. Used the sheet from the cot, twisted to make a rope."

"Dear God." She let him pull her into his lap, no longer caring about appropriateness. "Why? What did the letter say?"

"Well, it shed a bit more light, and confirmed Orm's involvement. Parnell wrote that a quick death by hanging was better than the living death he'd have on Orm's farm if his employer came after him for his failure. And also something about opium. He had seen what opium did to Orm's workers, and would rather take his chances in hell."

A cold spike of horror lanced through Eliza. Parnell had feared Orm so much he died rather than face whatever consequences the man might dole out. What sort of monster could this man be, and how could they hope to survive if he was bent on destroying them?

"Orm sounds worse than I ever imagined. Worlds worse."

"Agreed. There is one small—very small—bright side to today's events. Parnell's suicide note lent more credence to our theory than any of us could have done by merely trying to convince the sheriff it was true. The sheriff has asked any of us who are willing to push on to Salt Lake City to alert the garrison there. There's no land telegraph line between the two cities, it's out of radio telegraphy range and any of us would arrive faster than a courier on horseback."

"There's no one closer to help?"

He shook his head. "No one big enough. Only smaller outposts, a few dozen soldiers apiece at most. They don't have the manpower or equipment to investigate and stand up against Orm's men if it comes to that. Not if he's got sky pirates to waste on a bombing raid. And if he's making enough money from his illegal opium trade to fund all this sabotage, the ladies' Temperance Society, the whole mad scheme, we must be talking about a sizeable farm. It must be a large area with a lot of workers."

"Many of whom may be enslaved former opium addicts. Not very daunting. How loyal to Orm could they be?"

"They're probably not all slaves. He'd need enforcers, foremen."

"True." Eliza yawned, trying and failing to stifle it. "Pardon me."

Matthew wrapped his arms more tightly around her and pressed a kiss to her temple. "You need to sleep, and I need to leave before somebody finds us out."

"Hold me a moment longer?"

He did, and she rested her head on his shoulder. She thought, *just for a moment . . .*

Seventeen

Eliza still looked tired and pale when she entered the hotel lobby at sunrise, and Matthew wanted very much to kiss her. Those two things were foremost in his mind, and it galled him that he could do nothing about either of them. Couldn't even hold her hand, with the temperance ladies close enough to stare into the ground story windows. He orbited her as though she were the sun, drawn in by her pull but unable to get any closer than his fixed distance.

Her mind was on other things, however. "Miss Speck has the influenza. One of the maids found her lying on the floor in her room this morning, delirious with fever. Doctor Miller's already been to see her." She sat down on the round bench in the middle of the surprisingly ornate space, and Matthew joined her.

"Damn. And Cantlebury?"

"He's with her now, I think. He didn't look ill but I don't know if he plans to go on without her. I didn't speak with him; I found all this out from the maid."

He'd been looking at a map, and she reached over as she

spoke to tip it toward herself. It was a large detail of the land to be covered on the air legs, with stops marked and his own notations added. Eliza traced the dotted line of the route from Colorado Springs to that night's nameless checkpoint.

"They say Salt Lake's as far west as the commercial airships dare to go, and only a few of them at that because they don't like to cross the plains for fear of piracy." He laid a fingertip on the page, barely brushing hers, then continuing on from Salt Lake to Elk City. "Beyond Salt Lake, the pirates rule the air with little challenge from authorities."

"And on beyond that, there be dragons." She lowered her voice to a murmur. "Thank you for putting me to bed last night. I'm sorry I fell asleep on you."

"My dear lady, you may fall asleep on me any time you like. I wouldn't recommend doing it while the manic ladies' poppy brigade is out in force, however." He nodded discreetly toward the window. Even this early, there were women with placards assembling in the street, and a mounted policeman had taken up a station by the front of the hotel.

"I'll be glad to see the last of them. They do seem a bit chastened this morning, however. The maid informed me that some of the ladies were quite taken aback by what happened to poor Miss Davis, and they lost their heart for picketing."

"Informative maid."

"She was indeed." She bent to the map again, studying the region he'd outlined in red. "It seems such a small obstacle, compared to the size of the continent. This one place, holding all the Dominions back from coast-to-coast travel. The alleged foul vapors and disappearing dirigibles over California. Pirates in the air to the east. The Spanish to the south, and to the north nothing but freezing weather, fur trappers and hostile natives. It all comes down to the Sierra passage, doesn't it? If Orm has been orchestrating things to prevent people traveling there, think of the possibilities if he's exposed and stopped. This is the part where I expect you'll tell me I should quit because it isn't safe to go on."

Matthew smiled despite himself. He had wanted to. That didn't mean he *would*. "I've learned that on your personal map, beyond that line there be dragons. I'm not a complete idiot. And you seem every bit as likely to prevail as any of the rest of us. You're in a vanishingly small group of survivors, after all."

"I hear we are again reduced this morning," Madame Barsteau said, greeting them with a dismal wave as she crossed the lobby and joined them on the bench. "We'll be four, setting out. Lavinia insisted that Cantlebury not give up his chance. He'll be down shortly."

"How are you feeling, Madame?" Eliza asked.

"Tired. Angry for Cecily. Nostalgic . . . no, the meaning is different. I think you say 'homesick.'"

Eliza put a hand on the older woman's shoulder, then, impetuously, embraced her. "Just a few more days now and we'll be on our way home by fast clipper."

Madame Barsteau returned the hug for a few moments, then straightened and gathered herself. "As you say. Here is Mr. Cantlebury. Ah, and a rally official."

Mr. Nesbitt, one of the rally committee's representatives, reached them just as Cantlebury did, then stood turning his hat nervously in his hands. He'd all but ruined the brim of what appeared to have been a rather nice derby.

"A very good morning to you all, you remaining four. I trust you all know that today begins the air leg of the Sky and Steam Rally. From this point forward, all progress to San Francisco must be made by airship, whether dirigible or balloon, rather than by ground travel. I'll remind you all that upon the arrival of the final competitor at the penultimate stop, Carson City, your running time tallies will be sorted and your overall placement by time will determine departure order handicaps for the following morning when you embark for San Francisco. Racers will depart at ten minute intervals."

"Yes, yes, we remember, man," Cantlebury told him. "We only want to know our current rankings. Unless anyone else needed to hear more about the handicapping?"

Having been reassured by the others that they agreed with Cantlebury, Mr. Nesbitt pulled out the official time tally. "The current standings have Miss Eliza Hardison in the lead, followed by Mr. Matthew Pence and Madame Jeannette Barsteau at a tie, then Miss Lavinia Speck and finally Mr. Edmund Cantlebury.

"No Miss Speck," Eliza informed him. "Influenza."

"Ah, I see." He pushed his spectacles up his nose and pulled a pencil from some hidden pocket, making a careful note on the tally page. "As for this morning, departure will be in one hour's time from the town square. A coach will arrive in approximately thirty minutes to take you all there, so you may access your vehicles for your airship equipment. And on a more personal note," he added, with a self-conscious throat-clearing, "though I may be out of order for saying so, and I'm not sure I'd like my employers to know I've said this, I should like to apologize for the very odd turn things have taken in this rally. After reading the summary report I received from the post express rider this morning, I am simply astonished and horrified. While these events are always a risky enterprise, never in all my years have I seen anything quite like this. While I admire you tremendously for your desire to persevere, I will also say it's within my authority to call the race off. Are you all four quite sure you want to continue?"

They all nodded, though none of them did so with much enthusiasm.

"Very well. Best of luck to each of you, and I'll see you at the starting line."

As they had all already breakfasted and packed, it was

a question of waiting thirty minutes for their ride. Whitcombe arrived before then, greeting them with a face that looked better rested than any of theirs.

"If you'll all come into the private dining room," he requested, "the sheriff and I have put together a going-away package for each of you."

The "package" consisted of revolvers and ammunition, which all four of them accepted despite the extra weight it entailed.

IT WAS MORE of a starting box than a line. The four vehicles had been parked at the corners of the town common, a patch of sickly grass that hadn't really recovered from winter yet. The flowerbeds that edged the square were pretty, however, full of pansies and other bright flowers.

The El Dorado Foundation ladies seemed diminished both in number and volume, Eliza was pleased to notice. The group with signs had mainly congregated along one side of the square, and a heavy police presence kept them relatively subdued.

Why a temperance society? Eliza couldn't help worrying over that tidbit, wondering why on earth a supposed opium kingpin would want to bankroll such an enterprise. The ladies were fundamentally opposed to everything he was trying to achieve, as far as she could tell. And it seemed too convenient, too pat, that the organization had also taken so vehemently against the rally.

One of the placards read, ONLY ANGELS AND BIRDS WERE MEANT TO FLY. Eliza was glad she wasn't of that mindset. For one thing, it completely discounted other creatures like bats and those ballooning spiders. For another, she was looking forward to going aloft, leaving these drab, angry women and all her other concerns on the ground and soaring high above it all. She was also starting to sweat inside her fur-lined flight suit, and was eager to get into the air in order to cool off. But the mayor must make a statement first, then the other rally official, whose name she'd forgotten, and finally Mr. Nesbitt with the official announcement of rankings.

The ladies booed Eliza when her name was called, and some hissed, but she was used to that now. One of them, however, pitched a fist-sized rock at her steam car, startling her and leaving an ugly scratched dent in the freshly washed red paint. She turned her attention away from them, very deliberately, and ignored the scuffle of hooves and the shouts as one of the policemen sought the stone-thrower.

She had a flight checklist to go through and a semi-rigid dirigible to inflate. And Eliza always loved this part, the unfurling of the primary balloon. She focused on that, on making sure everything was in its proper place and her harness fittings and panniers were secure.

Although her airship was modeled on Charlotte's tiny craft, *Gossamer Wing*, Eliza's ship had several important differences. Improved steering and pitch control, by the addition of ballonets. A harness system that allowed Eliza to stand upright while launching, then latch the cradle into the horizontal position once she was airborne. Other minor refinements. But the biggest change was that unlike Charlotte, Eliza didn't choose to have her balloon blend tastefully into the blue of the sky.

Once the pilot was lit and the balloon began to billow and rise, the crowd gasped. No subtlety, no ladylike pinkish tint here. The ship was the unabashed vermilion of a Chinese lantern, complete with figured black and gold designs near the base and top to increase the resemblance. It was one tradition from the old country her grandmother's family had retained, and that Eliza Chen had passed down to her children and grandchildren, the symbolic meaning of this particular red. The crowd saw brazen, lustful scarlet, but Eliza saw good fortune and happiness.

"My *Firebird*," she whispered as the craft expanded to its full grounded inflation, just enough to fill the balloon without pulling her off the ground. "Well done, Dexter."

Looking across the square, she saw Matthew's somewhat larger balloon rising, revealing its horizontal gradations of green, from the fresh clear color of a budding spring leaf to the deep hue of a pine branch. They lent his bullet-shaped ship something of an organic air.

Cantlebury's balloon was more traditional in shape, with vertical panels of bright blue, orange and yellow, and all the subtlety of a circus tent. Eliza felt more cheerful just looking at it. And Madame Barsteau's craft earned another gasp from the ladies, a more appreciative one this time. The design of the silk was clearly couture inspired, and utterly French. On a background of crisp white, a design of black filigree swirls stood out in stark detail, and the color scheme was continued in the glossy black of the craft's small basket. It was an elegant and stunning ball gown, transformed into a dirigible. Eliza wanted to applaud.

She and Matthew would have an immediate advantage, she realized. Both Barsteau and Cantlebury relied on tethers to moor their crafts, and wouldn't lift off as quickly. She followed Matthew's lead, quickly getting her bearings and turning her ship west-northwest, in the direction they must head. Then it was simply a matter of buckling herself into the harness and waiting for the starting pistol, her fingers ready at the altitude control to fully inflate the balloon and be on her way. Eliza found her hand was trembling; she hadn't been this nervous since their initial start from New York.

That seemed a lifetime ago, and she could hardly believe it hadn't even been a full week. She glanced at Matthew again, trying to remember what it was like to dislike him. To be irritated when he drew near, instead of calmed and excited at the same time. She wasn't even sure when her perspective had changed. But it had, and now everything was different.

"Fly safely, Matthew," she whispered, just before the starter pistol fired.

And they were off.

Eighteen

MAJESTIC. THE WORD kept popping into Eliza's mind, each time she caught sight of a new vista, a higher ridge, a more dramatic river valley. She'd heard that parts of the Spanish territory south of the Dominions were even more stunning, a desert land of fantasy colors and jaw-dropping canyon systems. But this . . . she'd read, seen some artwork, studied topographical maps galore, but she simply hadn't grasped how *big* it all was until she saw it from the air. Even flying low, below the clouds and the risk of ear damage, she could see for miles when she topped the rises, and the mountains seemed to go on forever.

As the plains dwindled behind her, the crests and snow-topped peaks grew higher. After the first few hours of being too in awe to notice much else besides the view, she realized she was growing quite cold. At the same time, the uncomfortable pressure in her eardrums grew to a stabbing pain, despite the special plugs Dexter had designed to help her adjust to the changes in altitude.

I should have gotten those implants, like Charlotte

suggested. It had seemed so extreme, not to mention costly, considering the air portion of the rally lasted less than a week. Tonight's nameless checkpoint camp, then Salt Lake City. From there, they continued to Elk City, then had another two-day window to reach Carson City on the western side of the Sierras. At least, whoever remained in the race would continue in that order, before the final sprint to San Francisco.

Matthew had taken the lead from the start, and she'd stayed within eyeshot of him all day. It grew surreal by afternoon, seeing his balloon and sometimes nearing enough to see Matthew himself, but not being able to speak to him. They should have incorporated some sort of short-range communication devices into their airships, she thought. Then she remembered that at the time they were preparing for the race, Matthew Pence was the *last* person she would have wanted to talk to, even by radio telegraph. When exactly her opinion had changed, she wasn't quite sure, but now she found his concern more endearing than annoying. Somehow everything he did now seemed *right.*

Her thoughts drifted to the night in the barn, how he'd touched her. How she'd touched him, and that had been unexpectedly entertaining. The whole interlude had been not only sensual and exciting but *fun*, playful, and sweet at the same time. The sort of thing a girl could grow used to. And then at the end, had he really said he loved her? Perhaps she had dreamed that part, after all.

But thinking of the hotel room, how he'd held her as she fell asleep, then tucked her into bed without waking her, she suspected it was no dream. She still wasn't sure how she felt about it. What it meant to her.

The sky was fairly clear but the wind was fitful, sometimes aiding their progress and sometimes slowing them. The last few hours were excruciating in a way Eliza had never anticipated, with the sun glaring straight into her eyes. Even her darkened helmet visor wasn't quite enough to prevent a sun-dazzled headache by the time night began to fall.

She nearly cried in relief when she saw Matthew's balloon, silhouetted against the last of the fading light, sinking toward the signal fire that marked their checkpoint.

Charlotte had warned her about landing after a long trip, even with the improved harness arrangement. But when Eliza released the clip to slide into a vertical position to land on her feet, she realized she was in trouble before she even touched down. Cold and exhausted, for the last few hours she had neglected the series of subtle posture shifts and stretches that relieved the pressure from the harness.

She couldn't feel her feet. She hit the ground and kept on going, nearly pitching forward on her face, then falling ignominiously backwards when the balloon caught a final updraft and tugged her upward at the last moment.

"Well, damn."

"Eliza!"

"I'm fine," she called from beneath the layers of silk, as she frantically pushed them aloft again until she could kill the flame entirely.

"What in the—where *are* you under there? Oh, *there* you are. My goodness, not the smoothest landing I've ever seen you perform." He bundled the puffy red balloon up and into his arms, clearing the rigging so she could handle it safely.

"You're one to talk. I've seen you tip straight on your back trying to land in that chair."

"You sound grumpy, darling. Is it pain? Would you like me to kiss it better?"

She glanced to one side, where the rally official was fast approaching them to check her in officially. "Maybe later."

"Now, now, Mr. Pence. Remember the racers aren't supposed to interfere with one another's equipment." The man was barely visible in his thick parka with its fur-lined hood. "Miss Eliza Hardison, yes? Initial here, please. Thank you."

Eliza stabbed the pen toward the check-in form in something that resembled her initials, then attempted to stand. She sat down harder than she had on the landing.

"Owwww . . ."

"Are you all right, Miss?"

"Pins and needles, Miss Hardison?" Matthew knelt beside her, extending a hand carefully toward one of her ankles.

"No, no, don't touch. It feels like bees swarming up my legs. It'll pass."

"Do you require a medic?" the official asked.

She shook her head, focusing on detaching the rest of her harness and rigging to take her mind off her legs while the stinging buzz and general sense of humiliation subsided. Her hands were shaking, fingers dull with cold, complicating the task. The official finally took himself back to the fireside, a spot Eliza was eager to reach herself.

"No pirates," Matthew commented, removing his gloves and blowing on his fingers in a vain attempt to warm them. "I didn't expect to make it here unmolested, did you?"

She freed the last of the clips holding her to her rigging with a sound of triumph and began stuffing the deflated balloon into a specially designed pouch on the harness. "No, I didn't, but I'm not complaining. Are there guards here? What if they attack by night?"

Matthew shook his head. "Two rally officials, a medic and a cook. A pair of hostlers for the mule teams and wagons that brought them all here. Armed with rifles but they won't be able to do much against pirates in the dark. None of us will. Do you think you can stand now?"

She nodded and took the hand he offered as he rose. Her feet still tingled, but they would work again. And tomorrow she'd know to be more careful.

The race officials had finished giving Matthew and Eliza a quick tour of the camp facilities, and they'd availed themselves of such, when Cantlebury touched down. It was full dark by then, and his first words filled them with foreboding.

"Madame Barsteau fell behind a few hours ago and I lost

sight of her. I think she may have had to land, it looked like she was having mechanical trouble. Hard to tell through my spyglass."

In any other race, they would probably have rejoiced at the news that one more tough competitor was out of the running. But at some point between ground and sky, the four of them had begun to feel like a unit, the last surviving representatives. At least Eliza felt so, and the two men seemed to as well.

"I should have turned around. I'm too far behind on time to win this anyway, I could have gone back and looked for her. Made sure she was all right." He finished powering down his equipment and hopped from the balloon's basket to gather the silk.

"And then kept right on going afterward, until you arrived at the previous checkpoint? Your heart's back in Colorado Springs, Edmund," Matthew pointed out. "But Lavinia will be well by the time you get back there from San Francisco. I don't think she'd approve of your giving up at this point."

"She told me as much," Cantlebury admitted as he stowed his gear, securing it all in the basket with a tarpaulin. "Said if I didn't at least try to finish, she wouldn't have me back. Then she said something rather unkind about my poor wife, but I think that was the delirium talking."

Eliza blinked. "Did you say your w—"

"Let's see if there's any food available, shall we?" Matthew suggested a bit too loudly and cheerfully.

Cantlebury reached under his tarp and retrieved a heavy fur mantle, slinging it around his shoulders as he headed for the campfire and the meal that presumably awaited the racers.

"Tell you later," Matthew whispered apologetically. "It's not what you think."

She decided not to worry about it until after she'd eaten.

And warmed herself up. And possibly slept for eight or ten hours.

"It isn't a secret, by the way," Matthew said much, much later.

Eliza looked at him, obviously unsure what he was talking about.

"Cantlebury's wife."

"Oh."

The gentleman himself had retired to his insulated tent immediately after dinner, leaving the other two warming themselves by the fire. The rally officials were in their own tent, along with the medic. The cook and hostlers were either asleep or up to quiet pursuits of their own in the covered wagon. Matthew was as alone with Eliza as he was likely to get that evening.

"It probably hasn't escaped your notice that Cantlebury isn't your typical model of upper-class scion."

To her credit, Eliza didn't seem uncomfortable about the subject. She merely shrugged and smiled. "I've met worse specimens. You're not going to try to excuse him on that basis, are you?"

"No, no. That part is relevant, however. When Cantlebury was born, things went poorly all around. He was the first of twin brothers, and they were born too early. His mother nearly died. Edmund nearly died. His little brother was healthy enough. Perfect, in fact, except for having been born over an hour *after* Edmund. Clearly documented, witnessed by too many people to pretend after the fact that the healthy, normal baby had come out first. But not to worry, the doctor assured the Cantleburys that their new defective heir wasn't likely to live long. Cantlebury tells me his father was much cheered by this, and still shuns that doctor out of resentment whenever he meets him in the street."

"Because he was wrong about the baby living?"

"More because he was wrong about the baby dying. Also about his next prediction, which was that the child would almost certainly be an imbecile, and it would be easy enough to have him declared incompetent and unfit to be heir. And that he might have gotten through infancy, but he was unlikely to live to school age. To his father's horror, Edmund turned out to be an exceedingly bright little boy. And his tutor told *everyone*."

"So no incompetency?" She poked the fire with a stick, raising a shower of sparks that glowed amber against the black night. "And he was still alive. I take it this is all still relevant to the wife?"

"It is. Should we call them out to build this up some more? If Madame Barseau is still looking for the camp, she'll be having enough trouble navigating in the dark."

"After the story."

"Right. So the elder Cantlebury was stuck with this heir he was convinced would be unsuitable—because he's an idiot, Cantlebury's father, did I mention? However, he finally realized he had a cousin with a solution to his problem. This cousin had only one child, and his wife couldn't have more. He was stuck with a daughter, Margaret, who had been born with her own set of problems. A palsied hand, a limp, difficulty speaking clearly. And simple, although she's very sweet, is Meggie. Not much taller than Cantlebury. She's five or so years older than he is but she'll always be a child, really. The fathers thought, 'Perfect.' They'd match up their two problems and at least keep the money in the family, because the doctors kept assuring them that these children were both bound to die sooner rather than later. A betrothal was made."

Eliza stared at him, horrified. "What was *wrong* with them?"

"The children or their fathers?"

"The fathers. Monsters, both of them."

Matthew pondered that. "Short-sighted and pessimistic,

I think. But in their way, they *were* only trying to do what they thought was best for their families, if not best for the two people most directly affected. Anyway, the crux of it is, at the age of fourteen Cantlebury was told by his father that as the heir, he had certain responsibilities, and if he wanted to come into his money one day he'd have to marry someone suitable and sign a thick stack of documents about what would happen to that money if anybody died. Even as smart as Cantlebury was, there isn't much a boy of fourteen can do about these things. He was legally old enough to marry, Meggie was more than old enough, and neither of them had any clue about their parents' ulterior motives."

"So that's his wife?"

"Both of them keep stubbornly refusing to expire. Once Edmund was old enough to pursue legal action on his own, of course he looked into an annulment. They'd never . . . well, he had grounds, let's just put it that way. Then he realized it would be disastrous for Meggie if he abandoned her. Her parents would have her put in an asylum in a heartbeat without his protection, and her heart would be broken besides. She adores Edmund, and in his way he adores her. She's like a little sister to him. She lives at his country house with dozens of servants who are absolutely loyal to their little mistress, and he'd never be able to face them down either. So."

"But where does that leave Lavinia? It doesn't seem honorable to ask her to give up so much. It may not be his fault, but he's still a married man."

"Well, for one thing, the elder Specks have threatened to disown Lavinia if she shames them by marrying a grotesque who left his former wife under suspicious circumstances. I know, I know, but they're fixed in their thinking. They'd rather ignore the affair they must know she's having, than be forced to acknowledge Edmund as their son-in-law. So there's that. And for another thing, Edmund offered Lavinia marriage more than once early on, and she refused for reasons that had nothing to do with her family. He was prepared to hire the best lawyers, do whatever it took to ensure things could remain safe and constant for Meggie if he had the marriage annulled. Lavinia finally told him she couldn't decide until she'd met this infamous wife for herself. They went to visit Meggie, and the three of them had a picnic in the garden and played tiddlywinks. Meggie's very quick with her good hand. Edmund says that on the drive back to Oxford, Lavinia cried for a solid hour and told him he was never to ask her to marry him again as long as Meggie lived."

He anticipated Eliza's reaction and had his handkerchief ready before she asked for it. She took it with a quiet sniffle.

"It's horrible and sad, but beautiful. It would have been much simpler to hate him for philandering, and think of Lavinia as a fool for love."

"They are fools for one another." And Matthew knew exactly how they both felt, because he'd joined their ranks now. A fool, a moth to Eliza's flame. He burned for her, and wondered if he'd ever be able to quench that particular fire.

"Let's go see about the signal fire. Then I'm for some sleep. Perhaps the hot rocks and extra blankets will warm the rest of me. This fire hasn't quite conquered the chill."

I could conquer it for you, he thought wistfully. The camp was too small and the tents far too closely arranged for them to risk it, however.

"Today was like a strange dream," Eliza said as she stood up, stretching.

Matthew sighed and rose to join her. "At least it was a dream without any pirates in it."

WHEN ELIZA WOKE, it was to the sounds of sleepy talk by the campfire, the dull clink of utensils against enameled tin plates and the jingle of harnesses as the mules were hitched to the wagon.

She dressed quickly, cursing the cold from the moment she left her nest of blankets until she was safely shrouded in layers of goose down, silk and wool. Exiting her tent, she saw Madame Barsteau at the fireside, looking windburned and exhausted but otherwise unharmed.

"You made it!"

"Oui. Here, and no further, I fear. My air intake has malfunctioned, and my boiler nearly exploded before I was able to land and attempt to repair it. I had to put a stick there to keep it open, in the end. The valve had snapped."

Accepting a heaping plate of eggs and potatoes from the cook, Eliza sat next to the older woman. "More sabotage?"

"Just a part I should have replaced sooner. My own fault. I don't often participate in air rallies. I think this was probably my last."

The initial relief of seeing Madame Barsteau alive had blinded Eliza to some details. Now she saw the bandages on her feet, the angry red marking the tip of her nose and the top of one ear.

"Were you injured, Madame?"

"Frostbite. The medic thinks I may lose a few toes before all is said and done. In truth, I was surprised to wake up at all this morning, so I count the toes as a small enough price to pay. My fingers are all quite well, and apparently my nose and ears will recover. Those I was able to keep just warm enough. The funny thing is, I was able to finish my temporary repair, launch my dirigible by myself—though I did have to cut the tether lines—and navigate accurately for two hours before it was even properly dawn. I didn't even notice the pain until I stepped out and saw the medic waiting."

"We do what we must, I suppose. So where will you go from here?"

Madame Barsteau nodded in the direction of the men's tents, where Cantlebury had just emerged. Swathed in fur again, he looked like a wooly creature of the forest. But Matthew had explained that the cold was particularly dangerous to Cantlebury, whose stature and poor circulation put him at higher risk of hypothermia and frostbite. Eliza hoped the fur was enough.

"Mr. Cantlebury and I spoke earlier. I shall return with these gentlemen here to Colorado Springs, to convalesce along with Lavinia. Assuming she's no longer contagious, of course. Otherwise I will convalesce *near* her and communicate at a distance. They offered me Salt Lake City, but I chose the opposite direction. In this way, I gain a companion to stave off the boredom of waiting to see if my toes will drop off, and Cantlebury is reassured that somebody is looking after his lady love."

"I'll miss you," Eliza told her. It was the truth. She'd come to admire Madame Barsteau's spirit, and appreciate her sharp, dry wit. She also didn't relish the knowledge that without Madame, they were down to three competitors with five days left in the race.

"We'll meet again in New York. I plan to stay until it grows too hot to bear, which I expect will be sometime in July."

Eliza nodded, still sad but resigned.

Matthew came out of his tent, already in his flight gear just as Cantlebury was. The gentlemen, it seemed, had already breakfasted. Eliza was the last to rise, and once she was ready, they set off for Salt Lake City. The three of them.

Nineteen

To everyone's surprise and cautious relief, Salt Lake and Elk Cities were both hospitable and blessedly free of Temperance Society ladies. Nobody was blown up, shot at or crashed into. The weather held and promised to be somewhat warmer over the last few days of the race as they moved westward over the highest of the mountains.

After the decent accommodations at Salt Lake, and the rough but adequate housing at Elk City, Matthew had grown complacent enough to feel rather let down by the amenities at their next stop. Lake's Crossing was a grimy, dismal enclave of humanity stuck on the side of a mountain near a mine, and the one thing he could say in favor of the inn was that it appeared to be the cleanest place in town.

As they supped on bland, potato-thickened stew in front of a somewhat measly fire in the inn's small common room, Eliza told him to look on the bright side. "We've certainly slept in worse conditions during this race. At least the bedding appears free of not only bedbugs but fleas. Not sure I can say the same about those hay bales on the night of the storm."

"You had hay bales?" Cantlebury exclaimed. "Lucky. I slept in my vehicle that night. To the extent I slept at all, which is to say not much."

"Your night of roughing it sounds better than Madame Barsteau's," countered Eliza. "At least you were in no fear of freezing to death."

"True, true. It's all relative."

A local walked into the room, glancing about with wide, deranged looking eyes before settling his attention on the threesome by the fire. "Who're you? Don't know you."

Standing, Matthew sketched a short bow. "Matthew Pence. One of the rally drivers. Were you looking for anyone in particular, sir? We've been here for some time now and nobody else has come in."

The man trembled with more than the cold. Though obviously a miner, by his dusty costume and goggles, he seemed barely fit to be walking about on his own.

"Where's Jimmy?" he demanded, his voice filled with panic and suspicion. He started toward them, his entire body shaking. With rage or a terrible neurological condition, Matthew couldn't tell.

"Um . . . I'm terribly sorry but I don't know a Jimmy." Matthew edged between Eliza and the crazy miner, trying not to be too noticeable. He knew Cantlebury still had his pistol handy, but his own was in his room with his equipment. From the corner of his eye, he saw Eliza pick up an andiron from its rack and begin to poke the embers idly. Her grip on the handle was relaxed but firm, like a sword fighter's. *Smart girl.*

"Cletis, there you are." The stout, rosy woman who kept the inn rounded the corner into the room and faced off against the worrisome intruder. "Now I told you we had special guests tonight and not to come around, don't you remember that?"

"But . . . But Jimmy. Mavis, I have to see Jimmy tonight."

"You just come on with me. Jimmy came earlier and left

you something. It's in my office. Come on, now." She waited until he'd made his shuddering, anxious way from the room, then spared a glance at her guests. "You folks need anything else tonight?"

Her face was round and pleasant, but her eyes were hard and no smile could hide that. Matthew looked at Eliza and Edmund, lifting a brow in query.

"Miss Hardison, Mr. Cantlebury? Anything?" They shook their heads, and he relayed their answer and gave her their collective thanks. Once she was gone he sat down again heavily, plucking his trencher and bowl from the settle beside him. "And what, I wonder, did Jimmy leave for our friend Cletis, that he was so anxious to get?"

"Something for his nerves, one hopes," Cantlebury suggested.

"Opium," Eliza said bluntly. "I'm not exactly guessing. I went down to the front desk to ask Mrs. Brinks if she had a needle and thread, and inadvertently overheard her accepting delivery from someone I can only assume was Jimmy. He was quite miffed to alter his usual schedule, which I gather involves sitting here receiving his customers one at a time like a doctor—"

"Or a tax collector," quipped Cantlebury.

"He referred to them as 'patients,' but if he's a doctor, he only has one remedy to prescribe. Mrs. Brinks complained about the quality of the last batch, full of debris, didn't look like it had been filtered at all from raw. Jimmy assured her this lot would be superior."

"I'd say your guess was educated, at the least. But why didn't you tell me sooner, Eliza? Us, I mean."

"Wanted to wait until we'd at least had something to eat. But I'm glad I did wait, because it gave me time to think. I don't blame them, Matthew," she said earnestly. "For taking the opium. Look around at the few people you've seen in town. The vast majority of them are clearly ill. Cletis was no exception. I don't think we were seeing opium addiction alone there."

"What else, then?"

"I know the answer to this one," Cantlebury volunteered. "That place they all work at calls itself the Silver River Mine, but that's a play on words. They're not mining silver, they're mining quicksilver. These men are all suffering from various degrees of mercury poisoning. I've seen it before. The Trans-China Rally runs directly through a village much like this one. There, it *was* doctors prescribing opium for the sufferers. A tincture, like laudanum. It calms their nerves, helps ease the tremors and quiets the stomach enough to allow them to eat."

"And makes them a more docile workforce, no doubt," she added with a cynicism Matthew hated to hear. "Less likely to complain."

"True. And many of them simply worked until they fell dead or ran too mad to continue laboring. They had no choice if they wanted to feed their families. The bosses encouraged the opium habit. It kept the workers even more dependent, after all, and allowed the bosses to make good use of them awhile longer."

Matthew considered his friend. "You either spent some time there, or asked a lot of questions."

"The latter. And I was glad not to spend time there. The quicksilver gets to everyone eventually, it's in the groundwater. In their food."

"Mr. Cantlebury, say that again," Eliza requested.

"The quicksilver is in their food?"

"No, earlier—about why the bosses in China encouraged the opium habit."

"It made the miners dependent and kept them useful longer."

Matthew could almost see the gears turning in Eliza's brain before she spoke again. "It's just like Parnell's suicide note. You say the workers in China took a tincture of opium but were still able to be of use as miners?"

"Well, most of it isn't highly skilled labor. Some of it takes strength, but if you're paying your workers next to nothing anyway it doesn't cut into profits too much to hire more of them to help get the job done."

She nodded, thinking some more. "And if you're paying them nothing at all, it's even more lucrative."

"You really think Orm is using opium-addled kidnap victims to man his farms? Using them as slave labor? I know that's what you suggested to that general in Salt Lake, Matthew, but I thought it was just to get them enthused enough to investigate. It seems so fanciful."

"Probably not to the victims," Matthew pointed out. "Eliza, are you suggesting he doesn't simply press-gang the opium addicts, force them into slave labor, but actually keeps them addicted?"

"Think about it. It's as Cantlebury said, they would become dependent on him for the opium to ease their symptoms. Withdrawal symptoms, in this case. As a dilution, perhaps in the food, it would be pitifully easy to distribute, and a worker would have to starve himself to resist ingesting more of the drug. As slaves, he wouldn't have to pay them, just feed and house them, and not very well. He can always get more as long as the opium dens are operating, and as he controls the flow of the drug that seems likely."

"What if they escaped and told someone?" Cantlebury argued. "The inherent flaws in this business model are glaringly obvious."

"I'm not suggesting he's sane," Eliza said. "But he is clever. What happens if somebody tries to escape? Unless they escape with a supply of opium to keep them going, they begin to have withdrawals within a day or so, correct? Perhaps sooner. They'd either die in the mountains or be forced to find their way back for more. Opium eaters aren't known for their initiative, anyway, are they? I suspect they'd stay once they knew what would happen if they attempted to leave. And that's assuming they're even lucid enough to know what's being done to them. The sober ones, the guards and so forth, are complicit in a continent-wide scheme of kidnapping and forced drug addiction, not to mention the illegal drug trade. It's in their interest to remain loyal to Orm and keep his secrets for him."

"And all the while they'd be producing more opium for him to use in keeping them enslaved. That's more than devious, it's vile." Matthew pushed his food away, his appetite suddenly gone. "What's more, I think Orm enjoys the risks. He courts being found out, it's a game to him. The more outrageous the behavior, the more likely to lead to his exposure, the more thrilling the sport becomes."

"Two more days. I wonder if Carson City is any better than Lake's Crossing?" mused Cantlebury.

"Don't let Mrs. Brinks hear you speculate like that," Eliza warned. "You wouldn't want to be knocked out of the race by means of a swiftly wielded rolling pin to the head. She seems quite content with her little village."

"Yes, because apparently she's its drug kingpin," Matthew pointed out. "The biggest, strongest fish in a very small pond."

"Bolt your doors tonight, children. 'Ware the bogeywoman." Cantlebury had started kneading his thighs, working out the cramps that tended to strike him after a day of exercise.

Matthew nodded in agreement. "But first shall I ask the bogeywoman to send you up some hot water bottles?"

The small man grinned, his old devilish charm surfacing. "Pence, you always were a prince among men."

LIKE ALL IDYLLS, the racers' days of quiet soaring through peaceful skies had to come to an end.

Eliza, in the lead, spotted the first pirate craft shortly

after noon. She was headed almost due west at that point, but when she saw the ominous black-sailed wind balloon to the north, she risked edging slightly to the south. Noting the course correction, she gauged her fuel levels and decided to chance flying a bit faster.

A stiff, choppy breeze slowed her down, and she had to struggle to control the pitch of her tiny dirigible against the buffeting gusts. The landscape below, while still awe-inspiring, was less starkly beautiful than the mountains farther to the east had been. Only rare patches of snow topped these lower peaks, and there was more grass visible, with fewer rocky crags. This, she decided, was *pretty* rather than beautiful. Green meadows filled with wildflowers, sweeping up into crests that looked more inviting than forbidding. Most young society ladies would probably want to paint the vista. Eliza just wanted to spot the pirates, and didn't like that the mountains made it hard to do so. Too many places for them to hide, to rise up unexpectedly.

The ship to her north maintained a steady distance. Matthew and Cantlebury seemed to have taken her example and altered course as well. They approached her slowly, Cantlebury slipping into the lead and dropping altitude slightly. Looking for a place to land if they had to, Eliza surmised. Matthew was behind her, and when she glanced into the curved mirror that allowed her a panoramic rear view, she saw with horror that a second pirate ship was gaining on him, rising swiftly from a valley and pushing to within a few hundred feet of them. The northerly ship began to close in as well, forcing them to tack south once more.

Eliza felt for her borrowed revolver, finding it secure in the storage pocket on the harness. She had a knife in her boot as well. The small pistol she'd started out with was stowed in a shoulder holster; it rubbed uncomfortably with the rigging straps, but she felt reassured by it.

This isn't how I expected to die. As soon as the thought surfaced, she tried to quell it, to replace it with something else. *Perhaps we really will find Phineas,* or *perhaps these aren't pirates at all, but simple farmers out to dust their crops. With black sails. And crews of a dozen or more apiece.*

She knew panic had set in when she realized she was trying to jolly herself out of it. Badly.

"With crop dusters like that, those must be some pretty impressive fields," she said aloud, her words whipping away on the wind. She followed Cantlebury as he skimmed up a steep rise. He'd disappeared over the crest by the time she reached the top, and her first instinct was to scan the air and find him again.

She forgot all about Cantlebury for a moment as her brain tried to give meaning to the view before her.

It was endless. A sea of gold, broken only by occasional islands of red or pink. More than she had imagined, more than her worst fears. The scope of it was simply too much for her to comprehend.

But she knew one thing. They *were* some pretty impressive fields.

MATTHEW KNEW THEY were being herded, steered by the pirates. With no effective way to combat them, however, he didn't see much choice but to let himself be steered. Cantlebury had taken up a position in front of and below Eliza, so at least they were flanking the party member who was arguably most vulnerable, but he didn't know what good it would really do. Eliza's body was completely exposed on her suspended rigging. With no basket to hide in, she'd be utterly open to attack.

Of course, Matthew wasn't fooling himself into thinking he or Cantlebury were much better off. Cantlebury's basket was wicker, and Matthew's chair arrangement was wicker and light wood. Nothing that would stop a bullet any better than Eliza's leather harness. Their only real hope was to outrun or outmaneuver the pirate ships somehow, but Matthew lost all hope of that when he topped the rise, searched for the other two balloons and instead saw poppies. A whole world of them. From his vantage point he could see the mouth of the next valley to the north; it too shone golden, as did the valleys to the south and west.

He swore a vow in that moment to never again say something was a dream come true. This was his dream come to vivid life, and he would give anything for it not to be. As in the dream, the fact that it was largely beautiful to look at made it even more horrifying. They hadn't seen pirates earlier, he realized, because Orm had been biding his time; failing to intercept them earlier, the Baron had simply waited for the remaining racers to come to him.

Cantlebury's carnival-bright silks were a hopelessly easy target. Matthew almost felt it was a foregone conclusion when he heard the shots, saw his friend's balloon begin to billow as it lost hot air and altitude. Too fast, by far, for safety. He turned in the direction Cantlebury fell, and wondered how far he could make it before—

He heard the "ping" and felt the rush of air before he heard the gunfire. He ducked, cursing, straining the limits of the belts that held him in place as he tried to avoid the jet of steam shooting from a tiny nick in his boiler. The bullet hadn't gone in, but it had creased the metal enough for it to give under the pressure. His balloon could keep him aloft, but without the engine for his propeller he'd be stranded in the air without propulsion. Deciding quickly, he aimed for the patch of poppies where Cantlebury's balloon was slowly sinking. It was at least a quarter mile away and he wouldn't make it, but at least he could put himself closer. The thin, hissing needle of steam was already slowing, its pitch lowering as the pressure dropped.

He cut the gas and unhooked all but one of his straps, holding the buckle until he was inches from the ground, and then ripping it free and leaping from the basket chair to roll

This, everything you see out there, is *my* treasure. *My* hills paved with gold."

"Your El Dorado," she supplied meekly.

"Precisely."

"They're not all gold, though," she pointed out. "Some are red and pink, and I saw some white patches when I was flying in. Do the different varieties have different applications? If you don't mind my asking." The dastardly villains in bad novels always explained these things at some length when they planned to kill a character, so she thought it wouldn't hurt to ask.

"Ask away, my dear child. After all, you won't live to tell anyone." He was quite cheerful about this, and she began to grasp just how insane Orm must truly be. "The golden poppies are my own creation, a special hybrid created specifically to thrive in this environment. It has the hardiness of the native flowers of this region and parts south of here, and all the potency of the varieties one finds in Asia. And some other very nice qualities I find useful."

Gathering herself, pretending it was a game, she smiled in what she hoped was an encouraging way. "Such as?"

"It quells anxiety without necessarily putting the user to sleep. *Papaver somniferum*, the opium poppy we all know and love so well, is primarily useful as a sedative. The drug made from the common opium varieties slows the user down, system by system. Respiration, digestion, the nerves. Really, they're all but useless once they're under. Might as well be dead. But *my* poppy keeps them up, keeps them moving. They still feel little pain, and I gather things are rather dreamlike for them most of the day. Quite a bad dream, I suppose, for these poor creatures here." He pointed again, this time at another line of ragged, trudging workers. "But it works out so very well for me. They have practically no appetite, they're content with gruel, which is an excellent delivery method for the tincture, and they're incredibly biddable. Dose them a bit more heavily for their off shift—I'm not a monster, after all, they do need their rest—and they'll sleep like babies."

"Babies who've been dosed with laudanum."

"Yes, yes. And the best part is, while it's certainly as brutally addictive as any of its better known cousins, my hybrid can be used for much longer before the effects are noticeably reduced. Users don't build up a tolerance nearly as quickly, especially at low, steady doses. Why, some of these workers last for years before they wear out and need replacing."

The quick look he flashed her was all too sane. He knew exactly what he was saying, and the effect it was likely to have on her. Determined not to give him the satisfaction of being right, Eliza said the opposite of what was on her mind.

"So it's practical as well as brilliant. Why the secrecy, then? It seems as if you'd want people to know about your discovery."

"Oh, you were doing so well, girl, but you overplayed your hand there. Obviously people can't know. Trade secrets, for one thing. And for another, drug magnates are not known for their open and sharing dispositions. We're all mad as hatters and quite, quite paranoid. Besides, as you pointed out yourself, there are factors of practicality to consider. Who do you think benefits most from the continued lack of viable commercial land and air travel from New York to San Francisco?"

Terrified as she was, Eliza tried to think, focusing on the logic rather than the setting. If people can't travel or ship goods by land or air they must use other means, and the only current means was—"Companies who run cargo and passenger ships along the southern passage."

"Very *good*!" He tapped her nose with one finger as though she were a child. "Right on the nose!"

"And you also have a financial interest in one or more of those companies."

"Smarter and smarter, this girl. I do indeed."

This is far too big for me to handle. There it was, plain and simple. Eliza knew her limitations, and this was beyond them. She was only twenty-three and other than Vassar this was her first extended trip away from home. She was good with machines and high-toned rhetoric about workers' rights, she enjoyed daring fashions and she probably wanted to marry Matthew Pence. The last thought struck her with painful clarity, now that it was too late. When she was utterly truthful with herself, with no time left for pretenses, one of the few things on her mind was Matthew and how she wanted to spend her life with him. Losing him would be one of her greatest regrets, because he simply mattered more to her than all the things she'd thought so important back in New York.

But it was hardly the time for introspection. While at least one of these thoughts about herself was a surprise and a revelation, none of them suggested she should be able to single-handedly defeat a multinational drug lord who also owned an important shipping concern.

In a way, coming to this realization was a relief. The die was cast, and she simply couldn't do anything about her fate other than face it calmly and bravely, with whatever dignity she could muster.

"One last question, before you kill me?"

"Oh, that won't happen until tomorrow or so. Plenty of time. One more question before I have you bundled away into a cozy cell for the night, let us say."

"I still don't understand why you would fund a temperance society. They fight against the very business you depend on, and raise the public's awareness about the dangers of opium addiction. Shouldn't that sort of organization be the last thing you'd want to contend with?"

He grinned and clapped his hands together, clearly thrilled with her final topic. "Oh, my dear ladies of perpetual indignation. Nothing amuses me so well as writing the quarterly pamphlet for distribution. I have the pirates airdrop copies over the outlying farms, sometimes. Can you really not guess the benefit to me? How disappointing. It's the simplest thing of all, Miss Hardison. *Free advertising.* If I establish a new opium house in some town with a branch of the Temperance Society in it, I can count on my ladies to broadcast its location to everyone in that town within days, sometimes hours. Nobody is better at sniffing out moral turpitude than a self-righteous biddy. And do you know, they never once consider their very lamentable success rate? Of course the ladies came in handy for opposing the rally, as well. Fringe benefit. And all at minimal cost to me. A few handbills four times a year, and some trumped-up charter documents and cheap brass pins, and I have a ready-made force of thousands of women who will help me to promote pretty much whatever I like. It pays for itself a hundred times over."

"A fine return for your investment, sir."

"Yes. And now, Miss Hardison, I must send you along with these gentlemen." He waved to the guards by the door, and they flanked Eliza instantly. "Tomorrow you will begin the final chapter in this story, and you should know it will be greater than you imagined. You'll be dead by the time it ends, by slow poison most likely, but that shouldn't be too painful and I suspect you'll lose consciousness before the worst parts. You see, I plan to put you in your airship and send you along to San Francisco, per your original plan. Sadly, you won't have quite enough fuel to make it there. And when the investigators find your body in the wreckage, you will appear to have died from the infamous toxic gases these mountains are known to emit. Or so the medical examiner will conclude. Your name will be famous the world over. I wouldn't be at all surprised if the whole episode ended up immortalized in song. And the same fate for poor little Cantlebury, though I think I'll send him back in the direction of Colorado Springs and his lady love. A little romance is always good to punch up the emotional response, don't you think?"

She had no answer for him. Fortunately, he didn't seem to expect one.

Twenty-one

Matthew had thrown up at some point. He knew that, sadly, because of the taste.

"I didn't eat a thing, I'm not that stupid," he insisted, to no one in particular.

Cantlebury answered him. "Shut up, Pence, you're raving again. If you talk about the lemon biscuits again I'll have to beat you fully unconscious."

"You'll have to do what?"

"What? Wait, are you awake?"

Apparently he wasn't, because a period of dull darkness followed, and then he woke again to the sound of Cantlebury muttering something about his wife and Lavinia Speck.

"Should've insisted, you know? Meggie wouldn't even have to know. I'm not sure she's even aware we're married as it is. And I know Lavinia's family would get used to the idea in time. I'm charming, right? I could charm them into accepting me."

"You're a silver-tongued devil," Matthew confirmed in a hoarse, parched rattle.

"Ye gods, your breath is foul, Pence. Here, have some water. It seems to be merely water. A shame. I wouldn't have turned down a spot of opium right now."

Matthew drank, limiting himself to small sips until he was certain his stomach would accept the offering.

"What time is it?"

"No idea. One of those henchmen nicked my pocket watch when he relieved me of my pistol. It's nearly dark, though. Why the bloody hell did you eat the lemon biscuit, Matthew? You must have known it would be drugged."

"I *didn't*," Matthew insisted. "Didn't I tell you already? Look, you see?" He pulled his shirt askew to reveal one shoulder, where a puncture wound was clearly visible.

"They shot you up?"

"I felt a sting when we got out of the lorry, but I thought it was just a spike of that hemp rope poking into me. I suppose I was lucky they didn't hit a vein. It went into the muscle so it took longer to kick in. I lasted all the way up to Orm's office before I keeled over."

"And you never even got to try the lemon biscuits."

"A tragedy. From what little I recall they looked quite promising. So what have you learned during your stay in this delightful place? Anything useful?"

Cantlebury rolled his eyes. "Yes, my vast network of spies has informed me that this is one of many similar cells in a large building that smells rank beyond belief. It seems to be a dormitory for those poor bastards in rags, as well as their keepers. They tried to feed me some of the slop they give those drugged chaps, but as I didn't actually *want* to become one of those chaps despite my earlier jesting, I dumped it down the privy. Which, as you can no doubt tell by following your nose, is that hole in the corner."

"Have you tried the window?"

"Sadly, the bunk is bolted to the wall, and they didn't see fit to provide me with a ladder."

"Oh, right. Sorry. Let me." He slid from the bottom bunk

where he'd slept off his unwanted opium dose, and tried to stand. Unsuccessfully. "In a bit. I'll try it in a bit."

"Take your time, I'm not going anywhere." Cantlebury had liberated a rough, grimy-looking blanket from the bunk and folded it into a pad. He sat on it against the wall farthest from the privy, arms resting on his knees.

On his third try, Matthew managed to stand and make his way to the window wall, reaching as high as he could and feeling his way along the bottom for a latch. Then he climbed to the top bunk and studied the window from that vantage, discovering that the latch was quite simple but located on the outside of the window, presumably to keep the occupants from doing exactly what he was attempting to do.

"I don't suppose you have a hairpin or anything like that?"

"Fresh out," Cantlebury replied.

"If I had something long and thin I could pop the latch and boost you out, then climb out after you."

"That's a wonderful plan. Except for the part where it requires something long and thin, which we don't have."

The door rattled and two guards entered. One of them held a syringe, and the other was very, very large.

"Now lad," the one with the needle said to Matthew. "We can do this the easy way, or we can do this Bob's way. This here's Bob."

"I gathered as much."

Matthew sighed and slid down from the bunk. It was shaping up to be an unpleasant night. He wasn't sure whether to be glad he would sleep through most of it.

IT WAS SO simple, Eliza was concerned it was a trap. Any child with a pocket knife could have sprung that window, which was why she waited a solid hour before even attempting it.

When she finally got up the nerve, leaning over to the window from the top bunk in a feat of acrobatics, the latch slid smoothly to one side with a simple nudge of her knife blade. She let it fall back into place, stowed the knife back in her boot, and returned to the bunk to consider her options.

From what she'd seen on her limited tour through the building, men and women were thrown in together indiscriminately, eight or ten to a room. They appeared to rotate workers on staggered shifts every few hours, though she had no idea whether that continued through the night. All the rooms appeared to be full; workers exited, and more entered to fill it.

Eliza's cell, with its two bunks, was down a side hallway that sported mostly open doors and an odor that was generally less appalling. Some of the rooms held what appeared to be personal belongings. Guards' rooms, it seemed. Hers was definitely a cell, with its floor privy and no bed linens other than scratchy, flea-ridden blankets. Perhaps the guards simply liked to keep the troublemakers close, or perhaps this was the only available space, but the reason didn't matter. If Matthew and Cantlebury had also been lodged in one of these it should be easy enough to find them. The trick would be avoiding the guards—and if the men were drugged or incapacitated, perhaps they wouldn't warrant two guards outside their door as Eliza had.

Around sunset, a bowl of gruel and a glass of water were offered to her through a slot in the door. She took both and placed them carefully on the floor, wishing the gruel were edible. She'd managed to suppress her hunger and thirst until she actually had food and drink in front of her, but now she wasn't sure how long she'd be able to resist. The water, perhaps? It looked clean and clear, and she smelled nothing suspicious. Deciding the risk was worth it, she took a drop on her finger and tasted it. Nothing. No sweet, cloying taste of laudanum or the bitterness of other opiate tinctures, just . . . water. For a moment she considered Orm's threat of a slow poison, but the timing of that had sounded important to him. Surely he wouldn't hang that on whether or not she chanced a drink of water. She risked a sip, waited a few minutes for ill effects, then took another mouthful when she was fairly sure it was untainted. It was the best thing she had ever tasted.

Night had fallen while she worried over how and when she was to be poisoned. She could go now, when the path under the window was clear but her movements would stand out against the wall, or she could wait until a crowd of drugged workers were shuffling by, but risk being spotted by one of their guards.

Now. Because if it wasn't now, she would lose her nerve. After a final sip of water, Eliza climbed the bunk, slipped the latch again with her knife, and propped the window up with the fingers of one hand while she stowed the blade and made her move. It was neither easy nor graceful, but from the bunk she managed to work her head and shoulders through the small opening, and then scramble her way out once she saw the coast was clear. Aside from one moment when she feared she would lose her grip and land on her head, the whole thing went surprisingly well. She even managed to keep the window from slamming shut, lest the sound alert her door guards to the activity inside the room.

Knife again in hand, Eliza crouched low to the wall, skirting the building and peering around the corner to the front door. It was unguarded. A lost-looking worker shambled by carrying a yoke with two full water buckets, and she waited for him to pass out of sight beyond the next building before she peeked into the window next to the door. No guards on the inside either. Apparently Orm relied heavily on his perimeter defenses. The front door was latched from the outside, but it was a simple sliding latch, not a lock. Clearly the opium-addicted workers were not considered an escape risk. The generally lax security boded well for her prospect of finding Matthew and Cantlebury unguarded.

Eliza took a final glance around to make sure she hadn't been seen, then slipped the latch and simply walked into the front door. She recognized the way from her first trip, and it was an easy enough matter to find the corridor her cell had been in. She would start her search close to there, but not too close; she wanted to save the issue with the door guards until she had no other choice.

Along the way she peeked into some of the communal rooms, where the workers slept off their dosed gruel while waiting to be called for their next shift. Orm had said it was like a dream to them, but she could only imagine it was a nightmare. As a child she'd been given laudanum once for a stomach ailment, and it robbed her of all sense of time, turning the days and nights into an endless indistinguishable wheel. Two days, she'd been dosed with the stuff. It had seemed like an eternity. Was that what all these poor people were suffering now, an eternity of hell on earth for their sin of falling prey to opium addiction?

"I don't believe in sin," Eliza whispered to one anonymous group as she watched them sleep through the little square window. "I'll send help for you."

Then she continued down the hall to find Matthew and Cantlebury.

She came close to being spotted once, when she passed a door to one of the guard's rooms just as the occupant was crossing the floor. She flattened herself to the wall and waited, heart pounding, as his footsteps neared.

He was only closing the door. Almost sick with relief, Eliza went on, her knees shaking so hard they threatened to buckle under her.

Her cell had been near the end of the corridor. She snuck past the opening without being spotted, and started her search with the next hallway. No guards stood outside doorways, and her spirits sank as she started peeking into doors and checking locks. But in the end, she found them. Matthew and Cantlebury were all the way at the end of the hall, in the very last cell on the first side she checked. As with the other locks, this one was pathetically simple, though it did ostensibly require a key. Eliza used a hairpin to let herself in, and another to keep it from latching shut behind her.

"Hello," she greeted Mr. Cantlebury cheerfully.

After a moment in which he stared at her with wonder, he composed himself again. "About time, Miss Hardison. I was beginning to think you'd never arrive. Now help me with Matthew and tell me which way we're carrying him."

Matthew was sitting up, eyes half-open, a dreamy smile on his face. She'd never seen him completely drunk, but she suspected this was similar to the look. He was more pleasant and amiable than she would have thought, and the smile held some secret knowledge in it. When he saw Eliza he grinned wider and whispered, "I'm the large predator."

"I take it he's still drugged?" She worried for his health, but not too much. He looked quite happy, at least, and she envied that state not a little.

"Drugged again. It's beginning to wear off now, though. Whatever they're giving him seems to act more like laudanum than opium. Doesn't last very long, and he comes and goes while it's active. I was foolish enough to take a few spoonfuls of gruel, but I'm over the symptoms now. I've been faking it ever since when they come in to shoot him up. Obviously they don't think I'm much of a threat. Whatever they're giving him seems stronger than what the poor slaves are getting. He doesn't seem to mind it much."

"It may be some specialty of the house. Apparently Lord Orm grows his own varieties. I think I've used up all the luck I care to on the corridors. Your cell window is on the outer wall, yes?"

"I believe so."

"Lemon biscuit," Matthew muttered.

Eliza pondered her choices. "Did you happen to see if anyone picked up our airships, or did they leave them behind?"

"I didn't see anyone take mine. I don't think the basket would have fit in the lorry, anyway. Matthew says his was smashed, or at least I think that's what he's been babbling about."

"It was, but it should still be functional. His balloon will need patching, and so will his boiler. And he'll need water for that. My ship's intact, I just bundled it and hid it under his. So if we could sneak back up the valley to find them, now while it's still dark, perhaps we can make some quick patches, just enough to get us out of here. I'm not sure of the way, but working together, perhaps we can find it."

"I can find it," Cantlebury assured her. "I always know which direction I'm heading. Also, I wasn't tied up nearly as well as the two of you were, and I was able to look out the back window of the lorry a few times when they drove from my ship to yours. If my poor wreck is still there, we'd certainly have plenty of silk for patches. Although if the holes are small enough, I also have some pre-cut patches and this wonderful fibrous goo that Lavinia came up with. Faster than sewing."

"Perfect. Now the only problem left is how to get Matthew up and out of that window."

"Eliza?"

"Yes, Matthew, I'm here."

"Oh, all right then. I love you, you know."

She sighed. She knew, but it was problematic in so many ways for Matthew to say it aloud. "Yes, I know. Let's get you on your feet and out this window. And not a word out of you, Cantlebury."

"Madam, I wouldn't dream of it."

THE WINDOW TURNED out to be the easy part. The tricky bit was herding Matthew along without rousing the guards, particularly when he spotted the crescent moon and wanted to sing to it.

"No singing," Cantlebury hissed, huffing along as fast as he could while Matthew and Eliza stumbled along behind. Matthew's arm was heavy on her shoulders, and it was all she could do to stay upright.

"But it's so beautiful," he protested. "You're so beautiful too. I could recite some poetry to you instead."

"As long as you do it *quietly*," said Cantlebury.

"Don't encourage him. Matthew, do you even remember any poetry at the moment?"

"No."

"There, you see."

"I was going to make some up. About the hailstorm and the barn. Do you remember the—"

"Vividly. How about a nice poem about flowers instead?"

Cantlebury snickered. "I'd like to hear about the barn, myself."

"There were no ponies in it, alas," she told him, hoping to quell his enthusiasm.

"The sky, it falls, like heavy balls," Matthew began. "Upon the drivers, full of *woe*."

Eliza groaned. "Dear sweet merciful God in heaven."

"Nature's fury all unleash'd keeps us from where we want to *go*. This humble barn is all that stands 'twixt us and Gaia's vengeful wrath . . ."

"Ah, invocation of Gaia, nice touch," Cantlebury quipped. "I'll let Professor McCullough know you haven't forgotten your classics, next time I see him."

"So, grateful for it we must be . . . though one might wish it had a bath. The end."

"Bloody brilliant," was Cantlebury's assessment.

"Very tasteful," Eliza pronounced it. She was relieved and somewhat astonished that he'd kept it so. And absurdly touched that he'd just extemporized a poem to her. *A very bad poem*, she reminded herself fiercely, to no avail.

"I need to sleep now."

He nearly managed it, slumping halfway to the ground

and almost pulling her down with him. But Eliza pinched him hard, and Cantlebury splashed his face with a handful of the water from the bucket he carried. They'd taken it from the worker Eliza had seen, who was making another slow, shuffling trip to a well outside the wall when they passed by. She hoped the poor man wouldn't be in trouble for losing the bucket. They'd crept up and taken it when he wasn't looking, or more to the point, when he had seemed lost in rapt contemplation of the moon while he paused in pulling up the other full bucket for his yoke. Perhaps, she speculated, he had gone on to sing about it.

CANTLEBURY HADN'T LIED. He really could always tell exactly where he was, and his balloon was still stretched across the poppy field where he'd last seen it. The fields themselves had turned out to be blessedly empty, free of both the stupefied workers and their overseers.

Scrambling in the overturned basket, Cantlebury gathered a few surviving supplies.

"They've ransacked it, I think, and a few things were smashed when I came down. But here's the repair kit, tool box. Oh, my hamper!"

The broken wine bottle inside had not sullied the sausage or cheese that also dwelled in Cantlebury's hamper, and the trio ate ravenously as they trekked the last short distance to the wreck of Matthew's airship. It was unmolested, with Eliza's packed bundle still securely underneath it.

Matthew, unfortunately, was violently ill shortly after they finished the food, his stomach still reacting from the last dose of opium.

"It takes some like that," Cantlebury said with a philosophical shrug. "At least he can sleep for a bit while we patch this up. Time for some of Lavinia's miraculous goo."

Eliza found Matthew's discarded flight suit and pillowed his head on it, then set about putting his boiler to rights. A welding torch and proper metal patch would have been better, of course, or even a new boiler. But Cantlebury assured her that a square of tin nipped from the pail, secured with the fiber adhesive substance, would do the job well enough for a few hours. Eliza was impressed by the stuff, which adhered to both silk and metal equally well, and dried almost instantly.

"The trick is to avoid getting it on your fingers. Now, it would hold better still if it had an hour or two to cure, of course. But I say we give it fifteen minutes, then get the hell out of here. If you'll excuse me."

"I think it was called for. This place is like hell for those poor people. I hate leaving them all behind. And we never looked for Phineas. I feel like we've let down Barnabas and every other person who's lost a loved one to Orm."

Cantlebury reached for her hand, squeezing it gently. "Eliza, if Phineas were one of those sad creatures, he's gone already. All the parts that made him who he was, at least. I have no idea what's in that special preparation of Orm's, but to the extent I believe in souls at all, I believe that drug has destroyed the souls of these people. The best thing we can do is find a way to get word to the authorities, to make sure that the troops from Salt Lake really do march down here to rout this bastard out. As far as what will happen to the workers after that . . . I'm not sure I want to know."

"I want to know. I *need* to know. I'm going to do everything I can to get back here and help them. Those quicksilver miners too. Not through speeches or monographs or photos, but by *doing* things. Helping them to get well, to find other work somehow. There will be something I can do, and I will."

"Strangely, I believe you."

She chuckled. "Thank you. I'll remember that later on when I'm doubting myself."

"Let's see if we can rouse the dangerous predator from his nap, shall we?"

"Please forget you heard . . . everything Matthew has said while under the influence of that stuff."

"No. He's happy. I don't want to forget any of that, I like seeing my friends happy."

Eliza smiled and walked over to Matthew, shaking his shoulder gently. "Matthew, wake up. Time to go."

He snored and smacked his lips.

Cantlebury was more direct. He strode over to his friend and aimed a swift kick at the sole of his boot. "Pence. Up."

"What?" Matthew sat up, swaying and blinking. "I was dreaming about biscuits. Oh, where the bloody hell am I now?"

Eliza coughed gently into her fist, drawing his attention.

"Oh. I thought I'd dreamed you too."

"No. Can you stand up? It's time for us to go now."

He stood up, stumbling toward his battered airship. "Cantlebury's going to have to sit in my lap, isn't he? Damn."

"Could be worse," his friend said.

"I don't see how."

A shrill alarm pierced the night, and even at a few miles distance the three could see lights going on all over the castle compound.

"I'll blame you for that later," Cantlebury said. "Go, go, go."

Eliza helped them onto the rigging, Matthew urging her all the while to leave them and get herself in the air. She finished strapping them in before stepping into her harness and shrugging on the pack.

"We did fill your boiler, yes?"

"Yes, yes, *go*!"

Thanking Dexter for making her own ship a much simpler affair than Matthew's, she flicked the starter on her spirit lamp as Matthew turned the valve on his helium tank. The two balloons began to billow and fill in tandem, and they cleared the ground just as Eliza spotted the mounted riders pelting along the valley toward them.

Cranking the heat to full and crossing her fingers for luck, Eliza hauled on the rudder control and took a sharp turn west as she twirled up into the cool dark air. A shot flew past her, splitting the night with a singing whistle but somehow missing her.

Matthew's green silks were directly below her, and she could hear the chug of the propeller engine and the roar of his helium tank releasing too quickly as it took him higher.

More shots followed, but they were already out of range. The airships swept up and over the western ridge, crossed a silent valley filled with more poppies, then two more, before finally reaching the far side of Orm's holdings and soaring over the clear, safe ridges in the direction of Carson City.

TWENTY-TWO

ONLY THE DARK saved them, making it too hard for the sky pirates to track them over the mountains. They kept their airships low, lest the makeshift repairs fail and force them down. When they did land, however, it wasn't the repairs that did it.

"Cantlebury has the plague," Matthew called to Eliza as she stepped from her harness. They had come down on the outskirts of a small town, and the sun was just rising over the mountains behind them.

"It's not the plague," their friend said in a pathetically weak voice.

"Might as well be."

"At least you seem to have recovered," Eliza said.

Matthew shrugged. "I have a bad head, but I'll survive."

From the nearest building, an old man emerged, pointing a shotgun at them and approaching slowly.

"I assume I'll survive," he amended, raising his hands in the air and nodding to Eliza to do the same. "Good morning, sir. Does your town have a doctor?"

"Not for pirates." The man spit to one side and shifted the tobacco in his mouth with a suspicious air. "Never seen a girl pirate before. Or balloons like those two."

"We're not pirates, sir," Eliza explained. "We're part of the Sky and Steam Rally. You've heard of it?"

He nodded slowly, then jerked his head toward Cantlebury, who still reclined against Matthew's basket chair. "What's that one, then? The mascot?"

"Our colleague Mr. Edmund Cantlebury, another of the drivers in the rally. He's been taken ill and can't continue. Please, he needs medical care. We can pay you handsomely."

Still holding the shotgun at the ready with one hand, the gruff-looking fellow leaned down and placed a hand on Cantlebury's forehead, then felt for the pulse in his neck. Sighing, he gestured to Matthew and handed off the gun. "Hold that. How long ago did he start feeling it?" Taking one knee, he lifted Cantlebury's eyelids one at a time, cursing softly at the lack of light.

"About two hours? It's difficult to say, we were flying in the dark."

The man frowned and sniffed. "Vomiting?"

"Ah, no," Matthew said. "That was me. It's a long story. I'm quite well now, however."

"Rough night?"

"Something like that."

Eliza stepped forward. "You're the doctor, aren't you?"

He nodded, beard waggling as he smiled and chuckled. "Doctor John Belton. Also the mayor. And right now I guess I'm the sheriff too, since the real sheriff is sleeping off a bender over at the saloon. Your friend's fever needs to come down. Any idea what he's sick with?"

Sharing a quick glance first, Matthew and Eliza nodded in unison.

"It's the influenza," she confessed. "Several of the racers have been struck. Including Mr. Cantlebury's . . . fiancée."

The doctor seemed to mull that over. "So you drop down

from the sky with no warning, carrying a man with a virulently contagious disease and ask the first person you see to take care of him until you send help? Is that about the size of it?"

"And we'll pay you," Eliza reminded him.

"Do the racers always fly at night? I thought you all were supposed to land in Carson City yesterday, and be on your way to San Francisco by now. At least that's what the schedule in the San Francisco paper said. We get it a week or so behind here, but we do read it."

Matthew had already surmised that the doctor was smarter than he looked. Now he was certain of it. He decided to cut to the heart of the matter. "Are you Lord Orm's man?"

The doctor sneered and spit again, a thick brown wad of contempt. "There's a lady present, so I can't say what I'm really thinking, but the short answer is 'no.'"

"I'm probably thinking the same thing," Eliza told him. "Orm shot us down and took us prisoner yesterday. We barely escaped with our lives, and I suspect now it's daylight, his pirates will be after us again soon. We *must* get to Carson City. But Mr. Cantlebury will never make it there, and even if he does, the longer he stays with Mr. Pence, the more likely that Mr. Pence will be infected too."

"You're probably both infected already, this strain just seems to have a long incubation period. You're ticking time bombs," the doctor told her, but not unkindly. "But you're young and strong, and should pull through a bout of flu all right. Your friend here, I'm not as sure, but he'll live if I have anything to say about it. Help me get him into the house, then you two can be on your way. No offense, but I want you long gone by the time those pirates come looking."

THEY CAUGHT A tail wind and Eliza had started to believe they might reach Carson City after all, when she tried to adjust her course slightly south a few hours later and her airship didn't respond. She jiggled the control, pulled the lever again, but the ballonet still didn't respond by deflating as it should to send the ship in the desired direction.

She tried a gentle movement to the right, and the craft responded beautifully.

"*Damn*."

She could hardly make it to Carson City, much less San Francisco, if she had to do a full circle every time she needed to veer left. If nothing else, she simply didn't have the fuel for it.

Eliza's dirigible was slightly ahead of Matthew's and he followed her down to the ground. They landed by a copse of trees, with a charming runoff stream gurgling nearby. They hadn't seen a town or even an isolated cabin in miles.

"Now what?"

"I can't turn left." She tugged at the balloon as it deflated, flattening it along the ground as best she could, twisting it so the defective ballonet would be spread on top. And there it was, plain as day, a frayed tear in the silk. That bullet from Orm's henchman hadn't missed her after all, but had grazed the ballonet. The pressure must have been tugging at the scrape and widening it ever since, until it finally shredded open at the weakest point.

The tear was long, longer than any of her patches or the scraps left in Cantlebury's kit. Too long for her to sew quickly, and the silk would likely fray again from all the needle holes if she tried to darn an area that large.

After an hour of examining it from every angle, laying out patches in different combinations and considering the small amount of fiber goo remaining, Eliza threw her hands in the air. "That's it, then. It's over. I concede defeat."

She was fairly certain she'd never spoken those words in her life. They tasted bitter and unwelcome.

"Come and sit down. Have some luncheon. You'll feel better for it."

"Luncheon?"

Her stomach growled in a manner most indelicate, reminding her she hadn't eaten since the discovery of Cantlebury's hamper last night. Apparently, Matthew and Cantlebury had brought it along.

"We're down to the wine-soaked things now. But everything was wrapped in cheesecloth or linen, so at least we can be sure there's no glass in the packets."

Wine-infused dried apricots turned out to be surprisingly good. The dried, cured beef strips were not quite as delicious with their impromptu burgundy sauce, but Eliza ate several anyway. Chewing on the tough meat satisfied some craving she didn't know she'd had, the desire to really tear into a meal.

Investigating the stream, they found the water icy and clean, and almost miraculously refreshing.

"You can have the last of the cheese if you like. For some reason I can't stomach the idea of it."

Eliza considered telling Matthew about some of his less dignified moments of the night before, but decided against it. "I'll save it for later."

"Very well, suit yourself. Now that we've lunched, and presumably feel better . . . ?"

She nodded happily. There might not be much to celebrate, but food *had* helped. Now they sat under a tree, enjoying the quiet and the cool breeze, and that helped too.

"Right, then. I think you're missing a few obvious possible solutions to your airship problem, Eliza."

"What solutions? I can't patch it piecemeal. It'll never hold, and I'd be here for days trying to sew it anyway. One big patch would do it, with some stitching and the last of the goo, but I don't see any other way to manage it. I might as well hang my balloon over this branch for a tent right now and send you on your way as soon as it's dark."

Matthew leaned back against the tree, tilting his head to study the low-hanging branch she'd gestured to. "This would be a decent spot for a tent. But you're missing the point. We *have* silk. A ton of it. Right there." He pointed at his own airship, with its green balloon folded inside the basket. "Or just take my ship, and let me use your balloon for the tent. Either way, you need to move on to San Francisco."

If her anger hadn't spent itself on more important things, Eliza knew it would have flared up again. After all this time, after the change she thought she'd seen in the way Matthew viewed her, for him to play the chivalry card now was simply too much to bear.

"We're still competitors, Matthew. The only two left. You may not care, but I do. I don't want to give Orm the satisfaction of stopping the rally entirely. Only one of us can make it to San Francisco, and obviously it should be the one who still has a working vehicle. I won't accept a win based solely on your deciding to be noble."

"My working vehicle has been carrying an extra payload and is nearly out of fuel and helium," he explained. "I'm not being noble, just practical. I wouldn't make it to Carson City. Carrying Cantlebury, plus stopping to let him out,and lifting off again, took up any reserves I might have drawn on. But you're only a little over half my weight. You could make it there easily in my ship. Or in your own, if you borrow the silk. You should still have plenty of fuel left. Hot air is more efficient that way, and your *Firebird* is particularly well designed."

"Thank you. The ballonet placement was my idea. Dexter started with the same design as *Gossamer Wing*, but he'd planned to add to the weight with a more traditional rudder arrangement and smaller directional ballonets. I didn't like it, it felt clunky in the air. So I convinced him I could control the pitch just as well this way." She nudged at the silk's edge with one booted toe, suddenly shy and awkward as she realized she and Matthew were finally alone together. It wasn't quite the setting she'd imagined.

He stepped closer and slid his toe adjacent to hers, tapping the side of her boot with his own. "I remember. You're very good at that, you know. Taking existing designs, testing them and then improving on them. And you're also clever with fabric. I'm not very good with soft materials. I should lure you from Hardison House and put you to work on my designs."

He twined his fingers with hers as he spoke, and Eliza returned the pressure. It was as comforting as it was exciting. Just standing on a hillside, alone with a man. With Matthew.

"Lure me? It's not as though I work for Dexter."

"You're driving his steam car and airship. You field-tested vehicles for him, helped modify his designs. Or at least modify his modifications, as I believe the *Gossamer Wing* was originally conceived by some poor nameless naval researcher in a secret lab somewhere."

Now he was trying to flatter her. Why wasn't she full of umbrage? "He was nameless then. I think he's Lord Admiral Davis McCollough now."

"Interesting. So will you consider it?"

"Cannibalizing your balloon?" Was there some other subject she'd missed? It was hard to say. His fingers and flattery were very distracting.

He shook his head. "That too, but I meant coming to work for me. After all this is done, I mean. And after you've helped liberate the opium slaves. Or perhaps you could do that and work for me on an alternating basis. Job by job, as it were."

She turned to look at him, craning her neck because he stood so close. "You're serious, aren't you?"

"Yes. Quite serious. You wouldn't have to be an employee if you prefer not. A partner, perhaps? A consultant? I don't know, I'd always imagined . . . a partner, I suppose. Somebody to come with me to Europa when I had business there, who would also appreciate the artwork and so forth. Someone to make terrible puns with in the workshop. Just *someone*."

"And to share your bed?"

He looked up at the branch again. "I've always sort of assumed the *someone* would be my wife, so yes. But as you won't marry me, I suppose I'll have to work scandal management into my business plan."

"What a foursome we'd be, you and me with Cantlebury and Lavinia. Nobody would have us."

"We'd have each other."

Eliza thought back to the day before, in Orm's office, certain she was about to die. That strange peace had come over her, and part of it had been the shredding down of self-delusion to reveal her to herself. She did want to marry Matthew, although she wasn't sure what marriage was. What they could make it. She also knew that regardless of what she'd tried to think, her first reaction to the tale of Cantlebury and Lavinia hadn't been to congratulate them on their willingness to embrace life beyond society's limits. No, her heart had broken for them because they were in love and couldn't marry. Whether she liked it or not, she saw that as the happy ending.

Could she like it, with Matthew? People were always saying things were different when it was with this person or that person, different with your own children, different when you're in love. But in Eliza's experience it all looked the same. Charlotte was happy with Dexter, but their last trip to Europa had been their honeymoon, and now Charlotte seemed to spend most of her time balancing the household accounts and overseeing the installation of the rose gardens. Sometimes she visited the workshop, it was true.

"Charlotte and Dexter would probably still receive us," Eliza mused. "Charlotte can get away with anything. She makes the fashion."

"Which is strange, because she spent years as a recluse. At least as far as society knew."

"Matthew, what *did* Charlotte do before she and Dexter married?"

"Government work," he said quickly.

"Yes, but what kind of work? It wasn't just decoding messages, was it?"

He smiled. "It's just speculation on my part, I don't *know* anything. And if you ever, for one second, mention a word of this to either Charlotte or Dexter, I'll . . . I don't know, but there will be dire consequences for you."

"Understood. Now you *must* tell me."

Matthew sat up and glanced around ostentatiously, as if there were anybody within fifty miles to overhear them. "I'm reasonably certain she was a spy."

"A *what*?"

"A spy. You know, derring-do, secret capers, intelligence gathering. International espionage."

Eliza wasn't sure what she'd expected, but it wasn't *that*. The more she considered the possibility, however, the more sense it made. The way Charlotte had spoken of a whole career about which Eliza knew nothing. A career she'd given up entirely, as far as anybody knew, but if she was a spy then perhaps she was still doing it. Who would ever know? Added to that were Charlotte's unique skills, so different from most elegantly bred ladies of their acquaintance. How had the staid Lord Darmont's daughter become an expert pilot of a secret dirigible prototype, after all? Why was Charlotte such a crack shot with any weapon she put her hand to?

And if she truly was retired, perhaps she found it relaxing to tally pillowcases and double-check the housekeeper's arithmetic, after spending all that time at high alert, in constant danger. Even a few days of danger had been almost too much for Eliza to take. She could understand wanting a change. Safety, predictability. Simple fun.

"Matthew, if your wife is haring off to the continent with you and helping design your engines, who will see to the home? Hire the servants, make sure there's furniture in all the rooms? Who keeps the household ledger and handles the correspondence? Who minds the children or sees to it that they have the right nannies and governesses and tutors?

That's what wives *do*. They're too busy to play in the workshop and go to France."

He gave her an amiable, patient smile, the one she used to want to smack off his face. Still did, just a little. "My wife won't be. Except I thought I wouldn't have one, because we were planning to be scandalous instead."

"It isn't that I *want* to be scandalous."

She *wanted* him. If only it didn't have to be so complicated.

Still smiling, he leaned over to rest his forehead against hers, pushing strands of hair out of her face so he could cup his palms to her cheeks. He brushed a kiss over her lips, soft as air, then pressed his lips to her hairline.

"You're thinking too hard about this. Let's get started on that patch, then we can make the tent and have a rest before nightfall."

ELIZA SLEPT FITFULLY, dreaming of poison and flowers. Great brass stairwells rose to the clouds, moving on gears as tall as an elephant, powered by a wheel with a hundred opium slaves in rags. She ran over marble and jumped, then found herself flying over a field of poppies. Blood red, beautiful, alluring. If she fell, she would die, because she'd been poisoned and time was running out. Only by moving could she stay alive.

"Eliza."

Matthew was with her, flying alongside. Then he started to fall, and she tried to scream, to warn him, but he only looked back at her and smiled.

"Eliza! Time to wake up."

He was shaking her shoulder. Night was falling outside their green silk shelter.

"I'm awake."

"You should see the last of the sunset. It's spectacular."

She dutifully peered out of the makeshift structure to

view the western sky, and found herself agreeing with him. It was nearly gone, but still lovely, all crimson and violet against the encroaching deep indigo.

There was still enough light to find her way to the creek, and she returned feeling much refreshed.

"The patch has set," Matthew told her. "Should be safe enough."

He frowned down at the rigging of her airship, arms folded over his chest, looking miserable.

"Matthew?" Eliza laid a hand on his chest, feeling his strong heartbeat. She'd come to a decision, sometime between drowsiness and sleep, and had awakened still knowing it was the right decision. "I'll wait awhile longer, until well after full dark. Come back inside the tent with me."

Twenty-three

"I SHOULD STAY out here and stand watch. Go and rest some more if you need to."

"No. I'd like you to help me with something," Eliza insisted.

"With what? All the equipment's out here!"

She tugged his arm, laughing. "*Matthew*. I want you to help me . . . gather rosebuds while I may."

He was silent for a long moment. Long enough for Eliza to grow nervous. Finally he asked quietly, "Are you saying what I think you're saying?"

"Probably." She pulled on him again, loosing one of his arms and gripping his hand. "Come inside the tent and make love to me."

He stood his ground, resisting her efforts to lead him. "Say you'll marry me."

"I won't make you any promises."

"I love you."

"I love *you*, Matthew. But we can decide for ourselves what that means. And we don't have to decide right now."

"We might find ourselves faced with a decision fairly soon if we accidentally bring a third party into this. I'm not going to sire any bastards, Eliza."

Embarrassment flashed in her cheeks, hot and awful. She'd been aiming for a seduction and landed herself in a lecture. The worst part was, he was absolutely right. That didn't change how much she wanted him.

"I could die," she said, knowing as she said it that she shouldn't. The "don't-let-me-die-a-virgin" ploy was the last resort of seducers everywhere, and it cheapened her to use it.

"That was a very low blow."

"I know, I'm sorry. This isn't going like I thought it would."

He relented on his physical opposition and stepped in, pulling her into his arms. She hugged his waist, feeling safe and as though things would be all right, even though she knew it wasn't so.

"How did you think it would go, then? Just curious."

"I thought it would take less thinking, for one thing. That I would ask and you would agree, and then we wouldn't have to think for a while."

Matthew stroked her back, and the intimate gesture inflamed as much as it soothed. Eliza held him closer, wishing she weren't quite so susceptible.

"It deserves some thought. I've thought about little else for days, if you must know."

Giggling, she pushed back enough to see his face. "That's a different kind of thinking, and you know it."

"Oh, I do know it. Rest assured." He pressed against her, already hard, which frustrated Eliza even more.

"Please, Matthew?"

"No, you'll ruin me. I mustn't."

But something in his tone told her he was already halfway to capitulation. His tone, or the way he whimpered when she rose onto her toes, stroking against him.

"I promise if there's a baby, I will marry you. To protect your reputation."

Matthew groaned and bent his head. Eliza expected a kiss, but he stopped just short. "But we'd have to wait and see, to know for sure, wouldn't we?"

"Perhaps a month or so, I suppose."

He stroked his hands lower, cupping her buttocks and lifting her gently, squeezing, parting her legs with his thigh. "I don't want to wait and see. Agree to marry me anyway."

"I'll agree to think about it."

"Deal."

"Now? Please?"

He had her shirt half off before they even reached the tent, and she yanked it free impatiently as he started on her breeches.

"Boots," she reminded him, sitting down on the pad of silk scraps and flight clothes they'd rested on earlier. He helped her tug her boots off, then toed off his own and resumed his work undressing her until the job was done.

Eliza was slower, but then she was distracted. It had been days since they'd touched one another, and Matthew seemed determined to reacquaint himself with every inch of her.

"I've missed this," he said, kissing the part in question fondly. "And this. Oh, and I've particularly missed *that*. And . . . just roll over, if you would, darling? Oh, sweet gods how I've missed this. I mean it's not exactly hidden in those breeches, but still I much prefer seeing it in its natural state." He kissed her there too a firm smack of his lips on each cheek, before encouraging her to roll onto her back again.

"Are you quite finished with your reunion?" she asked, smirking.

"Not quite, my love. Here, let me wipe that look off your face." He cupped her between the legs and pressed a finger inside her, grinding his palm in a circle, and it was Matthew's turn to smirk while Eliza gasped.

"Use your mouth again, like you did in the barn," she pleaded, astonished at her own boldness. There wasn't time to be coy, though. It was now or never. Matthew, however, had plans of his own.

"I need fingers for this," he explained, edging a second one into her channel. It pulled, as it had the first time, and he frowned when Eliza winced. "All that time on a veloci-mobile, and it's still there. Astonishing. To hear the stories the thing's as fragile as a cobweb. One touch, and *bang*, it's gone and you're marrying the girl."

"*What*?"

"Your hymen. Maidenhead, what-have-you. It's quite ter-rifyingly intact, and I don't want to hurt you, so I'm stalling by doing this."

Really? At a time like this, he wanted to stop and have a conversation about the state of her hymen? "I think it's supposed to hurt, the first time. I'm not terrified, why should you be?"

"I'm terrified you'll blame me, regret this and never want to do it again."

He attempted a third finger, and Eliza grabbed his wrist. "Ouch."

"See?"

Look at him all concerned and anxious and trying to be considerate. How could I have ever not loved him? "Mat-thew, I think I need to have a little talk with Fred."

He pulled his hand away and sat back on his heels. "He's entirely at your disposal."

"I see that." She sat up and turned herself around, then leaned down and propped herself on her elbows, chin on hands, to face Fred squarely. It was dark, but she could see well enough for this. The trickiest part was not giggling. "Fred, I require your help. Matthew is being awfully reti-cent. I want him to make mad, passionate love to me, and he wants to have a conversation about anatomy. Do you have any suggestions for me?"

Matthew coughed, and Fred nodded. Eliza bit the inside

of her cheek to keep the laughter in as Matthew spoke. "He recommends you try getting in that same position you're in right now, only facing the other way. Fred's very single-minded. I've learned to be wary of his advice."

"I'll be cautious. Fred, I want you to know that whatever happens tonight, I won't blame you. I'll still be fond of you, and assuming I survive, I'll probably invite you over to play again. After all, the first time I went up in Charlotte's airship I got ten feet up, fell out of the harness and landed on my . . . lawn. That hurt quite a bit, but I gave it another try. And another after that. And look at me now."

"Oh, he is," Matthew avowed. "I am."

"I don't believe you," Eliza replied. "I don't believe you or Fred are sufficiently motivated."

She gave in to the impulse she'd had when she first bent down, and leaned forward to slip her lips over the tip of Matthew's penis, sliding her tongue over the tender skin and tasting salt and arousal. He cursed and wrapped his fingers in her hair, and she suspected she had just learned the best way to motivate Fred. She tried taking more into her mouth, but Matthew pulled her away and picked her up, flipping her onto her back and landing on top of her.

"Enough," he panted, rubbing himself against the crux of her thighs before shifting down again with another curse and planting his mouth against her sex. He drove her high, higher, *so close*, until she was lifting her hips into his face and clawing at the silk beneath them. When he stopped, she shouted her protest, but he had already moved again, and silenced her with a kiss. Rough at first, then tender as his fingers stole inside her body again. Not playing, this time, she realized. Making sure she was ready.

She was. She shifted, trying to get closer and bending her knees, and he moved himself into position, and—

"Ow! Bloody *hell*, that hurts!"

"Warned you."

She was already laughing, gasping against his shoulder

at how ridiculous it all was. He stilled his hips and grinned at her, kissing her a few times. Slowly, sweetly, as if time was a commodity they had in abundance. The sharp, startling pain ebbed to a dull sting, and Eliza made herself relax and assess things.

It hurt, yes. But she could see where it wouldn't always. That part was a nasty shock, but there were pleasant surprises along with it. The heat of Matthew's cock—she couldn't think of it as Fred when it was inside her—soothed the ache, filling and stretching her in a way that felt new but absolutely right.

Where their bodies met she felt the sting, but also a sweeter stimulation when he moved even a fraction of an inch. Inside her, outside her, even higher where his coarse hairs teased her clitoris.

"Is it all right now?" He whispered, feathering kisses over her cheekbone and down toward her ear.

"I think so."

He surged farther into her, a subtle flow of muscles beneath her hands. She'd thought he was already as deep as possible, but she'd been wrong. When he thrust a second time, then a third, she felt herself move by instinct, countering him. Accommodating him. Her body was reconstructing its awareness around him, turning itself into the perfect vessel for this precise activity, this exact moment.

"Ohhh . . ."

"Pain?" He asked, all concern again, his hips slowing. She responded by digging her fingernails into his buttocks.

"If you stop I will kill you."

"Oh. Good." And after a few seconds, *"So* good."

She started to complain again when he pushed to one elbow, peeling his sweaty upper body away from hers and leaving a chill behind. Then his hand moved between them, finding her clitoris and increasing the pressure there, and she forgot what she was upset about.

"Matthew?"

"I want you to come first."

"Isn't it cheating to do it like that?"

His laughing, taut belly shaking against his hand sent a shock wave through it into her. "No. Does it feel good?"

She gave him her reply in the form of an orgasm, tightening around him before she quite knew what was happening. It felt *too* good, like some sacred bliss not meant for mere mortals. Rippling through her, stroking every nerve ending with heat until she couldn't breathe or think or move. As it ebbed, she felt Matthew's tempo increase, his cock lengthen and stiffen even more inside her. He cried out her name as he came, spending himself on a final, shuddering thrust.

TWENTY-FOUR

ELIZA DISAPPEARED FROM view almost immediately, the delicate blue flame of the spirit lamp barely illuminating the red of her balloon. Matthew watched anyway, wishing for something better to happen. Something that didn't involve her having to leave his side and head off into dangers unknown. Or his having to wait here alone, possibly for days, to find out whether she'd made it.

He wanted her safely back, and he wanted her in his bed for as long as she could persuade her to stay there. Until they had to leave or starve. He supposed that was why hotel room service had been invented, to keep honeymooning couples from starving to death. So now he wanted Eliza back safely, in his bed, in a hotel with decent room service. Things were already getting complicated, and he'd only had sex with her the one time. That probably confirmed it had been a mistake, but Matthew didn't care. He would take her on her terms, scandalous or otherwise. Eliza was worth the complication.

Matthew sighed and looked back at his tent, which

looked more blue than green under the waxing moon. He pondered the improbability of flight, the marvel that they'd gotten this far at all. An owl hooted somewhere, and he thought of birds.

Then he thought of wings, and breaking a thing into its parts to start all over again, and the fact that he still had Cantlebury's toolbox. And the next moment, he set to work.

ELIZA DIDN'T LIKE Carson City one bit. Her view of the place might have been tempered by the fact that she'd grown accustomed to being greeted by cheering crowds when she arrived in a new town. True, not *all* the towns she'd been in recently and not *all* the crowd members were friendly. Some had been aggressively hostile. Eliza no longer cared much about winning, especially not to prove anything to Matthew. She knew what she'd gone through, and felt she had nothing left to prove to anyone about her general competence to take care of herself.

But even so, the absence of even a welcoming banner across the main road struck her as off-putting. The race was important. People, some of them her friends, had been injured or murdered along the way. The least they deserved was some recognition of the event they'd sacrificed so much for.

"It's as if these people don't care at all," she muttered, hiking up the street in the pre-dawn gloom with her bundled aircraft tucked under her arm. A woman on the wooden sidewalk did a double take, then stared at Eliza with a confused expression. There was a similar reaction from the sleepy boy minding the hitching post in front of the hotel, and from the hotel clerk himself. He procured the rally officials, who had been scheduled to leave with the afternoon mail coach, and backed them up as they explained things to Eliza. Beginning with the fact that she could not possibly be Eliza Hardison.

"Who else would I be? I demand that you clock my time and check me in so I can refuel and continue to San Francisco." It hadn't occurred to her that her very identity might be challenged. She would proceed without checking in if she could, but she needed that fuel if she was to make it to San Francisco and put a stop to Orm. She was the only one left to do it.

"But . . . the race is cancelled, miss. Because of the explosion. All the racers died. We had a letter," the official said, with a firm nod that nearly sent his glasses sliding off his nose.

"What explosion?"

"Over the Sierras. The last three got caught in one of those vapor fumes, one of their gas balloons caught fire and the whole thing went up. Fried to a crisp, all three of them, on the spot."

"And yet," she pointed out, "here I am. I'm not fried to a crisp, and neither are Mr. Pence or Mr. Cantlebury. Mr. Pence made it as far as the hills just east of here, and Mr. Cantlebury took ill. We dropped him off with the doctor in Belton."

"But we had a letter!" he repeated.

"From whom?"

"Lord Orm. Owns a big ranch up near where the gases start. Sent it by his own special messenger, and it had the rally committee seal and everything."

Eliza showed her rigging and balloon to the rally officials and asked again that they provide her fuel and let her sign the official check-in sheet.

"After all, if I'm not who I say I am, the race is cancelled anyway, so it won't matter. But if I'm telling the truth, and you refuse to let me sign and provide me my fuel, you've just compromised the outcome of the rally. And knowingly left two drivers stranded with no way to get to San Francisco or home. In that case, you'll have the entire committee and my sponsor, Baron Hardison, to answer to. Which option sounds more appealing, gentlemen?"

She had her check-in signed and her fuel tank filled within fifteen minutes, and was back in the air for the final leg of the rally.

MATTHEW DECIDED TO wait for dawn to test his creation out. It wouldn't do to spend all night and all his materials on the damn thing, then break an ankle tripping over a rock as he tried to launch it. Besides, it was most likely a death trap, and perhaps the morning light would bring some common sense with it and help him decide against trying it out at all.

He fell asleep waiting, and dreamed an explicit but ultimately frustrating dream of Eliza flying her dirigible clad only in her chemise. He woke to full daylight and a chorus of excessive bird song.

"Oh, shut up," he sniped at the harmless creatures, who paid him no mind and continued to trill and chirp merrily while he strapped himself in to the contraption.

Matthew suspected they were laughing at him, and he thought if he were a bird he'd probably be laughing too.

The curved framework of his balloon seat was lightweight metal, and it had been easy enough to pry away the wood and wicker, then straighten that piece into a large V shape. Scraps of wood from the rigging, unwound wicker bindings and a few stripped-down tree branches filled out the frame, and he had been able to cover it with silk handily. They'd run out of the wondrous fiber goo while patching Eliza's balloon, but he had needle and thread aplenty. The dawn light had found him stitching, testing, reinforcing, until the silk was securely in place. Then it was simply a question of attaching the wing to the framework he'd made by knocking down his balloon rigging and reassembling an abbreviated version of it. Taking a cue from Eliza's ship, he'd used his seat straps to create a harness like a mountain-climber might use, allowing him to run while launching the thing, then sit suspended by the harness, hanging on to a bar in front of him.

The birds might laugh, but Matthew was determined. He didn't merely *want* to go after Eliza. He *had* to, or die trying. It was very simple . . . though of course he hoped it wouldn't come to death. He sprinted down the hill at top speed, bouncing high a few times and coming down hard, but never quite managing to stay up. By the time he reached the flat before the next drop, his lungs were burning and his legs were jelly. He was hungry, thirsty, exhausted and in no shape for this, he decided.

He tried to pull up before the drop but momentum carried him forward, the wing bucked and he almost lost his grip, and then the hill fell away beneath his feet and Matthew was soaring away on an updraft, screaming at the top of his lungs.

ELIZA COULD BARELY land in front of San Francisco's primary government building for all the temperance ladies in the way. They crowded the official timekeepers, rushing past the barrier of posts and bunting that had been set up around a central grassy square. She didn't know what they hoped to accomplish, as she must land *somewhere*, and at the moment it seemed likely she'd wind up landing on one of their heads.

She pulled up and away from the grounds, hoping to give the officials time to clear a space, and that was when she saw the craft moored beside the graceful neoclassical Royal Governor's office. Wooden hull, a billowing clump of patched and dirty-looking ballonets and white sails. Replace white with black and arm the thing, and it would be unmistakably a pirate ship. As it was, it resembled a slightly disreputable but otherwise unremarkable sky schooner. With a golden poppy painted on its bow.

Drawing her spyglass from its tube on her rigging, Eliza

rose higher still and scanned the ship's decks. She saw unkempt pirates, and even a few filthy, rag-clad opium slaves. Those were working below the main deck, and probably invisible to anyone with a lower vantage point. Unless somebody recognized the craft or was looking for pirates, they'd probably never look closely enough to see the obviously suspicious crew. There was no sign of Orm.

Eliza looped slowly over the green, looking for a bandstand, a stage or other places where authority figures tended to linger. *There.* She put the skyglass up again and saw the race committee, marked with red and white sashes, seated on a dais and apparently grumbling to one another. They gestured toward the landing square, and up to Eliza's ship, but she saw no sign of anything being done to clear the area so she might land.

Orm was seated at the end of the row, wearing a gaudy lime green waistcoat and only slightly less gaudy dark green suit with gold piping that matched his gold lapel poppy. As she watched him through the glass, he looked up and gave her a little salute. Then he slipped the poppy free, flicked a switch on the side, and opened it to reveal a hidden compartment containing some kind of brown powder.

Snuff. He pulled one of the poppy petals, which turned out to be a tiny spoon. Then he dosed himself, saluted her again and put the ridiculous contraption back in its place.

She watched him lean over and speak to the committee members, saw them shake their heads and scowl at him. Orm shrugged and sat back again, crossing his arms. One of the members strode to the front of the stage and picked up a megaphone, aiming it directly toward her.

"Miss Eliza Hardison!" he shouted. "Miss Hardison, we must ask that you land and answer the charges brought against you, or we will be forced to allow the Royal Governor's Guard to intervene and bring you down."

Without a megaphone of her own, Eliza was forced to

yell through cupped hands and hope the old man could hear her over the crowd.

"I would love to land, sir, but my choices seem to be a tree, a rooftop or somebody's head."

A ripple of laughter went through the crowd, but it didn't reassure Eliza. What charges was she being called to answer? What had Orm told the committee? And hadn't *anyone* in San Francisco recognized a thinly disguised pirate ship when they saw it? Were they all willfully blind? Had they never traveled far enough east to encounter Orm's crews? *Probably both*, she considered ruefully. Orm had spent a great deal of time making sure people defaulted to the northeastern passage; the pirates couldn't be very busy these days.

"Clear the landing square! You there, with the placards, please remain outside the barriers!"

He seemed to like using the megaphone, as he shouted several more instructions through it before the square was sufficiently vacated.

"Harlot!" a few ladies called from the safe anonymity of the mob. Then, more ominously, "Murderess!"

"What are you all talking about?"

Nobody seemed to hear her, so she took advantage of the clear space to touch down, unsnapping her harness and resisting the urge to fall to her knees and kiss the ground. *Finished*. No matter what else, the whole misbegotten adventure was *over*, and Eliza couldn't remember being so relieved.

Except for the ostentatious guards bearing down on her from one corner of the grassy square. That part was less than a relief.

"What is the meaning of this?" she demanded, reasoning that by going on the offensive she would be in a position of greater strength.

The two leading guards took an arm each and simply

lifted her up, marching on out of the square with Eliza dangling ignominiously between them, facing backwards. Facing the crowd, in other words, some of whom were laughing at her.

Perfect. At least Matthew isn't here to see this . . . although I rather wish he could be here. Wherever he is, I only hope he's safe.

They came to a halt in unison, quite impressively, before the dais. The speaker wasn't quite as loud, so he must have abandoned his megaphone, for which she was thankful. She could only tell by hearing, as the guards still held her backwards.

"Miss Eliza Hardison, this gentleman has brought—oh, for heaven's sake, turn her around, you buffoons."

The guards scuffled about as though embarassed, putting Eliza down and turning her roughly by the shoulders to face the committee members and Orm.

"Better. Miss Eliza Hardison?"

"Yes, sir," she said politely, unable to curtsy with the guards once more gripping her upper arms.

The man frowned and turned to Orm. "My Lord, are you *quite* certain this is the person you mean to accuse? From the description given by you and the El Dorado Foundation workers, I was anticipating a painted Jezebel, and here we appear to have a little girl with her hair still in plaits."

"I had to use up all my hairpins," she explained. In truth, she was less than thrilled with her appearance, but for once perhaps looking younger than her age would work to her advantage. "Picking locks. While I was escaping Lord Orm's castle with Mr. Pence and Mr. Cantlebury."

"You see, sir?" Orm said, pouncing on her words instantly. "She names them even before we do, trying to deflect suspicion. How did she know who we were accusing her of killing?"

"You're accusing me of . . . *I beg your pardon*?"

"Miss Hardison, please. Lord Orm has raised very

serious accusation of multiple counts of murder, poisoning and arson. He's brought witnesses, evidence. I'm afraid we have no choice but to remand you into the custody of the guards and let them secure your person, pending a thorough investigation and trial."

"But Mr. Pence and Mr. Cantlebury aren't dead." *No. I left Matthew safe. He's alive, he has to be alive, because I love him. I need him. And Lavinia needs Cantlebury too. Please, please, let them not be dead.*

"Then where are they, Miss Hardison?"

"Hmph," one of the other committee members grunted. "Fair question."

The others took it up like a chorus. "Hmph." "Quite right." "Fair question." "Quite right."

"Mr. Cantlebury took ill with influenza and we had to find him a doctor. We took him to Belton. At least I think that's the name of the town. The doctor is also the mayor, and he's called Belton. And Mr. Pence is . . . well, to tell you the truth, I'm not sure, but I have the coordinates in my log. He's in a green silk tent on some hillside between Belton and Carson City."

Along with my heart and soul and everything I hold dear in this world, she nearly added. She tried to work out the timeline, to figure whether Orm would have even had time to find Matthew and Edmund, kill them and bring them here as evidence. It didn't fit. The pirates were fast, but not faster than the small dirigibles the racers flew. Their ship must have overflown Eliza and Matthew at some point, in order to make it to San Francisco ahead of Eliza. Orm must have left his castle shortly after he'd learned of the escape, and wouldn't have had time to double back. He hadn't found them. He was bluffing. Matthew was safe.

Relief washed over her, so powerful it made her dizzy. For a moment she was grateful for the large gentlemen holding her up by the arms. It wouldn't have done at all to go swooning to the ground just then.

"He crashed? Did you go to his aid?"

"The other way 'round. I had to land because of a tear in one of my ballonets, and he came to my aid. But he was running low on fuel and helium anyway, and didn't think he'd make it to Carson City. He made me use his balloon silk to patch my balloon, and I continued on."

Orm pointed at her again. "Creating a story in case we ask her why her balloon is patched with parts cannibalized from one of her dead competitors' airships. Next she'll be pointing fingers and claiming one of us is the killer. Gentlemen, I've told you I can supply a ship full of witnesses who *saw* this scarlet devil-woman lead her two colleagues in the path of a toxic gas jet, then ignite the jet to incinerate them."

"Oh, that's disgusting!" she exclaimed. "*That's* what you're saying I did? I didn't do anything of the sort, but I mean the very idea is appalling. How *dare* you! And you *are* the killer!"

"Aha! You see? Just as I said."

"Where are these witnesses of yours, Lord Orm?" the committee chairman demanded. "Let them confront her here and perhaps she'll go along to her fate more quietly."

Orm nodded, the smallest lift of his chin, and two men stepped onto the dais from the surrounding group of quasi-officials, timekeepers, medics and other race personnel. They were scruffy and thin, roughly clad, with the hard look of men who traded in death. Even among the rough-and-tumble citizens of San Francisco, their hardness stood out. Pirates, obviously. One of them even wore an eye patch.

The eye patch man looked from Orm to Eliza, and seemed torn. His face looked oddly familiar, but it wasn't until he began to lift the eyepatch that she realized where she'd seen him before. He must have seen the recognition on her face, because a look of alarm crossed his and he shook his head at her, finger to lips, silently begging her not to speak. Then he raised his eyes to the sky and, with a relief that was visible, lowered the patch and backed slowly off the stage. Eliza told herself that what she'd thought couldn't be correct. It was simply too far-fetched. Ridiculous, a hallucination brought on by nervous exhaustion.

She looked behind her and up, and saw what had brought him such ease. Her own heart lifted when she realized what she was looking at. She had never seen a more welcome sight.

Oh, thank God, it's Matthew. It's my Matthew.
What the hell is he flying?

THE GLIDER NEEDED more than a patch of grass to land safely, as was obvious to the crowd that scattered before the oncoming nose of Matthew's craft as he swooped down one side of the square. He finally coasted to a halt, using his feet to brake faster, and was unharnessed and running toward Eliza when the committee man wielded his megaphone again.

"Halt!" he shouted.

Matthew continued pelting toward Eliza.

"I said, halt!"

He finally stopped, gasping for air, and shouted back so the crowd could hear him, "Oh, sorry. Did you mean me?"

They were a fairly easy crowd, aside from the temperance group. They gave him a congenial, collective chuckle, clearly primed to get the maximum possible enjoyment from the day's events.

He waved, trotting the last few yards to join her. "Am I too late? Did I miss the ceremony? You're not wearing a medal or anything, so I suppose I'm in good time."

"And who are you, sir?" the aggrieved committee chair asked.

Before he could answer, Orm leapt forward. "Her accomplice. He'll claim to be Matthew Pence." He drew a revolver from his pocket and aimed it squarely at Matthew's head. "But he's only Miss Hardison's lackey."

"Here now," another of the committee said, irritation with Orm clear on his face. "You put that away. We don't do that sort of thing in the city, this isn't the wild frontier, you know."

Another chorus of harrumphing assent backed him up, and Orm reluctantly lowered his firearm. Eliza noted that he kept it cocked and out of the holster, however, and wished they'd taken it from him entirely.

"Young man, what is your name?" The elderly gentleman who'd objected to the pistol came to the front of the stand and peered down at Matthew. Despite his age, his bearing spoke of his patrician lineage, as did his House of Lords accent.

"It really is Matthew Pence, sir."

"Pence. Sir Paul Pence's boy, out of New York City? Your mother was one of the distant Vanderbilt cousins?"

"The same."

"I know your father, lad. He was great friends with my son when they were at Oxford. Used to come to the country estate for holidays. We still lived in Norfolk then. Pretty country."

"My Lord of Yarmouth? Your son is Winky Barrington? That is to say, Lord Barrington. My father used to tell the most amazing stories about your shooting parties, my Lord!"

"Ah, and my son used to tell me some humdingers about your father. The incident with the goldfish. How many was it? Fourteen? Sixteen?"

Matthew grinned. "Father now claims it was an even twenty, my Lord, but I believe the number has gone up over time."

The old man paused, then nodded. "No, it was always twenty. And you are who you say you are, Mr. Pence. Which means Miss Hardison has probably been telling the truth as well. Guards," he ordered in a voice that brooked no disagreement, "arrest Lord Orm!"

He stabbed his cane in Orm's direction, as if they might not know who he meant, but one of the men who'd been holding Eliza was already halfway across the dais.

He was barely in time to catch Orm, who'd seemed stunned for a moment, then darted toward the side of the platform as the crowd was still registering the new developments. He had no hope of escape, however. The burly guard caught him at the knees in a diving tackle, flattening him. A general scuffle ensued, and eventually a disheveled Orm was marched back to face the judges. The guard, whose ceremonial garb did not appear to include handcuffs, kept Orm from escaping by twisting one of the criminal's arms up behind his back at an angle that made even Matthew wince. Only a little, though.

"Oh, by the way," Matthew called up to the Earl of Yarmouth, "Lord Orm has cornered the illegal opium market in the Dominions. That's why he tried to stop us, and discredit Eliza. He has a huge growing operation up there in the mountains. Enormous, really. Mind-boggling. With slave labor. He held us hostage in his castle compound. Which was actually quite impressive, to give credit where it's due."

The Earl blinked and nodded. "This explains certain things."

The words *opium* and *slave labor* began to rustle through the crowd, a wave of shifting public opinion traveling audibly across the broad square.

"You'll regret this," Orm said to the group at large, then yanked out his strange poppy gadget and blew into the stem, producing a piercing whistle. He stared at the pirate ship, clearly expecting something of it, but the ship and its occupants failed to meet that expectation. Before he could whistle again, the guards had his free arm. The gadget flew from his hand and off the stage, landing near Eliza's feet. She picked it up and spun it in her fingers, examining it from all sides. It wasn't so bad, if one wasn't using it as a lapel pin. The workmanship was beautiful.

To the general delight of the audience, another tussle broke out between Orm and the guards who had stepped up to assist their comrade. It ended with four of the largest enforcers carrying Orm from the stage, one securing each limb, while the spectators hooted and catcalled at the villain.

"To the jail!" the cry went up. The refrain was echoed until the square rang with it, and at least half the audience followed the guards away. In their absence, the huge space seemed relatively empty and quiet, though it was still well populated.

Eliza fiddled with the poppy, trying to calm her frantic heartbeat and sort through all that had just occurred. The gadget truly was beautiful, as long as one ignored the source.

"It might look very fetching on a hat," she commented to Matthew, holding up the flower. He shrugged, not seeming to have a strong opinion either way.

The temperance ladies were milling around the square at a loss, baffled by the seeming downfall of their benefactor. Signs began to slip sideways and fall to the ground, followed by a litter of brass pins.

"Did they ever pronounce you the winner?"

Eliza shook her head, dizzy with relief once again. Probably with exhaustion too. "I expect they'll remember in due course. It doesn't really matter anymore, does it?"

"Well, the money would have been nice."

"I suppose. But it doesn't really *matter*."

"Still."

She turned to him and put her hands on his shoulders, clenching, trying to squeeze the understanding into him. "No. Matthew, when Orm started accusing me and I realized what he meant, for a brief time I thought he'd found you somehow. That he was going to produce your body, and Cantlebury's, to back up his claim. It only lasted a moment before I realized the timeline didn't work, he had to be lying, but that moment was enough to show me what I truly cared about. You survived. Orm didn't kill you. And that is the *only* thing that matters."

She rose up on her toes, pulled his head down to hers and kissed him soundly. Titters and scattered applause broke out in the crowd, but she didn't care. Matthew bent down enough to pick her up by the waist, lifting her and spinning her around once. When he set her down, she refused to let go. He shook his head and smiled, leaning down to rest his head on hers.

"You've just ruined me, you realize," he told her. "Everyone has seen me compromised. My virtue is indelibly stained."

Eliza nodded, returning his gaze with all the mock solemnity she could manage, though her heart was soaring and she felt like her entire being was made of smiles. She'd decided in Orm's office, really. The rest was just details. Her heart knew what it wanted, and when everything else seemed lost, her heart had yearned to be with this man.

"I suppose I'll just have to marry you, then."

"Make an honest man of me."

"Yes."

"I think that's my line. So . . . yes."

After a breathless, ecstatic moment, he kissed her again, scooping her off the ground and doing a thorough job before finally setting her down and nuzzling his nose against hers. And all was right with the world, which consisted of Eliza and Matthew and nothing else.

A gentle harrumphing from the dais drew their attention, and Eliza blushed when she realized the Earl was still standing there at the platform's edge. Now, however, he dandled a gilded medal from one hand and held a large faux check in the other.

"They remembered after all," Matthew whispered in her ear.

"Thank God," Eliza said. "It really is quite a bit of money, after all."

"But it doesn't matter?"

She winked at him and unwound her arms from his neck, striding eagerly toward the platform.

"Not in the least, my love," she called over her shoulder. "Not in the least!"

TWENTY-FIVE

THEY WERE ON the fast southern steam clipper, rounding Cape Horn, when Eliza finally remembered the other remarkable thing that had happened on the final day of the race.

"I've been meaning to tell you," she said, interrupting Matthew's investigation of the sensitive area behind her left knee.

"Hmm?"

"I have news for Barnabas. I'm not sure if I'm supposed to tell or not, but . . . this is going to sound mad. I don't know how I could have forgotten, it's been almost two weeks."

"I've been distracting you as frequently as possible," Matthew pointed out. "Myself too. I'm surprised I remember my own name. Tell me what you remember, and I'll tell you if I think it's mad or not."

"Come up here, then. I can't converse with you down there like that."

"Never seemed to stop you before." But he climbed up

the berth and plunked himself down next to her, nudging her head over to make room for his on the pillow.

"You have been a marvelous distraction, you know. I've hardly worried at all about Barnabas or Cantlebury or the others. I suppose I ought to feel guilty for that."

He gave her a squeeze. "They're fine. Barnabas is already home, and the rest are well on their way. This can't have been worth stopping for, Eliza. What is it?"

"I saw Phineas."

Matthew sat up and stared at her. "Come again?"

"At least I think I did. No, I told myself at the time it wasn't possible, but I'm still certain it was Phineas. I must have looked at that picture a thousand times. And he resembles Barnabas so strongly. There was no mistaking him."

"Why would you think you weren't supposed to tell me this? We're married now, you're supposed to tell me everything."

"My mother is never going to forgive me for that."

"Eliza," he said patiently, "we were *at sea*. We *had* to do it. That's why sea captains were invented, to perform spur-of-the-moment marriages so that couples could share cabins without the stewards giving them funny looks."

She rolled her eyes. "We could have taken separate cabins. And as for sea captains, I'm fairly certain there's also something in their duties about navigating and steering the ship."

"No, no. It's marriages, I'm telling you. So what made you think you couldn't tell me, darling? And where the hell did you see him?"

Eliza recalled that day with mixed emotions. Being accused of murder was horrific, a nightmare—but seeing Matthew safe had been little short of miraculous. And receiving her trophy and the prize money had been a dream come true. She'd gained financial independence in a single moment . . . and though she'd already decided to marry Matthew, she was glad to be doing so from the position of a woman with alternatives and resource of her own.

"I saw him in San Francisco. He was one of Orm's pirates. Only not really, I don't think. Right before you arrived, Orm had called two witnesses from his ship, who were supposed to accuse me of this murder by noxious gas incineration. They were obviously pirates, just as we'd seen before, and one of them was wearing an eye patch. He looked concerned, though, and then he started to take the eye patch off. That's when I recognized him. I was about to say his name, but he held a finger up to his lips and shook his head at me. Shushing me. He'd seen the glider. Then you arrived, and the next time I looked at the stage he was gone."

"How very odd. How could he have gone over to Orm's side? And when did he kick his opium habit?"

"I don't think it's odd at all, and I don't believe he was ever addicted to opium either. Matthew, I think Phineas is a spy."

"No . . ."

He stretched out beside her again, thinking it over with a deeply furrowed brow. A few seconds later he repeated himself. "No . . ."

"I think he was all set to save me by revealing himself and accusing Orm instead of giving false witness against me. That's why he was taking off the eye patch. Removing his disguise. But when he spotted you he knew he didn't have to. So he shushed me and melted away into the crowd instead."

"To preserve his cover."

"Exactly."

"When you put it that way it does make sense. A mad sort of sense."

"I believed you about Orm, and that was based on a dream. I saw an actual person."

Matthew rolled over and kissed her. "Fair enough. Actual person trumps dream. I'll add it to the rule book." He started working his way back down her body.

"What should we tell Barnabas?"

Lifting his head, he gave her a pouty frown. He hated it when she thwarted him after he'd already started, and now she'd thwarted him twice. "I'll think on it and we can discuss it later. But no more right now, because what's the rule?"

"No talking about other men once you're below the waist."

"Thank you. I appreciate your cooperation."

"Matthew?"

"Mmm?"

She raised her hands over her head and stretched languorously, because she knew how her new husband appreciated a good, languorous stretch. "Tell me again about the workshop you're going to build me."

He looked up long enough to grin at her. "With pleasure. It will be full of wonders. Worktables broad and wide enough to hold entire engine blocks. Built-in turntables with hand cranks. All of it ventilated with fans so you won't sweat too much in summer."

"I never sweat," she protested.

Matthew did one of those mysterious things with his fingers that electrified her spine and made it impossible to think clearly. "You're mistaken. You sweat often. In fact you're sweating right now, but I don't mind one bit."

"*More.*"

"About the workshop? Certainly. Our parts bins will be a marvel of organization to rival the finest libraries. What else? I'll custom build you a garage crawler with a down cushion, covered in velvet. Or perhaps silk brocade. Although leather might be easier to clean. Let's make it leather. Oh, and we should have one of those glass wall panels to show all the gears and wires for our chronometry and communication system. The system will be immense and cover the entire estate. Like Dexter and Charlotte's, but *even better.*"

"Matthew, *please . . .*"

"As if I could deny you."

Something like silence fell then, as they both grew too distracted to speak coherently.

SOME TIME LATER, Matthew felt a nudge against his shoulder and heard a beloved voice whisper, "And now tell me about all the *tools*."

READ ON FOR A SNEAK PEEK AT THE NEXT
STEAM AND SEDUCTION NOVEL
FROM DELPHINE DRYDEN

GILDED LILY

COMING JULY 2014 FROM BERKLEY SENSATION

THE HAT WAS too large, and it gave her away. Only to somebody looking hard, of course, but Freddie knew the risk was there. Someone looking hard, or someone who knew what they were looking for.

It was practicality, as much as vanity, that made her balk at cutting her hair off. As long as she kept it, she could blend seamlessly back into that other world. The world in which, ostensibly, she belonged. And it was far easier to disguise the hair than to explain its absence.

So for now, at least, she remained the plumpish, round-faced lad in the suspiciously oversized hat. Fred Merchant, tinker-makesmith extraordinaire. Quick and curious, clever with his hands, and known not to adhere to Marquess of Queensberry rules when cornered in a fight. Handy chap to know, bad chap to cross, such was the general consensus on the streets of London.

Chap whose bosoms have been strapped down far too long for one day. Freddie tucked an escaping auburn curl back under the outmoded black top hat, mindless of the engine grease on her fingers. She was sweating under the bandages and padding, the many layers of her disguise. The device in front of her was still in pieces, the purposeful array of parts revealing the order of their removal. She loved looking at them like that, their symmetry and sense. She could discern the purpose each component served in the whole, could already see where the flaw was. And she saw, as clearly as if the process were playing before her on a stereopticon, how it would all fit together and work again in the end. Where everything belonged, and how and why. The machine flew back together in her mind, whirring into seamless action.

"Wot, then? Beyond repair, is it, Fred?"

"Never." She spared a scowl for Dan Pinkerton, who always assumed things were beyond repair. "It's an easy fix, I just haven't time to finish today. And you know sod-all about steamers, Pink."

That last was reassurance for the client, the butcher, who had shown some dismay at Dan's assessment.

"You'll not get a farthing until that dog's running again," the butcher warned. "If I'm not making anything off it, you won't neither."

"I'll be back same time tomorrow," Freddie reassured him. "Finish it up in no time." The butcher depended on the mechanical "dog" to run the spit on which he roasted his newest product, ready-to-eat sliced meats. He'd taken a chance by setting it up as a spectacle in his shop window, to draw the attention of customers. The prospect of losing his competitive promotional edge was clearly weighing heavily on him, and it bothered Freddie as well. Her clients among the fishmongers were closing up shop left and right lately, the result of an unusually high rate of fishermen gone missing on the job and a simultaneous decline in the numbers of local fish schools. The rivalry between butcher shops had only heated up as trade shifted to place a higher demand on them in the absence of fish.

"Why not now?" the fat man demanded. "Pressing social engagement?"

Dan snorted into his glove, then tried to cover it with a cough. Freddie just smiled and shrugged. "When the Queen calls, Mister Armintrout."

He looked ready to take offense, then shrugged it off. Freddie was his only real option and they both knew it.

"Give her Majesty my best."

The laughter carried them outside, where Dan bustled Freddie onto the trap and down the lane in less than his usual time.

"You'll get caught, joking like that," he scolded once they were on the high street, safely ensconced in the noisy flow of traffic. The little trap bounced along the cobbles, tugged along behind the steam "pony" that Dan controlled with deft flicks of the levers in front of him. Most of London's flesh and blood horses were inured to the steam engines now, and didn't even shy at the noise and sudden bursts of speed from the surrounding vehicles.

"I'm bound to get caught eventually. I don't think cracking wise will make much difference one way or the other. Bloody hell, it's warm out here for April."

"You're sitting right in the steam. Told your father we needed a cowling on this thing when it was converted, but would he listen? And you shouldn't be using coarse language, it ain't ladylike."

"Don't be such a prig, Dan. You sound like my old nursemaid."

"Because your old nursemaid was my mum, or have you forgot?"

"How could I? You're the very image of her. Oh, bother. I've ruined these trousers with grease. My last. I don't suppose you could procure another pair for me tonight?"

"You're supposed to be saving your earnings, I thought. I'll get Mum to clean those ones."

"But they're not your size, won't she suspect?"

Dan's laugh rang out above the noise of the street. "You don't think she already knows? She knows everything, miss. She probably knew your scheme before you even thought of it yourself."

Freddie glanced around, a reflex with her now. "Don't call me that now."

"Right. Pardon, Fred old chap. Are we headed for your piece of skirt among the quality, my lad?" He swung wide to get around a slow horse-drawn carriage, then cut through a narrow gap between two cabs and down a quieter side street.

"Who's the coarse one now? Yes, to Lady Sophronia's." Freddie's closest friend and ally aside from Dan himself, Sophronia Wallingford could always be counted on to provide a hot bath and the loan of a maid when Freddie completed one of her little money-making ventures and needed to clean up before returning to proper society.

"Ah, the beautiful widow Wallingford." Dan let his voice deepen, and his rough accent managed to make even those few innocent words sound like lewd speculation. Freddie knew he teased to cover his genuine adoration of Sophie, a poignant longing that society would always make it impossible to requite. A footman could love a gentlewoman from afar all he liked, but the emotion could never bring him anything but empty daydreams and misery.

Freddie didn't know why Dan subjected himself to it, but she tried to be sympathetic while at the same time subtly discouraging him. "You wouldn't say that if you'd ever seen her before her maid was through with her in the morning."

She also didn't understand the embarrassed laugh and cough Dan hid in his glove, much like he'd done at old Armintrout's earlier. But that was Dan, he'd always had inscrutable moments as long as she'd known him. All her life, in fact. He was the big brother she'd never had, except that she'd more or less always had him.

A heavier than usual patch of traffic and slow-moving

pedestrians held them motionless for a few minutes, long enough for Freddie to grow anxious. The nearest walker, a youngish gentleman, had stopped alongside them. He stared in bewilderment from his map to the surrounding scenery, then in dismay at the cobbled road beneath their carriage.

"Haven't they ever heard of asphalt?" She heard him say into the lull, apparently to no one in particular. Clearly the street noise was too much for him. Delicate sensibilities, perhaps. Or he was a tourist; he had a foreign look about his clothes, an accent that hinted at time spent in the Dominions.

"They've started it north of the river," Dan remarked to him. "But it'll be a cold day for Lucifer before the nobs this far west allow that much change. Not to mention the smell when they lay it down. Nah, here it'll be cobbles and setts until they die, I'd wager."

Unheard-of cheek, especially coming from Dan who was usually so sober and proper. The tourist was obviously no commoner. But it was safe enough, Freddie supposed. The next moment the steam coach ahead of them lurched forward, and all was noise and motion once again. The puzzled, fresh-faced gentleman was lost in the crowd, left alone with his map to speculate on road surfaces and how to find his way through London. Freddie forgot him the moment he was out of view.

Wallingford House loomed ahead of them for a moment before Dan diverted the pony down another side street to the mews. They would enter as two rough tinker-makesmiths, then Dan would reemerge in his livery and return with the trap to Rutherford Murcheson's stately Mayfair residence only a few streets away.

Miss Frederique Murcheson would return home again only after attending a ball under the watchful eye of her friend and sometime chaperone, the Lady Sophronia Wallingford. With her mother now settled resolutely in France, and her father only in London occasionally for business, Freddie was able to get away with quite a lot—but sometimes even she couldn't weasel her way out of an important social occasion.

After all, when the Queen called . . .

BARNABAS STARED AT the map, then at the street in front of him, wishing for the dozenth time that he'd opted to unpack his dirigible and fly to his employer's home instead of taking the Metropolitan railway from the air ferry stop in Hillingdon, then walking to his final destination. It had seemed like a foolish waste of time to launch himself instead of taking advantage of the local transportation, but now he eyed the individual airships above with envy. He could have at least taken a taxicab, but he had the ridiculous notion that he knew the town well, and he'd judged the cab not worth the expense for such a short distance.

London was not as thickly populated as New York, but it sprawled for what seemed like endless miles. Ancient, meandering streets were overlaid by the new. What had seemed straightforward on the map was rendered meaningless by the scale, the bustle, and the overwhelming noise of steam cars and horse-drawn conveyances vying for space on old, cobbled roads or wood block paving. The few times he'd come to the city with friends during his Oxford days, it hadn't seemed so daunting. Or so cacophonous.

"Haven't they ever heard of asphalt?"

"They've started it north of the river," a voice commented from the nearest vehicle, a converted steam-drawn pony trap of a type that was still the height of fashion in New York. This one looked slightly down-at-heels, and its driver's and passenger's coats were frayed at the cuffs and collars. Tinkers, by the oil stains on their clothing and the box of tools at their feet. No expertise with fine clockwork, but they could likely repair an engine or a pump for anyone who couldn't afford a proper makesmith. Barnabas didn't begrudge them their living, but wondered how the local guilds viewed these independent competitors.

"Not to mention the smell when they lay it down. It'll be cobbles and setts until they die, I'd wager," the driver finished.

The trap disappeared like magic as the traffic suddenly picked up its pace, and Barnabas stared dumbly for far too long at the space the little cart had occupied. There was something odd about the trap's passenger that had diverted his attention from the driver almost instantly. He tried to pin it down, but was unable. Something, though. About the eyes and jaw line, the fit of the clothing . . .

A prodding hand jolted Barnabas from his bemused stupor, and he lashed out just in time to catch the wrist of his attempted pickpocket.

"Hey! Stop that!"

The boy dropped Barnabas's coin purse back into his pocket and escaped with a sharp twist of his hand against his intended victim's thumb. Obviously not the first time the youth had been in that situation. A cluster of other boys lurked near the next corner, looking too nonchalant.

More alert, Barnabas transferred all his valuables to safer inside pockets then returned his mind to the task at hand. He knew he was close to Mayfair, and the rough tinker's remark about nobs was confirmation. Rutherford Murcheson's house couldn't be too far off now. He should be able to find it in time to change and dress before the evening's festivities. Whether he would actually find it festive, trying to keep a watchful eye on Murcheson's wayward daughter, remained to be seen. At least it would be a relatively honest evening's work.

Rutherford Murcheson hadn't especially wanted Barnabas for the job of looking after his daughter. Barnabas had suspected as much from their correspondence, and his impression was confirmed by the man's edgy, dismissive demeanor when Barnabas had finally arrived at his tasteful Mayfair home.

"You resemble your brother," the older man said flatly after they'd shaken hands. "Are you going to disappoint me, as he did?"

Barnabas thought of Phineas, the younger brother who'd seemed destined to greatness in his military career before he allegedly succumbed to the lure of opium and fell off the map. "Who was he to you, sir, that you had any expectations of him?"

Murcheson was an industrialist, a manufacturer of clockwork devices and steam engines. Few knew of his other work, as a spymaster for the Crown. Barnabas himself had only learned this recently, and there was no reason young Lieutenant Phineas Smith-Grenville should have known it at all. But Barnabas had reason to believe there was much more to Phineas's disappearance than his family had been led to believe. Finding out the truth about his brother and restoring honor to his name was still his primary objective, regardless of what assignment Murcheson might make. His last attempt to locate Phineas had resulted only in more shame for the family, as it involved Barnabas performing very badly in the American Dominion Sky and Steam Rally. He'd made it no farther than the first rest stop before succumbing to influenza. His friend Eliza Hardison—now Eliza Pence—claimed to have spotted Phineas in San Francisco. But a more recent sighting by a former shipmate of Phineas's placed him in London, so here Barnabas was.

"Lieutenant Smith-Grenville was an unreliable operative. You have clearance to know this now. Your younger brother worked for me, and was meant to be in deep cover to infiltrate a ring of opium smugglers. Instead he fell victim to the poppy himself and disappeared into the western Dominions. Weak character. But my good friends Baron and Baroness Hardison assure me you're made of sterner stuff."

"I like to think my actions speak for my character, sir."

"I'd like to think so too, but I've little confidence. Your last major action was succumbing to influenza on the first day of the Sky and Steam Rally, dropping out of the race and wasting your family's substantial investment. Still, here you are, and I suppose I must make use of you. Incidentally, you'll find a trunk full of your brother's effects in your room. He'd left it in the keeping of his landlady, but it seemed fitting that you should have it. Perhaps you can deliver it to your family when you return to the Dominions, which I suspect will be sooner rather than later."

Murcheson's attitude was more than disheartening. The Hardisons had seemed so much more enthusiastic when they recruited Barnabas to their cause. The timing was perfect—his desire to search for Phineas in London, their European colleague's need for a fresh operative there with an upper-class background. They had assured him that just as their own blue-blood heritage had served them well in forming a cover story for espionage, Barnabas's social credentials made him ideal to pose as a young industrial dilettante abroad. A feckless fop of a son, perhaps, foisted off on the Makesmith Baron to train some sense into him. The story could be that the baron had assigned Barnabas the ridiculously easy but lucrative sinecure of finalizing some negotiations that had obviously been conducted months prior between the Baron himself and Rutherford Murcheson. Then Murcheson could instruct Barnabas as he saw fit. And compensate him, a necessity as Barnabas's father had refused to fund any further searching for Phineas following the rally debacle.

Barnabas had pointed out to his spymaster instructors—who included Charlotte, Lady Hardison and her father Viscount Darmont, much to his surprise—that he knew people in London. He couldn't appear *too* feckless, because he never had been before. At least he certainly hoped not. He was his father's heir, after all, current disagreement notwithstanding. Nor could he play the fop, when he'd been notoriously uninterested in things sartorial at Oxford.

"Ineffectual, then?" Charlotte had suggested.

"Can't I just be myself?"

They all looked at him as if he'd gone mad. Then Charlotte tilted her head, running her gaze up and down Barnabas as if seeing him in a new light. "It might work. No, let's consider this," she insisted when her colleagues raised their voices to object. "Who *is* Lord Barnabas Smith-Grenville? Look at him. He's cheerful, generally well-liked. He's quite earnest, but doesn't completely lack a sense of humor. Well enough connected, but hardly from a powerful family. Not a fashion plate or a Greek god, by any stretch. Meaning no offense, Barnabas."

"None taken, madam." But he found himself adjusting the shoulders of his coat and trying to recall when he'd last had his hair cut.

"None of those things are bad, none of them are particularly good. There's nothing on the surface that's—"

"Remarkable," the Viscount finished for his daughter, earning a glare from her. "I see it now. Or rather I don't, and neither will anybody else. He doesn't need a show to divert attention, because nobody's attention will be drawn to him in the first place."

"I'm not sure I'd go so far as to—" Barnabas attempted.

"Women will not swoon, captains of industry will not bow down, that sort of thing," the Viscount continued. "Just a perfectly nice chap, nothing more. Penny a pound."

"Precisely," Charlotte agreed, favoring Barnabas with a smile. "It's perfect."

"My boy, don't look so downtrodden," her father explained, leaning in and beaming at Barnabas. "We're not insulting you. On the contrary, we're paying you the highest compliment. In this business, unremarkable is the best thing you can possibly be."

Charlotte nodded. "Nobody will ever suspect you of derring-do, not in a million years. Which makes you the perfect spy."

But evidently the perfect spy was only fit for a job of personal busywork, more suited to an underling or footman in Barnabas's opinion. Spying on the boss's daughter, using his social graces to charm her into a false sense of security. When he found out Frederique Murcheson was his first assignment, Barnabas felt like he'd been had.

Murcheson claimed she was a security breach in the making and needed a tail. But now it seemed Murcheson didn't even trust him with following an errant, nosy, twenty-one-year-old girl. All because Phineas had let himself become addicted to opium.

"I'm not my brother, Mr. Murcheson." Barnabas let himself fall into the plummy, snooty tones of his upbringing. He was no misbehaving lieutenant; he was the eldest son and heir of an earl. Not a particularly important or powerful earl, true. But he still outranked a commoner in trade, at least in terms of social standing, and he had no compunction about reminding this man of that fact by his demeanor. "I was invited into Lady Hardison and Lord Darmont's confidence because they believed me capable of working well for the Crown. If you're not of the same opinion, I can simply—"

"Stop there, lad. Enough huffiness. You do the public school patter quite well, I'll give you that. If you want my good opinion, prove yourself. Everywhere my daughter goes, everyone she speaks to, you will know and report to me. But she mustn't suspect you. You must play the part of the fervent, well-intentioned suitor, do you understand? No matter how difficult you find that once you meet Frederique."

"Understood." What more could he say? It was clear any further reassurances from Barnabas would fall on uncaring ears. There was nothing left but to prove himself by outwitting and fooling this young woman into believing he was smitten enough to hound her every move, which ought to be simple enough. Wasn't that the primary concern of most young ladies during the social season, after all? Even the heiresses whose blood wasn't remotely blue. Except that this heiress was sounding less and less like the typical model.

"I suppose you ought to go attire yourself appropriately," Murcheson sniffed. "It is a birthday ball for a prince, after all."

Barnabas went, accompanied by a creeping sense of dread. What the hell had he gotten himself into?

A spy, an airship, and a simmering passion.

THE FIRST BOOK IN THE STEAM AND SEDUCTION SERIES

FROM
DELPHINE DRYDEN

GOSSAMER WING

A Steam and Seduction Novel

To make her mark as a spy, Charlotte Moncrieffe sets out to recover long-lost documents from the Palais Garnier in her stealth dirigible, the *Gossamer Wing*. Makesmith Baron Dexter Hardison is an ideal husband-imposter for Charlotte. But from their marriage of convenience comes a distraction: a passion that complicates an increasingly dangerous mission.

"Emotional and erotic."
—*Night Owl Reviews*

"Steampunk erotica at its best."
—*RT Book Reviews*

delphinedryden.com
facebook.com/delphinedryden
penguin.com

M1367T0913

"Meljean is now officially one of my favorite authors."
—Nalini Singh, *New York Times* bestselling author

FROM *NEW YORK TIMES* BESTSELLING AUTHOR
MELJEAN BROOK

Tethered
A TALE OF THE IRON SEAS

Surviving on the treacherous Iron Seas requires a heart of steel . . . but how can Yasmeen hope to survive when her heart has already been stolen by Archimedes Fox?

Tethered along the south dock of Port Fallow, Captain Yasmeen Corsair's magnificent new airship, *Lady Nergüi*, awaits its departure with adventurer and treasure-hunter Archimedes Fox. But Yasmeen has reason to worry when Miles Bilson, an acquaintance from Archimedes' earlier smuggling days, sends an urgent message requesting help.

With a past marked by betrayal, Archimedes wonders what his former partner could want—other than revenge. Yasmeen fears that Bilson could threaten everything Archimedes holds dear. Though both Archimedes and Yasmeen love the exhilaration of veering wildly off course, neither is prepared for where their newest risk will take them . . . or what it might cost them.

AVAILABLE FOR THE FIRST TIME DIGITALLY!

INCLUDES A PREVIEW OF MELJEAN BROOK'S *GUARDIAN DEMON*!

meljeanbrook.com
facebook.com/authormeljeanbrook
facebook.com/ProjectParanormalBooks
penguin.com

M1233T1212